WITCH'S SECRET

THE HEMLOCK CHRONICLES: BOOK FOUR

EMMA L. ADAMS

I walked through the wall, out of shadows and fog, humming the *Mission Impossible* theme. As a ghost, no door could keep me out, not even the sealed and guarded headquarters of Edinburgh's mage guild. 'Invisible spy' sounded more impressive than 'fugitive', so I'd take whatever entertainment I could get.

Okay, enough screwing around, Jas. You're on a mission.

The grey filter of the spirit realm turned the darkened halls into spectral corridors filled with shadows, but it'd take more than a little darkness to spook a necromancer. I scowled at the gilt-framed portrait of the esteemed Lord Sutherland on my right-hand side. Glossy black hair. A pleasant smile. Smooth features that made him look thirty years younger than his true age. No signs that he was anything other than the mage guild's respectable leader. He hid his crimes well.

I drifted out of the corridor and down the spiralling staircase into the lobby, spreading out my arms and pretending to glide along the banister. Really, we necromancers were wasting our talents getting poltergeists out of people's basements when there was a world of possibilities out there. I glided to a halt and flipped over in mid-air, bowing to an imaginary audience. *And you wonder why ghosts start to lose their minds after spending too long on the other side.*

A shadow fell across the lobby floor, and the lamps on the walls came on. They looked like old-fashioned lanterns, and, like everything in here, were probably worth more than a week's salary from my former job at the necromancer's guild.

I held my breath out of habit as Lord Sutherland passed by, though breathing was as unnecessary as caution considering he had no way of knowing I was here. He wore a dark shirt and trousers tailored to fit his tall, strong frame. Though I couldn't see the spells he wore on his wrists to hide his age, the faint tingle of witch magic stirred my senses even as a ghost.

Playing poltergeist had got old after my first few visits here, but I couldn't resist making the chandelier rattle by blowing air at it from above his head. The Mage Lord glanced up, a frown wrinkling his brow. Then a second figure came into view, a thin blond woman with a Mage Lord's knee-length coat. Lady Anders, another council member. The two were allies, so it made sense that he'd pick her as a confidant.

Go on. Spill all your secrets.

"Did you find them?" he asked her quietly.

"No," she said. "They're gone. Every last piece."

"Colton," said Lord Sutherland, spitting out the word like it was a curse. "I knew it."

"He stated his intent," said Lady Anders. "We have no

need of the shifters now."

"No, but I would have preferred to maintain access to the portal," he said. "It somewhat complicates things that the Twelve were able to remove the mirror from our possession."

Ha. Sounded like Vance and the rest of his council had succeeded in hiding all the pieces of Moonbeam—a stone that could control shifters against their will—so the mages couldn't use them any longer. And to add insult to injury, they'd also swiped the mirror Lord Sutherland's allies had been using to transport themselves into their secret bolt hole. I grinned, waggling my fingers behind Lord Sutherland's head.

Lady Anders's next words brought me to a halt. "Pity," she said. "If he'd kept the pieces, they would have been an easy way to dispose of him."

I wish I could dispose of you. It was no secret that the mages shamelessly murdered one another behind closed doors. They had it all—power, wealth, status—but the more they had, the more they craved. I might not have been in on the Council of Twelve's plans anymore, but the fewer dangerous magical artefacts Lord Sutherland and his allies got hold of, the better.

"As for Lady Montgomery," he said, "the guild should have sent me an answer by now. If I didn't know better, I'd say she's holding out on us."

A pang hit me at the sound of my former boss's name. I'd often wondered if she was the reason the mages had put their plans to force all supernaturals to add their names to a register on hold, but even Lady Montgomery didn't dare withdraw her public support of Lord Sutherland or else she'd be the next person he tried to 'dispose' of. At least, I assumed her support was a public show and no more. Pity I couldn't visit her and check, because the instant a necromancer spotted me, it was game over.

I missed the guild so much it was like a physical ache in my chest. I missed it all, even routine patrols, the smell of zombies, and the boring nights sitting in on three-hour-long summits in the freezing cold. I'd take a lifetime of archive duty if only I could turn back time and erase the chain of events which had led me here. But I knew better than to wish for what I couldn't have. Some doors, once opened, could never be closed.

"Maybe she already chose a side," Lady Anders said.

Shadows flickered on Lord Sutherland's smooth features as he moved into the lamplight. "Who? Colton's? He's back home in England. Besides, he knows the resources we have at our disposal. His hands are tied, and he knows it. So does she, if she has any sense. She'll come around."

My non-existent skin prickled. *What resources, exactly?* I'd suspected the ruling mages had other allies with immensely powerful magic. Like rogue witches. But they didn't bother me half as much as certain other foes.

Otherworldly ones.

Goose bumps ran up my arms, and magic shivered over my transparent skin.

"If you're sure," Lady Anders said. "If not, we'll move to take back what they stole from us."

"She has one chance," said Lord Sutherland. "Otherwise, we will need to give her an incentive to listen to us in future. She has no use for the artefact herself, and it belongs to us by right."

What are they talking about? The urge to warn Lady

Montgomery swiftly rose, then sank just as fast. She and Lord Sutherland were equals, and if she was one of the smartest people I knew. She must suspect he planned to act against her. Showing my face would bring an end to more than my own life.

Didn't mean I couldn't discourage him a little, though.

I concentrated on my hands, which lit up with blue light. Taking careful aim, I threw a handful of kinetic energy at the chandelier above his head.

I'd envisioned a dramatic crash, but instead, the chandelier blew to the side as though caught in a faint breeze. The tinkling sound caused both mages to look up.

"Did someone leave a window open?" Lord Sutherland's sharp gaze scanned the shadows around the staircase. He looked right through me, even when I gave him the finger. *Up yours, you murdering cockwaffle.*

Lady Anders stepped back into the shadows. "I will see you in the morning, Sir."

Shame I didn't have enough power to knock the chandelier on both their heads and make it look like an accident. After all, I wasn't a real ghost, and with my body lying several hundred miles away, there was nothing I could do to bring justice down upon this man. He showed no indication that he realised he was being haunted, but if anyone deserved to be terrorised by the mad poltergeists of all the people he'd murdered, it was him.

Another female figure appeared, casting no reflection in the mirrors lining the stairs and preventing me from following him up into the darkness. Her eyes shone in the gloom, grey-blue, like mine. At a distance, one might think the two of us were closely related. We shared the same dark brown hair, though I'd dyed mine black, and the same pale skin, which appeared even paler in Death's grey light. Behind each of us, however, lay something else. A shadow— or rather, a shade.

Evelyn Hemlock folded her arms and shouted, "Get out! Now!"

The manor's lobby disappeared, turning into a deserted living room lit only by the faint glow of a lamp set on the oak wood table beside the fireplace. I sucked in a painful breath, my heart hammering against my ribcage. Rolling to the side, I winced as ice cracked on my hands and feet. Soft carpet cushioned my body, but every bone ached with cold. The fire in the grate in front of me had gone out.

"What's the emergency?" Heart pounding, I scanned the living room, expecting to see the mages standing there waiting to pass judgement on me. But nobody else was here. Nobody living, that is.

Evelyn appeared floating in front of the empty grate, scowling at me. "The emergency is that if you starve to death, we'll both die. Or did you forget?"

"I'm not starving to death." I flicked more ice fragments off my chilled legs. "Maybe freezing, but I guess the fire went out while I was over in Death."

She drew in a breath and said, "You were in the bloody spirit realm for *sixteen hours*. You're lucky you haven't caught hypothermia."

My mouth fell open. "It was not sixteen hours. More like three."

Evelyn pouted her lips in an expression I'd come to know too well over the last few weeks. "Look, I'm a ghost, not a necromancer, but you can lose track of time on the other side of the veil. It blurs together. I should know, I lost several years. But unlike you, I can lose several years without dying in the real world."

Now she mentioned it, I was starving. Sixteen hours? How had that happened? In the spirit realm, I lost all physical sensation. It had its perks, but the downsides hit me all at once when I pushed to my feet and promptly fell over. Wincing, I managed to stand up by half-leaning on the sofa, found my stash of spells, and restarted the fire. Then I limped to the bathroom, gripping the wall to keep my balance.

The spirit realm had no clocks, no markers of the hours passing. After all, most people on the other side had no reason to keep track. I closed the bathroom door behind me, my gaze snagging on my reflection. I looked ghostlike, all the colour bleached out of my skin. Maybe Evelyn had a point. I'd seen necromancers who spent too long in the spirit realm fade out until one day they left their bodies behind and ended up joining the ghosts on the other side. *Oh, come on, I'm not that bad.* It wasn't like I had any other entertainment up here in the middle of nowhere. I didn't even have a phone signal most of the time.

By the time I'd emerged from the bathroom after a long, hot shower to banish the chill from my limbs, Evelyn was sitting on the rug in front of the fireplace, as though if she lingered close enough, some of the warmth would reach her.

"I hope it was worth it." She folded her arms across her chest. "Well?"

"Well what?"

Evelyn flipped over in the air, floating expectantly in front of me. "What did you hear from the mages?"

"Not enough for an arrest." I flopped onto the sofa again. "Good news, though—they won't be able to pull the same trick on the shifters as before. Vance and the others disposed of the Moonbeam pieces. They swiped the mirror, too."

"I'm glad the Mage Lord did something useful," she said. "Is he going to come and rescue us from this dismal hole?"

"We're practically living in luxury. Okay, 'living' is a bit of a stretch..." I broke off as she cast me an ugly look. Evelyn wasn't fond of me reminding her of her incorporeal state. I often found her trying to pick things up, the same way I did when I was haunting Edinburgh through the spirit realm—except her ghostly form was permanent.

A chill swept through the room from a crack somewhere in the walls, a reminder that Lady Harper's old house had been abandoned for at least a decade and if not for the wards on the outside, it would have fallen into disrepair years ago. Since the only source of warmth was the fireplace, I spent most of my time hanging out in the living room. Fine by me, since the other rooms were filled with too many ghosts, mostly of the metaphorical variety —Evelyn being the obvious exception. My former mentor had taken most of her secrets with her beyond the grave, and while I'd spent most of my limitless free time going through her old records, the pile of actual clues I'd accumulated was depressingly shallow.

One thing became abundantly clear with every passing day: I hadn't known Lady Alice Harper at all.

I rolled off the sofa and went to the kitchen to fetch a glass of water. Evelyn watched me, tracking my movements with her eyes. We both knew she wanted a body of her own, and if no other were available, she'd take mine. Considering we were bound to one another for as long as I lived, it was unlikely she'd ever have another option—unfortunately for both of us.

I sipped my water, meeting her stare across the living room. "Going to tell me why she's mad at me?"

"How would I know?" asked Evelyn. "Cordelia never tells me why she's angry. She just stares."

I drained the glass. "If anything, it should be you she's mad at. You blew our cover and got us kicked out of the city."

Her jaw locked. "The Hemlocks were sworn to secrecy in a world where the Mage Lords weren't ruled by a despot who makes deals with ancient gods. Times have changed."

"We still broke the law," I said. "Besides, we don't know how many Ancients he's working with, or what they're capable of. I wouldn't stake my friends' lives on it."

Evelyn raised her eyes to the ceiling. "You still put faith in them after they abandoned you? Did you learn nothing from your mentor's fate?"

"Lady Harper didn't have friends," I said. "And she was the most miserable person I knew. That's why I spent most of the last seven years avoiding her. But I guess you were asleep for most of it."

"Not sleeping," she corrected. "I had moments of consciousness, throughout your life, and I know that if you don't cut ties with your friends, they will perish in the war, Jas."

"There doesn't have to be a war." My hands clenched, magic sparking to the surface. At the sight of her magic in my hands, Evelyn's eyes narrowed. "If you hadn't decided to expose us, I could have been back at the guild right now, hunting zombies with Lloyd."

"That life was over for you the instant I awakened." Evelyn's eyes glowed blue-grey, a dark shadow appearing behind her.

"You don't get to dictate my life any more than Cordelia does, Evelyn," I said. "And if you even think of forcing me to abandon my friends, I'll make the next binding spell a permanent one."

Sparks leapt to her own hands, green light igniting. Tensing, I called on my own magic, which formed the shape of a glimmering semi-transparent whip covered in flickering runes.

Her eyes gleamed. "Try me."

I lashed the whip at her. She caught the end in her palm, dragging me towards her. I pulled, and so did she, catching both of us in a tug-of-war.

"You dare to use my own power against me?" she hissed.

"You *gave* me this power by choice." I yanked at the whip, which dissipated into nothingness, leaving Evelyn floating inches away from me. "You can't take it back now."

"It was hardly a choice," she said. "You were a proxy, nothing more. I'm the one who should have survived."

"But they killed you," I said. "The Hemlocks dealt the killing blow, at your command. Who did it, anyway? Cordelia? No, she was still cursed back then."

"They all were," she spat. "It was Lady Harper who performed the ritual, of course. It was she who bound both of us with our deaths."

Her words punched me in the chest. I staggered, my legs threatening to give out.

A nasty smile twisted her lips. "Are you really surprised?"

Well, no. Shocked, maybe, but not surprised.

I put the glass down and moved back to the sofa, my mind whirling. *Lady Harper performed the ritual that bound us?* Guess that explained why Evelyn had chosen to speak at Lady Harper's funeral when the two had barely known each other when Evelyn was alive.

"She's not a Hemlock witch." I addressed the fireplace. "How can she have performed the ritual without our magic?"

"She didn't need to," said Evelyn. "My own magic was enough, and with her help, I used my last breath to bind us."

The small hairs on my arms stood on end. Lady Harper had never talked about the invasion, only alluded to what she'd witnessed that night. Everyone knew she'd killed two Sidhe in person, and her entire family except for her granddaughter Wanda had died in the war. I owed her my life already, since she'd plucked me out of the witch orphanage and helped raise me, but I hadn't known Evelyn owed her a greater debt.

The last tangible thing my mentor had left in this world was the bond between Evelyn and me. A bond that kept us alive, saved us—and doomed us.

2

I awoke to strong daylight spilling across the living room floor through a gap in the hideous vomit-brown curtains, and a familiar chill telling me the fire had gone out again. I must have fallen asleep on the sofa, which was also a hideous vomit-brown in colour. Comfortable, though. My head felt muzzy with sleep, and by the light's intensity, it must be at least midday. I should probably eat, but living on instant noodles and dry cereal had got old after the first week of exile. Several weeks on and I was more starved for company than anything else. If only my Hemlock powers could conjure up a cheeseburger from Cassandra's Café.

"Get up." Evelyn prodded me in the side, which was downright disturbing coming from a ghost. "You're not spending another day in the spirit realm. I'm bored out of my mind."

"That's *why* I was in the spirit realm." I yawned and stretched. "Fugitive, remember?"

"I can't imagine I'll forget anytime soon," she said sourly.

"All right, no need to be rude." I padded to the bathroom to change into a fresh outfit. My hair had dried in an impressive bedhead, sticking up on one side. I'd stopped wearing my lip piercing, since I kept forgetting to take it out, and the black dye had started to fade from my hair as it grew out.

Slowly, I was starting to look more and more like a Hemlock witch. Next I'd be turning into a tree. *Jesus, I hope not.* Resembling a spirit realm junkie was bad enough.

Evelyn yelled from outside the bathroom door. "There's someone here to see you."

"What, someone living?" I finished dressing and ran to the front door so quickly that my legs forgot how to work again. I staggered against the door frame, catching my balance at the last second. Evelyn snickered, and I flipped her off.

I yanked the door open. "Please tell me you've come to exorcise a ghost."

"You or her?" said Lloyd, my best friend, lowering the hood of his necromancer coat to reveal his windswept locs.

I held onto the door frame for balance, shuffling aside to let him in. "Don't mind me, I just spent a bit too long on the other side and my legs forgot how to work."

Lloyd closed the door behind him and shook his head at me. "I can't leave you unattended without you getting into trouble, can I?"

"Is Vance not with you?" I'd hoped to warn him of what

Lord Sutherland had said, though it wasn't like he'd made a direct threat against the Council of Twelve. No, it was Lady Montgomery who needed a warning, but she probably already knew Lord Sutherland had his eye on her position as well. Still, I wished I could do something useful in my role as spy, rather than confirming what everyone already knew. If Lord Sutherland was hiding another Ancient behind the mages' backs, he had yet to let anything slip.

"Nope," said Lloyd. "The Mage Lord brought me here on his way to meet with someone in Aberdeen, and he said he'll pick me up in an hour."

Vance had the ability to teleport to my physical location, but since Lady Harper's house lay on the edge of a cliff on Scotland's coast, my other allies were beyond reach. Ivy Lane had gone to deal with an urgent situation in Faerie, while the other members of the Council of Twelve had gone back to their respective territories to form a plan on how to continue without the aid of Edinburgh's council. It didn't sound like they were making much progress.

"Good enough." I walked to the kitchen. "I was going to make something to eat. Cold cereal or soup out of a tin?"

He pulled a face. "Call it intuition, but I bought food with me. No wonder you look like you're channelling the Grim Reaper. You were skinny enough already."

I screwed up my forehead. "I don't need a lecture from you. I already had to listen to Evelyn bitch at me last night."

"Oh, I wasn't bitching at you," she said. "That was nothing. I'm just getting started."

Lloyd jumped. "She's just... visible all the time now? And she's the only company you have here?"

"I also have Lady Harper's priceless junk." I walked to the fireplace to move some of the boxes out of the way. "She owned enough antique crockery to host a medieval feast."

Lloyd sat down on the soft carpet in front of the fireplace and spread out a picnic of pastries and other snacks. "Cassandra's Café is almost going out of business without you there," he said, selecting a bacon sandwich. "Find anything useful in your mentor's junk?"

"Not so far." I grabbed a pastry. "Just the same shit we found before. The journal and the map."

"The journal nobody can read and the map that leads nowhere."

"That's Lady Harper for you." I took a huge bite of pastry, trying not to think of Evelyn's latest bombshell. She'd vanished when we'd sat down, perhaps due to our leaving her out of the conversation. "Turns out she's the one who did the soul binding spell."

His jaw dropped. "You're shitting me."

I swallowed another mouthful. "Evelyn was the one whose magic fuelled the ritual, but it was Lady Harper who made the final decision. I should have known. The other Hemlocks were already stuck in that cave."

"That is messed up." His gaze fell on the leather-bound book beside the fire. "Is that what her journal's about, d'you think?"

"No, she wrote in it nine years before the invasion," I said. "Thirty-one years ago, so before I was even born. Not that I can read it. Whatever code it is, there's no translation here."

He pulled the nearest box closer. "Gotta start somewhere. Have you finished checking this one yet?"

"Not before I lost the will to live," I said. "There are a lot of things we could be doing rather than this. Like dusting. This place is ninety per cent dust."

"Hey, it'll be worth it if we find something." He picked up a letter. "Man, she had a lot of correspondents."

That was true. Lady Harper's letters were short, crisp, and written in her infamous sprawling handwriting. Whenever I read them, I could hear her strident voice over my shoulder, telling me I just wasn't *trying* hard enough.

"I'm more interested in these cookies," I said, opening a bag.

"Isabel made them," he said. "Ivy said they're better than her handmade spells, if possible."

"Wow, really?" I bit into a cookie, and the taste of cinnamon flooded my mouth. "You've all been hanging out together while I'm stuck in no man's land, then?"

"I think Isabel's more interested in hanging out with her new witchy friend." He winked. "I know for a fact she's been sneaking up to Scotland for visits. She said she can't get through to you on the phone, but she managed to get through the forest without any trouble."

"So the Hemlocks have been pretending Evelyn and I don't exist?" I put the bag down and wiped my mouth. "Bloody cheek."

Since the last time I'd seen Isabel, she'd narrowly escaped being turned into a puppet by a deranged god, I'd have thought she'd want to avoid the city for a while. Then again, it sounded like she and Asher the witch had become close friends—or more than friends.

"Well, you *are* Edinburgh's most wanted," he said. "I always knew you'd make headlines."

I flicked a cookie crumb at him. "So you haven't run into any trouble since I left, then? No wayward zombies or annoying poltergeists?"

"So many zombies." He groaned. "Have you any idea what it's like trying to work with novices who can barely operate a summoning circle? I want my partner back."

"I'm right here," I said indistinctly through a mouthful of cookie. "I'll be back at your side when the guy who runs the mage guild forgets he wants me dead."

He winced. "Are you sure you're okay up here? I can fake a family emergency to get out of guild patrolling and come and stay here for a few days, if you want company."

"Don't worry about it," I said. "You've become way more maternal since I left."

"Someone has to look after the psychics."

"Thought that was Ilsa's job." I raised an eyebrow. "Unless you finally made a move on Morgan?"

"He remains oblivious." He cleared his throat. "Maybe when this blows over."

"We're in the Highlands. Nothing blows over. It turns into a storm that lasts for weeks."

I didn't *mind* the rain—I mean, I'd grown up in England then moved to Scotland—but the monotony had grown tedious, to say the least.

Lloyd ducked his head over the box of letters. "Man, it sounds like these Briar people really pissed Lady Harper off."

I looked up sharply. "Wait, did you say Briar?"

He picked the topmost letter out of the box. "Yeah, why? You know the name?"

"Yeah… the Briar Coven. I lived with them for the first year of my life." They'd also been the Hemlocks' allies, and Lady Harper had instructed them to keep an eye on me when I'd moved to Edinburgh. Yet when I'd gone looking for them, their house had been empty, and no trace of their coven had been left behind.

Lloyd handed me the letter and I scanned it. In typical brusque fashion, the letter read, *Not good enough. Tell the Briars I'm coming to pay them a visit. A. Harper.*

That was it. She hadn't signed the note, but the tone had my former mentor written all over it.

I put the yellowed piece of paper down. "The address says… Foxwood. Any idea where that is?"

Lloyd shook his head. "Nope, doesn't ring a bell. But I can look it up when I have a phone signal. The guild has records of most supernatural places, too."

"You know how secretive she was, though," I said. "Text Isabel when you have the chance. I'm ready to visit the forest and find out what Cordelia's hiding."

———

"You're wasting our time," said Evelyn.

"Can I hear something?" I stood on the hillside, wrapped in a warm coat with four layers underneath to stave off the chill of the Highlands. "It sounded like a whiny voice on the breeze."

Vance had whisked Lloyd away without sticking around to chat, but it was my idea to go through the forest. It was a testament to the grudge-holding power of the Hemlock witches that they'd let my mentor through and not me, even though I was their supposed saviour.

I didn't feel like much of a saviour, marooned there in no man's land. Frost coated the grass like icing sugar, and the sky was slate-grey, merging with the distant mountains. On my other side, the house clung to the cliff's edge, just high enough to avoid the spray of the waves lashing against the shore. Mist shrouded it from behind, making the whole place look otherworldly.

Rubbing my hands together to warm them, I focused on the thin, transparent line running along the hillside beneath us. While I could usually see the spirit lines better as a ghost, my Hemlock magic was tied to this particular spirit line, which cut through the middle of Scotland and England and linked to the Hemlock witches' home. Or it was supposed to, anyway. Despite the glow lighting my palms, no answer came from the other side of the line.

"You have some nerve lecturing me about not taking my duties seriously and then throwing a tantrum and shutting me out, Cordelia," I said aloud. "I thought I was your last hope."

The air shimmered, and a solid shape appeared, slamming into my padded coat. I grabbed my attacker by the scruff of its neck as its sharp teeth snapped inches from my ear. The small horned creature shrieked and kicked in my hands, its sour face twisted with hate. Some kind of faerie—a goblin.

"Where did you come from?"

Rather than answering, the goblin wriggled free from my grip and thrust upwards with a sharp knife. Stepping out of range, I called on my Hemlock magic and deflected his blade, sending it spinning away down the hillside.

Evelyn let out an impatient noise and lashed out. Magic sparked from her hands, forming a semi-transparent whip that cut off the goblin's head like a knife slicing through paper.

I gave Evelyn an exasperated look. "You didn't want to ask how he got into the forest before you decapitated him?"

"You were taking too long." She threw the last of her magic at the goblin's headless corpse.

Honestly. Evelyn and I understood one another better than ever before, but somehow that meant we argued more often. Almost like siblings, except for the part where Evelyn wanted to take over my body. I'd never had a sibling, so I assumed *that* wasn't normal, anyway.

I walked to the spot where the goblin had materialised from and searched for the traces of the forest's magic where it rippled through the spirit line. Grabbing the threads, I hissed, "If you don't let me into the forest, Cordelia, I'll take an axe to you."

The glow around my hands grew brighter, then the world fell out from underneath us. After the spirit realm, the fall seemed tame by comparison. The landing, not so much. I crashed in an undignified sprawl in a nest of tree roots, grateful for the layers I'd padded myself with for breaking my fall.

Pulling twigs out of my hair, I scrambled to my feet. "Thanks for that, Cordelia.'

"You should not be here," rumbled a female voice from the tree in front of me.

"Terrifying," I said. "You should consider a career in voiceover acting."

The tree warped before my eyes, becoming a stone sculpture with a pair of eyes staring down at me. On either side were the cramped walls of the Hemlocks' cave, covered in snaking tree roots. I never did figure out how many Hemlocks were trapped in those walls, but the others had stopped talking a long time ago.

A small figure covered in fur sat on a rock, baleful eyes blinking at me.

"I thought the Soul Collector killed you," I said to the fae creature.

"You thought wrong," she said in a raspy voice. Even the Hemlocks' half-faerie servant was angry with me? If anything, Evelyn had been responsible for my current fugitive status. She was the one who'd tried to murder the mage council.

"Why are there Unseelie fae in your forest?" I asked Cordelia. "A goblin just jumped out of the spirit line and attacked me."

"The fae are restless," Cordelia responded. "They feel the forces moving in this realm and others, and they grow fearful."

"Say what now?" I said. "Forces moving… like what?"

Cordelia didn't answer. It was amazing how a face stuck in a tree could look so much like an angry school-teacher. Or my former boss and head of Edinburgh's necromancer guild, Lady Montgomery.

"Have you heard from Ivy Lane lately?" asked Cordelia.

I blinked. "No. Last I heard, she was in Faerie. Why?"

"No reason."

Yeah, right. When the Hemlocks tried to avoid my questions, it meant they were sitting on something major. "Please, just give me a straight answer for once. Have you ever heard of a place called Foxwood?"

"No."

I stood my ground. "I found correspondence between Lady Harper and the Briar Coven, which marked Foxwood as their address. I'm guessing they didn't always live in Edinburgh?"

"I wouldn't know," she growled. "We were not local to you, during our human lives, and I haven't set eyes on anyone in the Briar Coven since before our imprisonment."

"Didn't the Briar witches bring me directly into the forest when I was nearly poisoned to death?"

"The Briar Coven brought you to the forest's boundary on Lady Harper's orders. We did not see them."

That's convenient. "Look, the leader of the Mage Lords might have made a deal with the monsters you gave up your magic to defeat," I said. "If I were you, I'd be trying to help me, not thwart me. The Briars might be the allies I need." I'd be unwise to pin my hopes on anyone, but the Hemlocks were a literal world away from mine. They couldn't remove the price on my head or make the mages forget they wanted me dead.

"I'm well aware, Jacinda, that the man is in communication with the Ancients," said Cordelia. "If anyone can thwart him, however, it's you."

"Are you feeling all right? Did you just praise me?"

Cordelia's pit-like eyes blinked. "I'll thank you to watch your tongue, Jacinda. You know our power runs in your veins and is limitless."

Evelyn made a small noise, barely audible.

Limitless? Not hardly. Okay, while Lord Sutherland possessed only one type of magic, his earth mage ability, my Hemlock magic could create any regular witch spell and pull apart the fabric of reality to boot. On paper, it sounded reasonable for me to be able to challenge him—except for one slight issue.

"He's working with witches himself, Cordelia," I told her. "He had one tied up in his dungeon who he forced to summon an Ancient. I bet if he had one god's name, he'll have others. I have no idea what powers they have or what they're capable of."

"Then you know what to do," she said. "Kill the mage."

"Kill the mage," I muttered to myself. "Sure, I'll just stride in and murder the most powerful man in Edinburgh."

"You have power over life and death," Evelyn pointed out. "He can't claim that much, at least."

You want me to haunt him to death? I knew the limits of my own power. I could set a zombie army loose on him. I could rattle the windows of his bedroom all night. But as a ghost, I was limited to the spirit realm alone.

I needed to be there in person.

"Look, I spent my teenage years with mages," I said. "I saw first-hand the lengths they go to protect themselves from potential assassination attempts. They go out in groups, they have reserve teams scattered throughout the city in strategic locations—and since he knows I survived, he'll have a crack team of witches on his side, too. Necromancy isn't much use against living people unless you're dealing with another necromancer or—" I broke off.

"Or?" Evelyn tilted her head, her eyes gleaming in a way I didn't like.

"You use blood magic," I finished. "That was a one-off."

I'd used blood magic to kill the Whisper, but I had no intention of making a habit of it. Blood magic had been outlawed since the mage council's inception. I was supposed to be clearing my name, not adding to the list of crimes on my head.

"It's your choice, Jacinda," Cordelia said.

"Look, it's Lord Sutherland who summons beasts from between the worlds on his days off," I said. "Blood magic —sacrificial magic—it's his area. I already set one deranged god loose by messing with the forces of nature and I'd rather not do it again."

Oh, I *wanted* to destroy Lord Sutherland. I despised him for everything he'd done to me, and to Isabel, and Wanda, and all the other people he'd hurt. There was nothing I wanted to do more than destroy him. But using blood magic? Tapping into the power of the gods myself? The risk wouldn't rebound on me, but on everyone else around me. The gods were unpredictable and dangerous, and more to the point, the Hemlocks ought to be entirely against using the magic whose roots lay in the realms they'd given their lives to protect the world against.

Instead of answering, Cordelia disappeared, and so did the cave, leaving Evelyn and me alone on a forest path.

"What's got into her this time?" I said to the empty silence. "I would have thought she'd rip my head off for suggesting using blood magic, considering it already wiped out one coven. I'm on the run and she suggests breaking more rules?"

"Exactly," said Evelyn. "You have nothing to lose."

"I think you mean *you* have nothing to lose," I said. "I still have friends out there, and I won't let them be collateral damage."

"There's a simple solution. Ditch them."

"Give it up," said a voice, and Isabel stepped out from

behind a tree. "You're not going to convince her, Evelyn. Jas doesn't abandon her friends."

"Damn right." I walked over and hugged her. Isabel was a couple of inches taller than me at five feet, slender and dark-skinned, with her hair braided with bright ribbons that matched the band-shaped spells decorating her wrists. She wore jeans and a denim jacket over a yellow shirt which looked downright unsuitable for the weather.

"Glad to see you, Jas," she said. "I got Lloyd's message."

"It's great to see you, too," I said. "The Hemlocks have been letting you in here and not me? I'm insulted."

She grinned. "Don't worry, we're not plotting behind your back."

"You know they think I should assassinate the mage council? That's their big idea."

She raised an eyebrow. "Don't they think the other mages would jail you for life if you did that?"

"I guess they think I have nothing to lose." Which was partially true—but I dreaded to think what the mages would do to my friends if I failed. "They don't seem to have considered that if there's nobody to take their place, someone worse might end up in power. Not to mention the mages might still have witch allies."

"That's my job," Isabel said. "I'm heading to Edinburgh now to look into ways of tracking and isolating the witches Lord Sutherland and his allies might be hiring to help them. Asher asked me—"

"And to think I thought you came to see me." I put on a mock-hurt expression.

She gave me another grin. "It *is* good to see you. But

you know, it's not safe for you to go too far from Lady Harper's place."

"Nobody knows I'm coming back into the city. It's fine." If anything, I'd welcome a tense game of hide-and-seek with the mages to break up the monotony. "Don't get me wrong, I'd still rather be at the guild, but at least I'm still alive."

I didn't mention the Hemlocks' suggestion that I use blood magic. Isabel had been forced to use it against her will when the Whisper had possessed her, and while she seemed none the worse for wear from the experience, I didn't need to burden her with the Hemlocks' latest absurd suggestion.

"I told Lloyd to wait for you somewhere that isn't the guild," she said. "He'll have texted you, but I guess you have no signal in the Highlands."

"Nope. Lady Harper's idea of paradise," I said. "Even the cows and sheep avoid the place, let alone the people." If you ignored the occasional goblin, anyway. "I just have to make a quick detour to Keir's house."

Keir didn't know I was coming, but he'd want me to tell him what I'd learned from Lord Sutherland. While he was a second's distance from me in the spirit realm, our situation had become somewhat complicated after the two of us had found Keir's missing brother held hostage along with Wanda in the other realm. Aiden's body was intact, but his soul was nowhere to be found. I hadn't thought it was possible for someone to survive without a soul, but then again, I was a walking impossibility myself. Aiden's presence meant Keir couldn't leave Edinburgh, especially as there was still the slim chance that the mages knew something about where Aiden's soul might be.

Yet another reason I needed to leave Lord Sutherland alive—for now.

"Good luck," Isabel said, as the forest disappeared, leaving us on the bridge outside Edinburgh's abandoned train station.

I drew in a breath of bitterly cold air and took in the sight of the city's peaked roofs, the castle on the hill overlooking the city, the grey sky. *Home.* I was home.

And possibly the most wanted person in the entire city.

3

Walking through Edinburgh's streets to Keir's apartment, I felt more ghostlike than my night-time jaunts through the mages' head-quarters, a stranger in the city I'd called home for the last seven years. I pulled up my hood, hoping the bulk of my winter coat would make me harder to recognise. I'd also removed my lip piercing but didn't bother with a disguise spell. If I ran into any senior necromancers, they'd be able to see right through to me in the spirit realm no matter how good my disguise might be.

I slowed as I reached the cul-de-sac where Keir lived, starting to regret my spurt of recklessness. Aside from Lloyd, Keir was the person I'd missed most in my exile, but being near him doubled the target on both our heads. His midnight visits every couple of days ought to make up for my lack of contact, yet I missed him in the same way I missed the necromancer guild.

The door opened a moment after I knocked. "Jas?" Keir's eyes widened. "You shouldn't have—"

"Fuck shouldn't." I was over the threshold and had my arms around him before he could say another word. He pushed the door closed with one hand and used the other to cup my face as he kissed me. A familiar coolness brushed me from head to toe, and his touch, both physical and otherwise, conjured memories of the all-too-brief stretches of time we'd stolen for ourselves in the last few weeks. Moments in the dead of night, filled with whispers and touches that left me giddy with pleasure. Since I'd accidentally bound our souls the first time he'd fed on me, I was the only person capable of satisfying Keir's vampire side. Yet something in his touch satisfied me as much as him, and when we broke apart, his eyes were aglow, his face flushed.

He released me and stepped back into the hall. "I'm hardly going to throw you out, now, am I?"

"I hope not." I tensed at a faint creaking noise above our heads. "Does anyone live upstairs?"

"Nobody else is home, don't worry," he said. "The upstairs apartment is owned by some rich dude who hasn't been here in years, and he has a private entrance round the back, anyway. This is just an old house that creaks a lot."

He beckoned me through a door into his ground-floor apartment. The living room was fairly spacious, and while some of the furniture was a little battered, I'd seen much worse.

A slightly open door at the end of the living room revealed Aiden's bedroom, now occupied by his soulless body. Keir's shoulders tensed as he saw where I was looking. My chest went tight. "Is he—?"

"No change," he said. "None. I don't know how long

he's been unconscious for, but he should have died of dehydration or starvation by now. It's like he's in a kind of stasis. A magical coma."

He crossed to the bedroom door, pushing it fully open. The books on the shelves, the rows of hand-stitched puppets—every item in the room was unchanged since his brother's disappearance eight years ago. Aiden Langford lay on the bed, his dark hair brushing his shoulders. He and Keir had the same defined cheekbones and long eyelashes, but Keir was an inch or two shorter with broader shoulders and a more solid build courtesy of his martial arts training. Aiden looked younger from this angle, too, though part of that was because Keir looked like he hadn't slept in a week, with dark half-moons under his eyes and his cheeks dotted with stubble. He swallowed hard as he lifted his brother's pale hand. "He has a pulse."

I took Aiden's hand, tentatively. His skin was cold, but not as cold as mine when I'd spent hours in the spirit realm. His breathing was quiet, steady. Yet when I tapped into Death, the only spirit aside from mine within the room was Keir's.

Aiden's was gone.

"I tried to feed him," Keir said. "Tried giving him water, too. Didn't work. It's like he's under a spell, but I can't see the cause."

"I can check," I said. "I didn't think to, last time I was here."

"I wouldn't have asked it of you," he said. "I don't think it'll do him any harm."

I dropped Aiden's hand and held my palms out over his body, feeling for any signs of a spell. A tingling sensation rubbed my fingertips. Magic. Not Hemlock magic, but familiar.

Trembling a little, I pulled down the collar of Aiden's shirt, revealing a mark etched onto his skin.

Blood magic.

Keir stiffened. "He… no. He can't be one of *them*."

"He's not," I said. "He's alive. Not a zombie." The mark looked exactly like the ones on the reanimated zombies held together by witch magic, but his heart was still beating, signalling that he'd never passed beyond the gates of Death.

"Can you remove it?" he whispered.

"Honestly? I don't dare," I admitted. "He might die, if the mark is what's preserving his body. His soul needs to be reattached first, when we find it."

"All right." He carefully lowered his brother's collar again, concealing the mark. "I don't want to make things worse. But if it's the same magic Lord Sutherland used…"

"He didn't," I said. "He forced a bunch of witches to, but he's not capable of using magic like that himself. I can take a photo of the mark and text it to Isabel so she can ask Asher if he recognises it, if you like. It's more his area of expertise than mine."

I dug in my pocket for my notepad, then remembered I'd left it in my necromancer coat back at Lady Harper's place. As for the fancy sketchbook and paints Keir had given me for Christmas, they were in my old room at the necromancer guild. I hadn't dared break in to retrieve them, because if I did, the boss would realise I was still alive.

"Ah—have you got a pen and paper?"

"Sure." He crossed to a set of drawers and opened the

top one, passing me an old notepad with faded pages and a blunt pencil.

I copied the mark on Aiden's shoulder onto a blank page. Then I snapped a picture and texted it to Isabel before ripping out the page and shoving it into my pocket.

"Keep the notepad," said Keir. "It's not like you to leave your art materials behind."

I shrugged, looking at Aiden again to avoid meeting Keir's eyes. "They're in my room at the guild. You know how that goes."

He pulled the covers up to his brother's neck so he looked as though he was merely sleeping. "If only a few weeks passed for him, then he's still twenty years old. I was seventeen when he disappeared and I'm older than he is now. I don't know if he'll even remember his time in stasis when he wakes up—let alone his life beforehand."

"He will," I said, more confidently than I really felt. "Trust me. When we bring the mages down, we'll force them to tell us everything."

The mages knew how to contact the gods. Maybe they knew how to bring back a soul that was beyond reach.

"When we bring them down?" Keir said. "You have a plan?"

"I wish," I said. "I've been spying on them for weeks and it's like they just dropped their old plans. The registry idea is gone, and I thought they were dead set on it."

The mages had wanted to put every single supernatural in the city on a list—not a popular idea, since a fair number of people wanted to avoid detection for a reason. The children of the invasion, like me, had no birth certificates or any formal identification, which protected our lives but also made it easy for people to disappear.

Like the Briar Coven, and like Leila Hemlock. And now, me.

"Who knows what they're thinking?" he said. "They've dropped their plan to turn the shifters against the rest of us, then?"

"They had to," I said. "Vance and the others got rid of the pieces of Moonbeam stone and buried them miles outside the city. I saw Lord Sutherland last night and he was pissed off about it."

"Too bad," said Keir. "Pity they couldn't bury him along with them."

"They could be plotting to and I wouldn't know," I said. "I've been stuck in Lady Harper's junk-filled old house, dying of boredom. Oh, I did find out one useful thing, though. The Briar witches might be in a place called Foxwood. Know it?"

"Nope," he said. "Not in Edinburgh?"

"Doesn't look that way." My phone buzzed. "That'll be Isabel."

"I'll search for Foxwood online." Keir pulled out his phone and I did likewise. As I'd suspected, a dozen messages and missed calls that hadn't been able to reach me up in the Highlands had crash-landed at once. I scrolled through a dozen texts from Isabel and Lloyd. No recent replies from Isabel on the spell affecting Aiden yet, though.

"Isabel's at the market," I said. "I'm sure she'll get back to me later. I'm supposed to meet Lloyd at South Bridge."

"Now?" He lowered his phone. "No, Foxwood doesn't come up when you run a search. Maybe it's a magically hidden location."

"The letter that mentioned the address was written

pre-invasion, so the faeries might have levelled it." And to think I'd thought I'd finally found a decent clue.

"Are you okay, though?" He moved closer to me, his hand brushing my shoulder. "I wish I could see you in person. I hate that you're taking the heat for everything Evelyn did. Someone ought to have prepared you for the possibility."

"They believed the best of her." Even Lady Harper. I nearly told him she was the one who'd bound Evelyn to me, but if I got started on that, I'd be here all day. "Lloyd is waiting for me. I don't want him to get ambushed by zombies when he's out there in the cold."

"I'll come with you."

"I really don't think—"

"Not in person."

"Oh." I nodded in understanding. He'd be there in spirit, if nothing else. That was the next best thing.

I walked out of Aiden's room and crossed to the living room window, seeing movement on the other side of the curtains. The spirit realm filled my vision, and I stiffened. Three people stood outside Keir's apartment.

Mages.

4

I jerked out of view of the window, hoping they hadn't spotted my shadow behind the curtains. Keir walked into the room, hands in his pockets.

"Relax," he murmured. "I've done this before."

How can he be so casual? The mages were barely two metres away from us.

Keir's gaze went distant as he tapped into the spirit realm. Turning on my own spirit sight, I followed as Keir floated free of his body, through the wall of the apartment building and down the winding road towards the river. A moment later, two bodies rose from the water, rotting hands grasping the shore to pull themselves onto the cobblestones. On unsteady feet, they both staggered in the direction of the nearest house.

Smart idea. The zombies were far enough away not draw attention to us, but close enough to cause a stir. When the humans inside the nearby house started screaming, Keir disappeared. So did I, blinking back into my body in time to see the mages outside the window turning in the direction of the screams.

"Nice going," I said. "How many zombies do you have, exactly?"

"A dozen at a time," he answered. "They decay so quickly it's a pain, but they're good for a quick diversion. Also, if the mages got any closer, the security spell would have turned on. It's an illusion charm."

"I didn't sense a spell outside," I said. "Some witch I am. Where'd you get it?"

"Asher," he answered. "I paid him a visit the other week and bought one of those fake-brick-wall illusions. He wasn't keen to sell anything to me, but he knows about —Aiden." He faltered on the last word.

"I'll help him," I said. "I promised I would, and when we find the Ancients, we'll get him back."

"Sure." His tone was quiet, his usual confidence gone.

I exhaled in a sigh. "I really have to go, Keir. If they come back—"

"I've got this," he said. "You think I haven't made contingency plans?"

"I wish I could say the same," I said. "There's nothing I can do to stop them hunting me. Unless I declare my allegiance to Lord Sutherland, and even then, he'll never forgive me for attacking his son."

"We don't need his forgiveness," said Keir. "We need him behind bars where he belongs."

"Couldn't agree more." I pulled out my phone, relieved to find I had a signal. "All right, I'm warning Lloyd."

"They haven't been near your friends," he added. "That I know of. I've been watching through the spirit realm."

Lloyd picked up the phone. "Hey, Jas."

"Lloyd, I can't meet you on the bridge," I said. "Sorry. The mages are out in the open. They were close to Keir's house. We need to meet somewhere less conspicuous."

"Shit. Okay, come to… you know Ilsa's address?"

"Yeah, I do." I'd passed by her place on the way back from missions before. "Okay. Be careful."

"I should be the one saying that." He hung up.

I released a steadying breath. *Right. They're not hunting my friends. I hope.*

"Ready?" Keir hugged me, his warm arms enveloping me from either side. His lips brushed mine, a swift but intense kiss. I longed for his warmth again the instant he let go, but if I hung out here all day, I'd be putting both of us in danger. Not to mention his brother.

"I'd say I'll be back later, but I don't know how long I'll be able to stay in the city," I said. "The last thing I want is to draw attention to you."

"Don't worry about me," he said. "The mages assume I'm no longer living in Edinburgh. Whenever I leave my apartment, I use a disguise. Besides, I'm used to living on the edge."

"I'd be mad *not* to worry." I pushed up my sleeve, sifting through the array of bands on my wrist to find a shadow spell. Not my best work, but I had to be sparing with my ingredients since I didn't have a regular supply anymore.

The mages were gone when I walked outside, but I still pulled up my hood under my shadowy disguise. The one upside to the mages' incapability of being subtle was that I'd see them coming a mile off. They couldn't seem to help flaunting their magic, and unlike necromancers, they could be fooled by the simplest of disguise spells.

Ilsa lived on a road lined with neat terraced brick houses, an ordinary-looking corner of the city which seemed untouched by the impact of the invasion. I knocked on the door, turning off the shadow spell when Ilsa answered.

"Look who it is." She stepped aside to let me in, her dark brown eyes widening a little. "You look like hell warmed over, Jas."

"Cheers." I waved at Lloyd over her shoulder. Ilsa was about my age, tall and curvy with long dark brown hair and pale skin. "Had a run-in with a few mages on the way. Don't worry, they didn't see me. Lloyd, you didn't run into anyone, did you?"

"Nope. Staying out of trouble." He grinned and embraced me. "Meaning I'm staying here now, when I can. Ilsa has a spare room."

"If you ever need somewhere to crash," Ilsa put in. "We have a vacancy for a new housemate."

"Seriously?" I followed him and Ilsa into the living room, where a sofa and a couple of armchairs grouped around a flat-screen TV. "Won't the guild kick up a fuss?"

"They assume I'll use the spare room when my sister comes to visit," Ilsa said. "Anyway, you can come and stay here anytime. Nobody will come looking."

"I owe you one." Guilt over potentially getting Keir and his brother into trouble kept me from staying over at his place, but I wouldn't say no to a bolt hole inside the city to lie low in if the mages came after me.

"There's nobody else in aside from us at the moment," Ilsa said, walking to the kitchen. "Want coffee?"

"That'd be great. Thank you." I sat down next to Lloyd on the sofa. "A safe house. That's what this is, right?"

In case the guild is under attack.

Lloyd gave another shrug. "I guess, but the mages never come to this neighbourhood. They were at Keir's, though?"

"He caused a diversion before they got too close," I said. "He also used an illusion spell to hide the place. Sounds like he's been paying visits to Asher. You know, Isabel's friend."

"Friend," he said, with a trace of a smirk on his face. "She sure spends a lot of time over at his place considering she lives hundreds of miles away."

"She does?" The Hemlocks must have been really mad at me. Or Evelyn. Let's face it, Evelyn deserved most of the blame. Not only had she blown our cover, she'd opened the spirit line and set a giant dragon loose in the city as well. It'd be nice if Cordelia admitted I'd had it right that Evelyn was a loose cannon and acknowledged that I'd made an effort to stop her, rather than shunning both of us.

Ilsa walked over, carrying three coffee mugs, and gave one to each of us before settling in the armchair on my right. "Who are you talking about?"

"Isabel." I checked my phone. "That reminds me, I need to talk to her. Keir's brother… he's under a blood magic spell."

Ilsa's eyes went wide. "Really?"

"Damn," said Lloyd. "Like those zombies we fought?"

"Kind of, but he's not dead." Aiden's situation was unlike anything I'd ever seen before. "His soul is gone, but his body is still alive. I thought Asher might recognise the symbol I found on him." I pulled out the crumpled paper and showed it to Ilsa.

"Doesn't look familiar," she said. "When I said I used blood magic, I meant a blood summoning, not witchcraft. That's not the same symbol the zombies had on them, is it?"

"No, but…" I dropped my voice. "His body is still functioning and alive, but Keir said he hasn't aged in eight years. Either that symbol put him into stasis and stopped him ageing, or he got stuck somewhere time doesn't pass in the same way as it does here."

Ilsa put down her coffee mug. "You mean like Faerie? Some liminal spaces are like that, too. You can spend a few minutes there and find it's been days or longer."

"And the witches' forest," I added. "I guess that other realm is the same. I know it's a long shot, but I'm certain Lord Sutherland knows more than he's letting on. He summoned an Ancient right there in his basement."

A thoughtful look came over Ilsa. She had an incurable instinct for seeing everything in an academic light. "If he does, then the mages have resources the guild doesn't. I've been combing the archives for weeks, but I've found nothing about that other realm at all."

"The archives are falling apart without you there, Jas," Lloyd said. "We have a weekly vigil in your honour, and the boss has turned your room into a shrine."

"Pfft. Now you mention it, what did you do with all my stuff?"

On my instructions, Lloyd had brought me some of my clothes, but it'd have looked suspicious if I'd taken too many of my personal possessions with me to Lady Harper's house.

"Relax, I made sure nobody touched anything," Lloyd said.

I drew my knees up to my chin, my insides churning with sudden emotion. I'd left my sketchbook, my paints that Keir had given me... everything. No wonder I felt like I'd left part of my*self* behind.

"The boss asks Lloyd about you at least once a week," said Ilsa, picking up her coffee mug again and taking a swig. "She's good at hiding it, but she misses her best assistant."

"But she knows why I come back." I gripped my own mug in both hands, savouring its warmth. "I expected the mages to be lording it over her for harbouring a criminal at the guild."

"Actually, it's been fairly quiet," said Lloyd. "The mages stopped the active search for you after the first week."

"I'm insulted," I said. "I thought I was Edinburgh's most wanted criminal. I killed the Whisper *and* the witch Lord Sutherland hired to summon her."

"Maybe that's why," Ilsa said. "If you killed Lord Sutherland's best witch, he'll have had to go looking for alternatives. Not to mention you exposed your magic in front of the council. He didn't know about your Hemlock power before, but now he's got to be on guard in case you use it against him."

"You sound like Cordelia," I said. "Maybe you're right, but if we take him down, there'll be a power vacuum and someone worse might take his place. That's what Vance keeps telling me, anyway. Not to mention, murder is kinda illegal. Cordelia doesn't care, but she doesn't have to deal with the backlash. Killing him won't remove the death sentence on my head."

"Cordelia?" said Ilsa, a quizzical look on her face.

"Jas's evil grandmother," said Lloyd.

"More like great-great aunt," I said. "She seems to think I should just march into the mages' headquarters and slaughter the entire council. I don't know about you, but I doubt that would improve the situation."

"Definitely not," Ilsa said. "But I think there's something to the idea of proving Lord Sutherland's guilt in a public setting. Make everyone see him for who he really is. Have you been into the mages' place recently?"

I knew she didn't mean in person, since Ilsa was one of two people who shared my ability to walk around the spirit realm at will.

"Yes, but there's nothing incriminating out in the open," I said. "Lord Sutherland is pissed that the mages took away the pieces of Moonbeam stone. Oh, and he thinks Lady Montgomery has something he wants, but he didn't actually say what it was."

"The boss knows he's a bastard." Lloyd drained the rest of his coffee. "You should hear the shit she says about him when she thinks nobody can hear."

"Wish I could join in." I checked my phone. "Oh yeah—have you heard of a place called Foxwood?"

"Did you say Foxwood?" Ilsa said.

"Yes… why, do you know it?"

"Foxwood is the name of the town I grew up in," said Ilsa. "It's a village way up in the Highlands—supernaturals only."

Well, damn. "Lady Harper sent a letter there thirty-one years ago, to someone going by the name Briar. Aka, the coven that saved my life. Ring any bells?"

"No." Her brow wrinkled. "The town isn't on any maps, but the mirror… if I knew where it was, I'd take you there."

"What, *the* mirror?" I said. "I thought it led to the other world, where I found Aiden and Wanda."

"It does," she said. "But it used to lead to Foxwood, too. Do you know what the mages did with the mirror after the battle?"

"Didn't they tell you?"

She shook her head. "I guess I'm not important enough."

"Likewise," added Lloyd.

"Great." Just when life threw me a bone, the bone reanimated itself and smacked me in the face. "How did they expect me to find them, then?"

"There's another way," said Ilsa. "The Ley Line also links up to Foxwood, but... didn't you hear what the mages did to the Ley Line?"

My heart sank. "What... what did they do?"

"They kind of *own* it now," said Lloyd.

"I'm sorry, what?" I blinked. "You can't own the Ley Line. What the bloody hell did the faeries have to say to that?"

"They don't know," said Ilsa. "The mages are restricting their control to this city only—for now, anyway. There's some kind of upheaval in Faerie distracting everyone at the moment, too. But there are patrols on the Ley Line all the way from the beach to Arthur's Seat."

"Damn." My shoulders slumped. "I guess it's not urgent enough to risk getting arrested. The Briar Coven—the coven who raised me—might have lived in Foxwood over three decades ago, and I thought they might be able to help me figure out how to bring down Lord Sutherland. Plus, Lady Harper knew them, and I thought—maybe they could help me make sense of the clues she left behind when she died."

Ilsa's brow furrowed. "But you've never met them in person?"

"Not while conscious," I said. "They left the city right after I found out they existed."

Which suggested they hadn't *wanted* me to find them. Still, Lady Harper had trusted them, when she trusted so few people. That must mean something.

"We can check out the Ley Line," Ilsa said.

Lloyd made a noise of protest. "Not with the mages swarming around, you won't."

"Through the spirit realm," I added. "They won't see me. I rattled the chandelier above Lord Sutherland's head last night and he had no idea I was there."

I hardly believed he had the nerve to claim the country's largest spirit line for his own, as though it wasn't the site where the faeries had invaded this realm twenty-two years ago. I'd assumed he had more sense, but this was the same guy who'd summoned an angry god in his own basement. The problem was, his ridiculous actions would affect much more than just him and his fellow mages.

"We'll do it upstairs, in my room," Ilsa said decisively, rising to her feet. "Don't look at me like that, Lloyd, Jas knows the risks."

"Jas has an unhealthy sense of what counts as risky." Lloyd gave me a look. "She's risking life and limb being here in the flesh as it is."

"I'm aware of that," I said. "You can just chill out downstairs and watch a movie, and you won't even realise we're gone."

"Exactly," Ilsa said, checking her phone. "My brother will be over in a minute if you want company."

"I—" Lloyd cut off, the hint of a flush darkening his cheeks. "Sure, whatever."

I gave him a wink, but Ilsa didn't seem to notice the tension in the air. Maybe Morgan himself wasn't the only person oblivious to Lloyd's crush on him.

We walked upstairs to Ilsa's room, which contained what looked like half the archives stacked on the shelves.

"Did you borrow *every* advanced textbook the guild had?" I asked.

"Only the ones I was allowed to." She grinned a little. "Sorry, I still haven't found anything about… your little problem. If you're still trying to solve it."

"Evelyn?" I shook my head. "Looks like we're stuck together for the long haul now. I wouldn't mind undoing the curse binding Keir and me, but it's not a priority for either of us."

Ilsa walked to the bookshelf and picked up several candles. "We'll do it the proper way."

Lloyd snorted from behind me. "For someone who loves books, you never do things *by* the book."

There seemed little point in using a spirit circle to anchor ourselves when Ilsa boasted the title of the Gatekeeper between life and death, while I had two souls and couldn't be dragged beyond the veil as long as I was bound to Evelyn. But I helped her lay out the candles to appease Lloyd.

As we placed the last candle in a circle of twelve around us, the doorbell rang.

"That'll be my brother," said Ilsa. "Best get into the spirit realm before he follows us."

"All right," said Lloyd. "Good luck in there, okay? Don't go treading on any evil spirits."

The candles lit up when Ilsa snapped her fingers, and I shifted out of my body. Ilsa appeared next to me, floating before the bookshelves. The house disappeared beneath a grey haze as the two of us floated through the ceiling. A breeze stirred my hair, and I found myself smiling. Sure, the living city was my home, but this empty haven had claimed part of me, too.

"There." Ilsa halted on the spot, pointing ahead.

The Ley Line shone brightly, a beacon of light cutting through the city. Sparks of light danced over the line, a living current of magic. Even most rogue necromancers wouldn't dare try a summoning in a place where the walls between the worlds were thin enough that monsters from Faerie could cross over in a heartbeat. The Line cut through Arthur's Seat, travelling north along the coastline. In the opposite direction, it angled west, disappearing over the border with England.

Ilsa and I dropped lower, above the hilly peak of Arthur's Seat. "That's where I used to cross over to go home," she murmured, pointing to the grass below. "The mages decided to set up a base right there on the cliff and pissed off all the local half-faeries in the process."

Sure enough, instead of a group of Summer faeries, several mages stood clustered together on the hillside, wearing thick cloaks to stave off the cold. The mages were grouped together every hundred metres or so along the Line right up to the beach.

"They can't actually do anything to the Line, can they?" I twisted to face Ilsa in the air. "Mage magic isn't affected by spirit lines."

Witch magic was a different story. And necromancy, come to that. Even shifters could be forced into animal form by Ley Line surges, as I'd learned recently.

"Watch out," said Evelyn, her voice sharp.

"What now?" I turned on the spot, facing my second soul. "Is it Faerie?"

Her brow wrinkled. "No… it's not Faerie."

Ilsa hissed out an exclamation as a dark spot appeared on the Ley Line, growing larger. Then, a patch of blue light detached itself from the Line, heading in our direction.

Crap. That can't be good.

5

Ilsa swore, tensing next to me. A glowing symbol appeared on her forehead, flickering around the edges: the name of one of the gods, the one who supplied her Gatekeeper's power.

The glowing shape drew closer, forming the outline of a humanoid shape with wing-like shapes extending from its shoulders.

"What the hell is that?" I whispered. "That's not a shade, is it?"

"No, it's a wraith," Ilsa said. "The mages screwed up the spirit realm when they claimed the Ley Line, so Faerie's ghosts are crossing over."

"I'm sorry, did you say that thing is a *faerie* ghost?"

"Yes, and regular necromancy won't work on it. I'm gonna have to deal with this one." Ilsa floated towards the glowing shape in the sky. "Hey, dickhead, over here!"

"Gatekeeper," said the wraith, in a guttural voice, sending a blast of vivid blue energy in our direction. It bounced clean off Ilsa and hit me instead. I flipped over in mid-air, winded, icy magic tingling in my bones.

"Sorry," Ilsa said over her shoulder. "Forgot to remind you—it'll still have the faerie magic it had when it was alive, and I'm immune to it."

Oh, bollocks.

I'd fought a wraith once before, but all I'd been able to do was hit it with kinetic power from a distance. Granted, I hadn't known I had Hemlock magic at the time, but I'd be a fool to let my magic anywhere near the Ley Line. Who knew what else might come out?

A bolt of energy blasted from Ilsa's hands, knocking the wraith back. I moved to her side to help out, but as I did so, my Hemlock magic flared to life with a crackle in my fingertips. Not directed at the wraith, but at Ilsa.

Whoa. I wheeled backwards, cutting an accusing look at Evelyn. "What the bloody hell are you doing?"

"I'm not doing anything." She floated free beside me, magic igniting in her own hands. "It's your fault for allying with people who willingly use the magic of our enemies."

"Ilsa isn't our enemy, Evelyn." My hands grew brighter with pulsing magic, drawn like the point of a compass towards Ilsa. Crap. *Stop that!*

If I got too close to her, my magic might actually hurt her. Evelyn didn't seem to be concerned with collateral damage at the best of times, and she'd been seconds from wiping out the entire mage council during our interroga-tion before Vance had teleported us out. This time, nobody could drag her away if she decided it was worth the risk of hurting our ally. I alone had any leverage over her.

I grabbed Evelyn's arm with a firm tug, pulling her backwards. She shot me a furious look, squirming out of my grip. Bursts of light came from below and I dropped my gaze. The wraith hadn't come alone. Three other glowing spots covered the slope of Arthur's Seat, and the mages conjured fire and lightning to fight against them. None of them paid me or Evelyn the slightest bit of attention, but Evelyn dropped in mid-air, her gaze fixed on a new target.

I flew lower, too, spotting a familiar sneering face beneath a mop of straw-coloured hair.

Neil Sutherland.

A spasm of hatred shot through me. He'd tried to murder Keir and I'd hit him with my Hemlock magic in retaliation, which had been the final catalyst to the death sentence on my head.

You tried to kill Keir, you bastard.

My hands tingled with power, and I fought the impulse to land a hit on him from above. As he fought the wraith, the swirling currents of the Ley Line rippled inches away from him. Damn, it was too risky. My magic added to a volatile spirit line was like dropping a firework onto a packed street.

Evelyn appeared beside me, taking aim. Magic poured from her hands and crashed into the wraith, sending it reeling back away from its target. Neil's eyes widened, and Evelyn readied another attack. The spirit line trembled, the flow of energy disrupted.

"Evelyn, don't hit the Line," I hissed. "Do you *want* another faerie invasion?"

"I want him dead," she said.

A torrent of power left her hands—heading directly

for the barrier between Faerie and Earth.

The Ley Line rippled, and I flew into the path of the magic, conjuring a shield. The two streams of energy collided, sending me flying back into the current of energy. I flipped head over heels and managed to still myself, but the battle raged below, undisturbed.

Evelyn whirled on me, her eyes blazing. "You bitch."

"I want that prick dead as much as you do, but I won't wreck the Ley Line to do it, Evelyn," I said. "You're not thinking clearly."

Dealing with the Ancients was impossible enough without provoking a war with Faerie on top of that. Evelyn should know better, but her furious magic continued to spark in my fingertips. Below, Neil had resumed his attack against the wraith—and he had company. My whole body went still at the sight of the cloaked figure approaching his son.

Lord Sutherland.

The tall mage moved at a brisk pace for someone who was at least seventy, his long cloak brushing the ground. The wraith turned on him, and a thrill of dark anticipation stirred inside me. *Go on. Finish both of them.*

The Mage Lord walked right up to the wraith and spoke a word, but the wind snatched it away. An instant later, the wraith turned around and was gone in a flash, as though fleeing a pack of hellhounds.

I remained still, mouth open in disbelief. *How did he do that?*

Ilsa's voice snapped me out of my shock. "Jas—we can't stay here. The boss is coming."

I dragged my gaze from Lord Sutherland and spotted another cloaked figure below. Lady Montgomery strode up the hill, approaching the Mage Lord and his son. I held my breath, sure she'd look up and see me, but she had eyes only for Lord Sutherland.

"We have no need of your help, Lady Montgomery," he said to her. "As you can see, we've dealt with the trouble."

"I'm glad to see it," said Lady Montgomery, in tones that suggested she wasn't. "We've had trouble with wraiths before, so I saw fit to send some of my people out here to check the Ley Line. I trust the extra patrols won't be a problem?"

"Do what you must," he said, waving a hand. "I understand that's your area of expertise… it must be useful, having one foot in both worlds at the same time."

"Bet he wants the spirit sight," Ilsa whispered in my ear, having apparently given up on her plan to get out of the boss's line of sight.

"I suppose," said Lady Montgomery icily. "I received your invitation this morning. Might I save time by asking you to explain what you wished to discuss with me rather than coming to see you later? I have quite a busy schedule to handle today."

"Why, of course, Lady Montgomery," said Lord Sutherland. "I assume you know there's a certain item which rightly belongs to the mages, and which the guild is known to have in its possession."

"Really?" Her tone remained as icy as a lake in winter. "I'm afraid I have no idea what you're talking about, Mage Lord."

"Pity." He shook his head. "Remember all that we have given you. We can withdraw that support just as quickly."

Lady Montgomery's shoulders tensed. She glanced up —and I blinked hard, willing myself to return to life.

I took in a deep breath, returning to consciousness in Ilsa's bedroom. Twelve faintly burning candles came into focus and I twitched my fingers, rubbing my hands together to get some sensation back into them. Beside me, Ilsa straightened upright.

"That went well." Ilsa stepped out of the circle and started to pick the candles up. "He's such a slimy old toad, isn't he?"

"Tell me about it." I helped her retrieve the candles, my numb hands fumbling. "He's blackmailing her."

"Relax, she's heard his bullshit before," Ilsa said. "As long as he doesn't actually *use* the Ley Line to summon anything, he's in the clear."

"Then how did he banish the wraith?" I returned two candles to Ilsa's bookshelf. "I didn't see him use magic. He just said a word."

"An Invocation," Ilsa said. "I'd bet my talisman on it."

"What, the name of one of the gods?" A chill raced down my back. He knew one name already—the name of the Whisper. And like in necromancy, if you knew a god's name, you could summon them. *Un*like in necromancy, just saying the word could destroy a person's mind, body and soul all at once. Lord Sutherland shouldn't be an exception, but it was hardly the first time he'd meddled with forces beyond his limited understanding.

"Maybe," Ilsa said. "What does he think Lady Montgomery has that belongs to him, though?"

"I..." I froze, my hand on the last candle. "Who do the Council of Twelve trust the most? And where's the safest place in the city to store a dangerous artefact?"

Her eyes rounded. "You don't think...?"

"I'm almost certain." The mirror formed a direct link

to the realm where the Whisper had come from: the realm of the Ancients. Of course Lord Sutherland would want to get his greasy hands on it after the Council of Twelves had moved it from sight.

"He might have meant some of Lady Montgomery's textbooks," Ilsa said. "They're valuable."

"He specified *one* thing at the guild that he wanted, and it sounded like they acquired it recently," I said. "If the mages try to take the mirror—"

"They won't, if they have any sense," said Ilsa.

"They summon and converse with evil gods. They don't."

"Fair point." She frowned. "What do you want to do? Take the mirror ourselves?"

"Can you imagine carrying that thing across the city in public?" I shook my head. "Guess that explains why he was so pissed about the Moonbeam, though. When the mages took the pieces away, they cut off his link to the gods' realm."

Aside from the pieces of the shattered Moonbeam, the only path into the other realm was the mirror. Maybe that was why Lord Sutherland's world domination plans appeared to be on hold, his claiming of the Ley Line aside. He needed to take back possession of the mirror to get what he really wanted.

"What exactly did he say when you eavesdropped on him last night?" she asked.

I thought back. "He mentioned giving the boss an incentive to hand it over. Whatever *that* means."

Someone rapped on the door. "Hey, we know you two are back," said Lloyd. "Let us into your top-secret meeting."

"It's not secret," said Ilsa, opening the door.

"Sure, like I believe that." Next to Lloyd, Ilsa's older brother Morgan peered into the room. He had the same dark brown hair and eyes as his sister did and while he'd gradually lost the gaunt, starved look he'd worn when he'd first shown up at the guild from living on the streets, his necromancer cloak still hung loosely on his thin frame. "Go on, tell us."

"Nothing to tell." Ilsa stepped out of her room. "Come on, let's head back downstairs."

"I'm not going to mess up your stuff, Ilsa," said Morgan.

"The last time I left my room unlocked, you decided to leave half a zombie on my bed," she said.

"You put a zombie in your sister's room?" Lloyd laughed all the way downstairs. "Nice going."

"Half of one. I couldn't leave it outside, could I?" Morgan sprawled on the sofa, propping his feet against the cushions. "Anyway, Mackie is being a bloody nightmare. I have to keep hauling her back from wandering near the Ley Line whenever she has a spare moment."

"Ah, crap," I said. "What's she doing that for? Because the mages are there?"

"Pretty much," he said. "She's pissed off about Lord Sutherland, and at this rate, she's going to snap and get herself arrested."

"I guess she didn't listen to my last lecture." Ilsa sat down in an armchair. "I tried talking her out of it, but it's hard to when she's right."

"No kidding," I said. "This fugitive crap is wearing thin. The mages are going after Lady Montgomery and I don't think they particularly care if they cause any damage to the rest of the guild in the process."

"What?" Morgan sat upright. "Nobody told me they were going after the boss."

"Because we just found out a few minutes ago," said Ilsa. "You can't tell Mackie. Not a word. You know why."

His mouth thinned. "Right, right, I'm the untrustworthy psychic. What made them choose to go after her now?"

"They need something from the guild," Ilsa said. "The mirror."

"Oh, shit, that thing?" Lloyd said. "I didn't know it was at the guild."

"I'm certain that's what Lord Sutherland wants," I said. "That's why he's holding back. I bet his resources were left in the other realm, and we took away his means of getting there."

"And he thinks he can walk into the guild and steal it?" Lloyd said incredulously. "Yeah, no, that's not happening."

"He won't do it himself," I said. "He'll send some underlings to try to bribe or threaten her. So we need to get in there first."

"You mean, us," Morgan put in. "You're—"

"A fugitive. I know." I nodded to Ilsa. "Can you find the mirror and protect it?"

"All right." Determination gleamed in her eyes. "I think our best bet is to lay a trap. Then we can hand the mages over to the boss, force a confession—"

"And they'll go right to jail," Lloyd said. "I'm not on the guild's rota today, but I can volunteer for something so the boss lets me patrol outside the doors."

"Won't the boss be suspicious?" I asked. "I mean, it's

not like you've ever volunteered for an extra mission in your life."

He stuck his tongue out at me. "Not all of us can be suck-ups."

"Didn't do me much good in the end, did it?" I rolled my eyes. "Whereabouts might Lady Montgomery hide an incriminating artefact?"

"In the dungeon," Morgan said. "She posted guards outside the front, but not the side entrance. It has its own protection, but Ilsa can get through it."

"You can?" I asked her.

"Yep. Perks of being Gatekeeper." She pushed a strand of hair out of her eyes as though to unconsciously trace the mark that appeared on her forehead whenever she entered the spirit realm. The mark of an Ancient.

My magic almost reacted against her.

It wasn't the first time my Hemlock powers had been triggered by an Ancient. It'd reacted against the Moonbeam pieces, but it'd never tried to strike down a person before. Both Ilsa and Ivy had talismans containing power belonging to the Ancients, and if my Hemlock magic decided *they* were the enemy… that could cause problems.

"What about you, Jas?" asked Lloyd.

"I'm going to the mages' place first," I said. "It's not warded against spirits and they won't know I'm spying on them. I'll tell Isabel first, though. Oh, and Keir, too."

Isabel still hadn't replied to my message about the blood magic symbol on Aiden's body, but we had bigger problems now. If the mages got back into the Ancients' realm, they wouldn't need the witches. They'd have all the power they needed to wipe us out.

6

"You're mad," Isabel said.

"I knew you'd say that." I'd texted her my plan on the walk to the market, where I'd found her waiting in the mouth of the cobbled alley leading to Asher's shop. Meanwhile, Ilsa, Morgan and Lloyd had headed to the guild to have a look around and see where Lady Montgomery might have hidden the mirror and prepare for the mages' attempted robbery.

"Asher might be able to help you," she said. "C'mon, you can ask him."

We walked down the alley to Asher's shop. The wooden door lay at a slightly crooked angle, fixed back into place after the zombies and the mages had knocked it off its hinges. Asher had been drawn into our drama entirely by accident when we'd contacted him to identify the signature on the spells the mages had used to control the shifters against their will.

Considering the trouble we'd brought to his doorstep, I didn't blame Asher for scowling at me when I walked in.

He sat behind the desk, resting his elbows on the half-open book in front of him. "I thought you were a fugitive."

"I am," I said. "Don't worry, nobody followed me here. Have the mages been around? They're not making trouble for you, are they?"

"Not at all," he said. "They just see me as a harmless old witch."

"You're not that old." He hardly looked a day over thirty, though there were flecks of white-grey in his short dark hair. Yet despite that, his light brown skin had lost the greyish cast it'd had the last time I'd seen him. The healing magic Evelyn had used had slowed whatever curse had backfired on him.

He grunted. "Pain ages you."

"You're still fighting that backfiring spell?" I didn't quite understand why Evelyn had used her healing magic on him. Sometimes she could be surprisingly considerate... and then on other occasions, she decided to blow up spirit lines and invite angry dragons into the city.

"I'm helping him," Isabel added. "We've been able to make some improvements."

"This foul stuff." He waved a small bottle of liquid. "I owe my life to it, mind, but I don't have to like it. What are you here for, Jas?"

"Did you find out what that symbol meant?" I asked Isabel as much as him. "The one I texted you?"

"Ah." She shifted from one foot to the other. "Uh, I was going to ask, but... we got distracted."

Asher cleared his throat. I raised an eyebrow at her but decided I didn't want to know.

Pulling the scrap of paper from my pocket, I unfolded it. "This symbol."

Asher took the paper. "What's this from?"

"It's the spell on Keir's brother," I explained. "I think it's keeping him in some kind of coma, but I want to check what the symbol actually means before I try to mess with it."

"Ah," he said. "Yes, that does look like a binding, but not one I've seen before."

My brief rush of hope dissipated. "You don't know what it means?"

He shook his head. "I don't know every symbol, especially the ones that don't exist in public record."

"That doesn't mean no records exist, though," Isabel added.

Dammit. I'd bet the mages had their own secret book of symbols. Maybe I'd be able to find their resources on my trip into their headquarters.

"All right." I took the paper back and folded it over. "Got any spells for stealth? Wouldn't hurt to get a ward neutraliser, too."

Asher arched a brow. "Breaking and entering, are you?"

"Kind of." I weighed the odds, then said, "Suppose I found out the Mage Lord was guilty of a crime and wanted to prove it… what kind of spell would be able to hold him? Not kill him. Trap him. His magic is too strong for a regular trapping spell. And he's an earth mage, so he can probably break any other type of binding, too."

"Maybe try throwing a net at him?"

"It's not funny," I said, irked. "I thought you were the best at what you do."

"Oh, I am." He lifted a thick leather book from a shelf

underneath his desk. "As I'm sure you found out when you used my spell to destroy an Ancient."

"Your spell? I thought you got it out of that book." I indicated the leather-covered volume he'd pulled out. "Wait, you're not saying you use it yourself? Blood magic?"

"Did I ever say I didn't?" He turned over the pages, which were stained in the residue of old spells.

"I thought you said the enemy forced your friends to raise the dead using blood magic against their will, but nobody in their right mind would use it otherwise," I said.

"That's not what I said." He turned to a fresh page. "The Orion League forced the Bloodroot Coven to use their magic to commit terrible crimes. They were active blood magic practitioners before then, like my own coven. If you have an issue with that, you're welcome to find another witch."

"I'm in no position to judge anyone for using illegal magic," I said, "but—it's dangerous, isn't it? Was it blood magic which backfired on you and hurt you?"

"It was," he said, with a slight cough. "A miscalculation on my part. I do have a regular spell you can use to break into the mages' headquarters, but if you fail, no spell can prevent the mages from using their own wards to trap you."

"I'll risk it," I said. "If I don't catch Lord Sutherland and bring him to justice, he'll go after the necromancers."

"Why not leave the guild to handle the mages?" he said. "You don't work for them anymore."

"I owe them my life." Lady Montgomery and the necromancers had given me a home when I'd come to Edinburgh alone, fleeing the Hemlock name. They'd welcomed me, given me a purpose, and now thanks to Lord Sutherland, their lives were in danger.

"I may be able to put something together which will help," Asher said. "But it'll cost you."

"Not an issue." Thanks to the fortune Lady Harper had left me, money was the least of my problems. Pity it'd take more than cash to buy my freedom. The mages had the power of the gods on their sides.

Asher went into the back room to set up the spell, leaving Isabel and me alone in the front.

"Spending a lot of time together, huh," I muttered. "And you got distracted? Really?"

She ducked her head. "He's... not like any other witch I've met."

"I can't say I've met another witch who used blood magic and gave themselves a fatal illness as backlash," I remarked.

"That's not... okay, he did," she admitted. "But he's learned a lot since then. He knows what getting caught will cost him."

I was more concerned with Isabel getting caught, considering she wasn't local and didn't have her fellow coven members waiting to defend her.

"What do the rest of your coven think about all this?" I asked.

"They don't know," Isabel said. "They think I'm away on official Council of Twelve business—which is technically true, more or less. I left my Second in charge. She's good at her job."

I released a breath, willing myself to relax. Asher wouldn't talk her into breaking the law. Isabel was way more sensible than that. The only reason she'd left me instructions on how to use that blood magic spell was because it was the only way to kill the Whisper.

Still—Cordelia's words kept coming back to me. She *wanted* me to use blood magic. Granted, I was already a fugitive, and it was no secret that my coven was steeped in ritual magic—like the binding that'd saved my life, for instance.

Asher emerged from the back room and handed me a fresh spell. He must have been taking lessons from Isabel, because it was band-shaped and striped in red and grey.

"What does this do?" I turned the spell over in my hands.

"It's one of my illusions," he said. "Won't hide you from the necromancers, but it can be enhanced for four different stealth options that can trick most wards, even the ones the mages use. Just twist it to change from one mode to the other."

"Thanks." I fished in my pocket for my spare cash. Lady Harper had hidden fistfuls of twenty-pound notes all over her house, and I'd stuffed my purse with them before leaving.

As I handed the cash over, my phone buzzed. Nodding to Isabel, I stepped away from the desk and answered the call.

"Hey, Jas," said Lloyd. "We ran into a slight hitch."

"Oh?"

"The mirror's not here," Ilsa's voice said in the background.

"Wait, it isn't?" I dropped my voice as Asher gave me a curious look. "Are you sure?"

"I used my spirit sight to search the whole building,"

Ilsa said. "It's not there. Not in the boss's office either—Morgan went and looked."

"You might know it," I said. "Are they hiding it in another location? I'm going to the mages first, regardless. If they're not going to break into the guild, I'd rather find out *where* they're targeting before we try to ambush them."

"Meet you there," Ilsa said. "If you're sure."

"I am," I said. "I don't know what they're playing at, but we'll stop them."

"Damn straight," said Lloyd. "Catch you later, Jas. Don't get arrested."

"I'll try not to." I hung up. No time to waste. I couldn't think of anywhere safer than the guild's headquarters, but what else could Lord Sutherland possibly want to steal from them other than the mirror?

I pushed up my sleeves and took stock of my spell inventory: healing spells, cleansing spells, shadow spells, trapping spells. Nothing too complex, aside from the new illusion spell.

"Does it have a time limit?" I asked Asher.

"An hour."

"Then I'll use this one first." I twisted my spare shadow spell, my body disappearing and blending into the dark shop. I'd save Asher's illusion charm for the last minute, if at all.

"Call me if you need me," Isabel said. Doubt shone on her face, displaying her inner struggle about whether or not to follow me, but I refused to let my friends take the heat for my recklessness. Besides, I wouldn't be alone.

"Jas," Keir whispered in my ear. "Are you sure about this?"

"Nope." I ducked out of the shop. "But you know,

desperate times call for kicking the shit out of mage apprentices."

"Wish I could be there in person," he said.

I reached out through the spirit realm, searching for Neil Sutherland's presence. It was easier to track someone I knew well, but meeting someone once was enough for me to be able to recognise them in the spirit realm. Especially when they'd pissed me off as much as Neil had.

Sure enough, I found Neil standing guard outside the mages' front gate, a waiting target.

"I'll grab a vessel," Keir said. "Then I'll keep an eye out. The place has some heavy wards outside."

"Not an issue." My new illusion spell waited on my wrist, tingling against my skin. Tricking wards was difficult, but while Asher might be a little unpredictable, he knew what he was doing with witchcraft.

I left Asher's place, hurrying through the market. The shadow spell made me invisible to anyone without the spirit sight, which would be enough to get me into the mages' place without being spotted. *I hope.* I hadn't counted on the mirror not being at the guild, though. Where was it, then? Surely the mages didn't already have it... right?

I came to a halt when a dead man stepped out of the alley in front of me. "Hey," it said, in Keir's voice. "Nice to see you, Jas."

"Nice to know you're taking this seriously." My heartbeat quickened as the front of the mages' place came into view, along with the slight, straw-haired figure standing in front of the warded gates.

A bright presence pinged on my radar. Oh, shit. Necromancers.

Ducking into the alley with Keir's vessel, I held myself out of sight.

"They aren't high-ranked," Keir murmured. "They can't sense us."

"Still." Three cloaked necromancers were walking towards the mages' guild in full view. "That's not a patrol, is it?"

A sharp suspicion gripped me. Keir swore softly, as though he'd had the same thought. Then his vessel moved before I could hiss out a warning. The dead man shambled past the entrance to the mages' place. Neil gave him a cursory glance, but Keir had picked a vessel who resembled a normal human and not one of the mages, so the others would think he was a harmless onlooker.

Unless one of the necromancers turned around.

The three of them approached Neil. As he moved to let them inside the gates, I shifted out of my body, unable to help myself. I had to know what they were doing in there. Had Lady Montgomery put them up to this? Only the senior necromancers had been allowed into the mages' headquarters even before they'd upped their security and withdrawn from the Council of Twelve.

There was one other explanation: the mages had insiders at the necromancer guild. Which meant...

"Keir," I whispered to him, in the spirit realm. "They already stole it."

"Figures," he said. "What do you want to do?"

I don't know. If I went ahead with my stealth mission, the three necromancers might spot me through the spirit realm, but I'd know if they were high-ranked, and they weren't.

I turned on my spirit sight again, sensing the necromancers' glowing forms inside the mages' headquarters. I'd bet Lord Sutherland couldn't get anyone with any real talent to betray Lady Montgomery. She was too smart to allow traitors to join the guild's highest ranks.

A smile formed. "The necromancers won't stay in there forever. When they come out, we'll *convince* them to confess to their crimes directly to Lady Montgomery."

It'd make my entire year if the testimony of a group of novice necromancers led to Lord Sutherland's arrest.

"I like the way you think," said Keir. "Want me to lure them out?"

"Let me text Ilsa first. She's already on the way."

I sent her a message and then waited a few minutes before leaving my body and floating up to the gates again. The mages' headquarters was an impressive sight from the outside, a grand old house with tall balconied windows and wards flickering over its whitewashed exterior.

A shuffling sound behind me heralded Keir's presence —or rather, the zombie he'd hijacked. He walked right past the mages' place again with exaggerated slowness.

This time, Neil stepped forward. "Hey, who are you?"

The zombie moved closer, until it stood inches away from the mage apprentice. Then Keir made its head lift up and look Neil in the eyes, rasping, "Brains."

Neil yelped and jumped backwards into the wards. "Help! Zombie!"

"Who doesn't carry salt these days?" I stifled a grin. Arrogant mage apprentices.

Neil pressed a hand to the mage mark on his arm, then faltered at the last second, perhaps because it'd hit him that the Mage Lord wouldn't appreciate being called out to deal with a single zombie, considering the necromancers already in the building. Lucky, because I'd forgotten he was wearing that pesky mage mark. If the Mage Lord himself showed up before Lady Montgomery did, then our plan would fall to pieces.

Three glowing lights in the spirit realm moved, and the oak doors to the mages' guild opened wide. The necromancers hurried out of the mages' headquarters in pursuit of the zombie. *Where is Ilsa?* She was supposed to show up before they came out. If the necromancers spotted either of us, we'd have to start from scratch.

Keir had other ideas. Smoothly avoiding Neil's half-hearted strike, he lunged at the three necromancers as they passed through the gates. One of them dropped like a stone as Keir's vampire power drained him. The second cried out a warning, only for the zombie to punch him in the mouth. Neil yelped and hid behind the wards as the zombie dove at the third necromancer. I'd seen Keir knock out someone with ease and he could have put all three necromancers on the ground in seconds, but that wasn't the goal. He wanted to draw attention, and nobody could cause a stir quite like a mostly-invisible vampire.

"Excuse me?" Ilsa's voice rang out. *There she is.* "What are you doing so far from your patrol route?"

She strode towards the necromancers, accompanied by two other cloaked figures. Clever. She must have been gathering more witnesses. That way, the necromancers wouldn't be able to hide that they'd been having clandestine meetings with the mages.

"There's a zombie," said the necromancer who'd hidden himself behind the gate.

"The three of you couldn't take out one zombie

between you?" Ilsa raised an eyebrow. Of course, she could see Keir floating behind the zombie, but she didn't give him so much as a glance.

Neil's head popped up. "You're the Gatekeeper, right? My dad would like to have a word with you. Would you like to come in?"

That was unexpected.

"It's got to be a trap," I hissed at Ilsa, but she ignored me. The mages wouldn't make an overt strike against the Gatekeeper, would they?

Ilsa hesitated for a second. Then she nodded to the other necromancers and walked past the fallen cloaked figures to the gate. "All right."

What's she playing at? Maybe she couldn't resist getting a look at what the mages were doing in there. Lord Sutherland hadn't called any meetings with non-mages since he'd pulled Edinburgh's entire mage council out of the Council of Twelve, and he pretended the other super-naturals didn't exist most of the time. That he'd been secretly conspiring with necromancer apprentices proved he hadn't forgotten us, but he must know Ilsa would never side with him over the necromancers.

Ilsa walked up to the stone steps leading into the mages' guild. *I hope she knows what she's doing.* Then again, there was no refusing an invitation from the Mage Lord himself. Ilsa must be nervous, but she walked confidently into the wide hall, her head high. Above, the chandelier gleamed, filling every inch of the hall with light.

"In here, Ilsa." Lord Sutherland's voice drifted from a half-open oak door, and my skin crawled.

Inside the otherwise empty council room, Lord Sutherland sat at the end of a long table, for all the world like he was waiting for the council who had yet to show up. His hands gleamed with spells, designed to make him look young, fresh, and harmless. My hands curled into fists, and while I could literally put a hand through his skull as a ghost, I didn't want to distract Ilsa. If he laid a hand on her, though…

"Ah, Ilsa." He rose to his feet, a false smile on his face. "You must forgive me for giving no warning before inviting you to speak to me. When I heard you were in the area, I couldn't resist. It sounds like your boss keeps you under her thumb."

"I wouldn't say that," Ilsa said, her voice calm. "I'm employed by the necromancer guild and the Council of Twelve, and you opted out of working with both."

"Is that what your supervisor told you?" he said. "I can assure you that we made every effort to attempt to cooperate with Lady Montgomery. Most unfortunately, she was not receptive to the idea."

"I know," said Ilsa. "I was there, remember? She's opposed to the idea of listing all supernaturals on a registry, for one."

"Oh, that's old news," he said, waving a hand. "I wish to extend a formal offer of cooperation directly to the Gatekeeper, then. That's you."

He packed an alarming amount of condescension into those two words, like he disbelieved that Ilsa had won the position fairly. Her shoulders stiffened and her expression shuttered, her hands clenching behind her back.

"I'm afraid I don't understand what you're offering," Ilsa said. "If you're asking me to approve of your registry plan, I can't do that."

"That isn't what I'm asking, Ilsa," he said, his tone deceptively soft. *You utter slimeball.*

"Then what?" Ilsa asked.

"I find myself in need of the cooperation of someone with necromantic capabilities," he said. "I heard you're one of the best the guild has to offer, and a comparative newcomer. You might have heard the mage guild employs other supernaturals on occasion, if we feel they would benefit."

"If you're asking me to work for you, I already have a job."

"Rest assured, this won't take away from your guild responsibilities," he said.

Damn, Ilsa. If I was in her position, I might have said yes, if I didn't hate the bastard too much to hide it. But if she turned him down, who knew what he'd do to her?

His smile was as cheap as the spells he wore, while his spirit was the typical faint grey of a human without the spirit sight. Except for the glowing blue light in his pocket, which brightened by the second.

Oh, hell.

I'd seen that glow before... but I'd thought all the spirit devices had been destroyed.

He's carrying a live bomb. Ilsa must be able to see it if she turned on her spirit sight, but even the Gatekeeper had no defence against a device that could both absorb and unleash spiritual energy. Human souls included. Those traitorous necromancers *had* already stolen from the guild—but it wasn't the mirror they held.

The light grew brighter as I drew closer, wishing I could reach through the spirit realm and take the device right back. My magic sparked to life, and Lord Sutherland's gaze snapped up. "Who is in here? Who did you bring?"

Ilsa shook her head. "I don't know what you—"

"Ilsa, get out of there!" I shouted, as the doors burst open and three mages ran in.

"Sir? What's going on?"

Lord Sutherland turned on the spot, his enhanced features twisting. "There's someone in here who shouldn't be," he snapped at the other mages. "Get them out. Now."

"Jas," Keir whispered from behind me. "We need to go."

Without warning, my breath choked, coldness seeping through me. The world disappeared as I was wrenched back into my body, into deep water. Drowning.

7

I kicked my way to the surface, spitting out a mouthful of water. How had I ended up in the river?

"What the hell, Evelyn?" I spat out more water, grasping the side of the bank with both hands.

"I saved your life," she snapped. "Your shadow spell ran out and those mages were seconds from finding you. What in the name of the gods were you doing in there?"

"The Mage Lord was about to steal Ilsa's soul." I pulled myself out of the water, shivering, my waterlogged jeans clinging to my legs. "He had that damned spirit device— they *did* already steal from the guild, but it wasn't the mirror they took."

The mages had the means of stealing anyone's soul they wanted to. I hadn't realised any of the devices had survived, and I'd bet those traitorous three necromancers had swiped them right when everyone was distracted by my escape. Dickheads.

Activating a drying spell on my drenched clothes, I

looked around to get my bearings. Evelyn must have run like hell to get me away. I pulled out my phone, which was deader than a zombie. "Thanks for that one, Evelyn."

"What did you want me to do, let them catch you?" she said. "You're welcome, by the way."

"Did the other necromancers Ilsa brought with her at least call Lady Montgomery and report those traitors?" I asked.

"I didn't see," said Evelyn. "I was more concerned with saving your ungrateful neck."

Since when was she concerned enough to take over my body for the sole purpose of helping me? Either she was scheming again, or at some point in the course of our tumultuous partnership, Evelyn had come to actually care about me.

That might be just as dangerous for both of us as the alternative.

A hand grabbed mine, with the familiar cold touch of a vampire. I spun around, then sagged with relief. "Keir."

He floated before me in the spirit realm, eyes wide. "I thought they took your soul."

"Sorry I disappeared," I said. "You can thank Evelyn for that. Is Ilsa okay?"

"Yeah, she ran for it," he said. "She knew he had that device in his pocket, but if she'd tried to take it—"

"He'd have used it on her," I said. "I think he felt my Hemlock magic react, too, but it's not like he could see me."

"Good," said Keir, his jaw tightening. "We should go."

"Not to the guild," I said. "I should make sure the mages didn't send a tail after Ilsa."

I also wanted to know if Lady Montgomery had

managed to get a confession out of those three traitorous novices, but I'd come too close to exposing myself once already. Lloyd would be worried about me, and thanks to Evelyn, I didn't have a working phone.

"Who do you think gave him those devices?" I whispered to Keir. "He either stole them from the guild or he has another vampire working for him."

"I'd say the guild." He floated alongside me in the spirit realm as I walked. "There isn't a vampire who'd go within a mile of the mages these days."

"Hmm." The Soul Collector had intended to use those devices to unleash enough energy to break the spirit lines, eventually succeeding in sneaking into the Hemlock witches' forest so he could steal the Ether Converter—a talisman that functioned as a jacked-up version of the same spirit devices. While he and Leila Hemlock were long gone, it wouldn't surprise me if the mages had taken over the so-called Society of Ley Hunters. "I can't believe he tried to recruit Ilsa. I guess he wanted to take the Gate-keeper out of the picture, since her family's linked with the Ley Line."

"And she can spy on him," he added. "Maybe he suspected someone was hanging around the mages' place, unseen."

"Maybe, but it's not like he can prove anything." Anger on Ilsa's behalf made my hands tingle with magic. She was as much at risk as I was now. And unlike me, she hadn't openly done anything wrong.

"I think he's systemically getting rid of anyone who can stand in his way," he said. "If he can't recruit them, he'll kill them."

"Maybe you're right, but who might he go after next? Morgan or Mackie?"

By the time I reached Ilsa's house, the sound of shouting echoed from inside. I knocked on the door three times before Lloyd opened it and yanked me into the hall.

"Guys, stop yelling!" he said to the others. "Jas is here."

"For god's sake, be reasonable, Morgan," Ilsa's voice drifted out of the living room. *Good. She's okay.*

"I'd say it's a perfectly reasonable for me to be ready to kick that mage into next week," Morgan said at full-volume.

"Brilliant idea," Lloyd said, "but not now. The guy's surrounded by guards and has a weapon that can steal souls. Not to mention, some of our people are traitors."

"Did the boss lock them up?" I asked.

"They got hauled back to the guild, but they're crying and saying they didn't do anything wrong," said Ilsa. "Jas, where did you disappear to?"

"Evelyn took over my body," I explained. "She decided to jump into the river to hide, and now my phone is broken on top of everything else. Did you tell the boss Lord Sutherland tried to recruit you?"

"Yes," said Ilsa. "I did, and she sent me home so she could put those three twats through a grilling on why they were at the mages' place. I hope she dragged them into Death and left them there."

"They deserve worse," Morgan said, his face pale and his fists clenched. "He had that soul-stealing device right in front of you and you didn't run?"

"I didn't know he had it until I walked into that room," Ilsa said. "Yes, I knew the risks, but we had to find proof."

"I'll get proof, all right," said Morgan. He made to march out of the living room, but Lloyd caught his arm.

"Easy." Lloyd tightened his grip. "I get it, but can you think of any scenario where you go up against the entire mage guild and walk out in one piece?"

Morgan scowled, but let Lloyd pull him away from the door. "He tried to kill you, Ilsa."

"Recruit me," Ilsa corrected. "And you know, I bet I'm not the only person they'll try to recruit if that's the game they're playing now."

Morgan swore. "You mean they'll go after Mackie again?"

"They can't touch her at the guild," said Ilsa. "Lady Montgomery won't stand for it. Just—everyone, chill out, okay? I'm fine."

A buzzing noise filled the room. Lloyd cleared his throat and got out his phone. "Jas, have you heard from Isabel?"

"No, but my phone's broken. Why?"

"I think she's in trouble." He tapped his phone screen.

A staticky voice filled the room. "Lloyd, tell Jas… Asher…" Isabel's voice cut out.

"They went after her, too." The mages had targeted my friends in two directions at once. Cursing them, I checked on my spells, which had been lucky to survive being drenched in the river.

"Oh, so it's okay if she goes charging off but not me?" Morgan said.

"Jas is pretty much invincible," said Lloyd, though he didn't look happy. "We'll all go. Safety in numbers."

"It's the mages, I'll bet," I said. "At this point, I assume everything bad that happens in this city is their fault."

Nobody had any argument for that. I led the way out of the house, closely followed by Ilsa, Morgan and Lloyd.

"If it's him," Morgan said, "I'm gonna kill him this time."

"It won't be," said Ilsa. "Even he can't be in two places at once—and he's a coward at that."

"Coward or not, he's not screwing around," I said. "Even I can lose my soul—or one of them, anyway. Lloyd, are you sure—?"

"Nowhere's safe, Jas," said Lloyd. "Isabel's my friend. We're coming with you."

"All right. I'll get Keir." I tapped into the spirit realm. "Keir, you around?"

He appeared floating in front of me. "Jas, are you okay?"

"The mages—I think they attacked Isabel and Asher. Can you take a look?"

"Sure thing." Keir disappeared, while I turned off my spirit sight and hurried down the deceptively quiet street. I couldn't believe how quickly things had got out of hand. I'd barely been back in the city a few hours and already the mages had targeted me on multiple angles at once.

The four of us walked at a fast pace, stopping occasionally to check the spirit realm for any signs of an ambush. The market was a bustle of activity both in the waking world and in the spirit realm, preventing me from tracking Isabel—wherever she was.

"Damn, I can't sense her in there," I muttered to Ilsa as we crossed the cobbled street towards the huddle of market stalls that formed the witches' main trading area. "Too many people."

"Let me try this." Lloyd pulled out his phone and tapped the screen. "If she's close, we'll hear her phone."

Morgan stopped walking. "Uh, the sky is moving." He pointed up at the sky, and a shadow descended over the market, edged in green light. A wraith.

"Crap," said Ilsa, the mark on her forehead igniting. "I've got this. You guys find Isabel."

Screams rang out as the witches in the crowd spotted the approaching wraith, but I kept running towards them until a barrier brought me to a halt. Several undead lay in a heap on the rain-slick cobbles, caught in a tangle of trapping spells. Oddly, nobody had thrown salt onto them yet.

"Hey," Lloyd said to the witches gathered around the zombies. "I'm a necromancer. Need our help?"

"No!" said one of the witches, her voice frantic. "She's my mother."

"She's dead, Annette," said another witch in gentle tones.

"Someone raised her." She turned accusing eyes onto our group—especially Lloyd, who wore his necromancer coat. "Your people did this."

"We didn't," Lloyd said. "If there's a rogue out there, we'll catch them. Can you deactivate those trapping spells so I can put them to rest?"

The witch gave a despairing sob. My stomach turned over. It wasn't the first time we'd had to destroy the reanimated bodies of someone's family members, but it didn't usually happen in such a public setting.

The witches' trapping spells flickered, the red lines disappearing. Then the undead straightened upright, facing the huddle of witches. I glimpsed familiar symbols etched onto their collarbones.

Oh, hell. This was the mages' work, all right—not that the other witches would know that.

"Uh, guys, step back!" I warned the witches. "They're stronger and faster than normal zombies. Use salt, and do it quickly before someone gets hurt."

"We'll handle them," Morgan said, throwing a canister of salt at the zombies. Two of their bodies dissolved, but the glowing light surrounding their reanimated forms didn't diminish. A familiar cold sensation rose within me. I checked the spirit realm and found myself face to face with a tall, human-shaped shadowy form, his hands reaching for Lloyd.

"Vampire!" I yelled.

Lloyd staggered forwards as the vampire drained him, and Morgan crashed headlong into him from the side. Since the vampire was a ghost, Morgan passed right through him, and he and Lloyd both fell into a pile of dismembered zombie parts.

"Hey, dickhead." Keir appeared in mid-air, his own shadowy hands glowing with blue light. "You're not welcome here."

The vampire's form became clearer, his sharp grey eyes darting between Keir and me. "It's too late for all of you," he said. "Just like that witch, you'll die."

That witch. "Did you take Isabel?"

The vampire didn't answer. Keir grabbed him from behind, gripping tightly, draining his life force. "Tell me," he said, his voice low, measured. "Where is Isabel?"

The vampire squirmed, his body fading. "I don't... know..."

"I'll track her." Trusting Keir to finish off the vampire, I turned back to the market. Lloyd had staggered to his feet next to Morgan, the two of them armed with salt shakers against the disintegrating undead, who were still flailing and grabbing at anyone they could reach. Nobody deserved to suffer like that. I called Hemlock magic to my hands, directing it at the symbols burning in their skin. *Release them.*

The dead fell, crumbling as the last of the blood magic let them go. "I'm sorry," I said to the witches. "They won't rise again. You can safely bury them now."

"Burn the bodies," Lloyd added, his face ashen. "Otherwise they might come back." Inching closer to me, he hissed, "I thought you were keeping a low profile. Where's Isabel?"

"I can't see a damn thing in the spirit realm." The wraith's presence filled the air with bolts of green magic, and since Ilsa was immune, all its attacks did was bounce off her and smash into the already-collapsing market stalls.

Closing my eyes, I searched the spirit realm for any trace of Isabel's presence. A flicker ignited, and I took a step backwards. "I think she's outside the market."

Lloyd glanced at the sobbing witches. "I'll take care of the dead. You—find her, okay?"

"Incoming!" yelled Ilsa, and a haze of green light crashed overhead, knocking a market stall over. The wraith followed, its shadowy form eagerly seeking the life below. Ilsa ran up alongside me. Light gleamed from her hands and her forehead, and my own magic sharply changed directions, honing in on her.

Not again.

Willing my magic to calm down, I backed away through the market, searching for Isabel's trace. Then I felt it again—a spark of life, not far from here. I broke into a run, cursing my legs for not being as fast as my spirit form. *Isabel!*

I halted in front of a broken-down old shop which looked like it hadn't been in use since before the invasion. Barely pausing to breathe, I kicked the door open.

Asher lay sprawled face-down on the wooden floor in front of the entrance. My stomach lurched at the sight of the blood, a thickening trail surrounding his body.

And a second body, lying inert on the wooden floorboards. Around it, twelve candles glowed, keeping a transparent figure caged. A ghost.

Isabel.

8

"No," I whispered.

"Jas," Isabel gasped, locking eyes with me. "Don't—you're the one they're after."

"You're the one they—"

Killed.

Isabel's body lay in the circle, her spirit hovering above it. Nobody could survive separation who wasn't a necromancer. The instant the circle disappeared—

No. She can't be dead. I won't let her be.

A cold blast of energy slammed into me from behind. I spun around, and a creature appeared from the shadows —humanoid but emaciated, its hands replaced with clawed talons. Crooked wings stuck out at sharp angles from its shoulder blades.

What in hell is that? It almost looked like a fury, but bigger, and it hadn't made a sound when it sneaked up on me. Shadows curled around it like tendrils of smoke.

Magic burned my palms, forming an iridescent, shimmering whip. I lashed the creature's throat—only it wasn't there anymore. "What the hell *was* that?"

"Some horrible cousin of the furies," Isabel said. "It can turn to shadows—Asher!"

The monster appeared from the shadows beside Asher, turning his limp body over with a claw.

"Get the hell away from my friends," I snarled, my hands lighting up with Hemlock magic.

At the sight of my magic, the monster vanished, becoming shadow once more. Damn, that was one hell of an annoying power.

I scanned the spirit realm but didn't see any signs of the new fury. I *did* see a bright spark above Asher's body. He was alive.

I stepped in his direction, and the winged monstrosity appeared from the shadows, solid claws piercing me in the side. I yelled aloud, hoping my thick clothes had prevented the wound from being fatal. I couldn't afford to die again, not with Isabel still caught in the trap.

With a hoarse cry, I stabbed upwards with my Hemlock magic, only for the fury to disappear into the shadows again.

I let my magic return to my hands, burning with a shimmering light. If I couldn't track the monster through the spirit realm, then it must leave a trace somewhere.

Enjoy hiding in shadow, do you? Let's see how you like this.

I pushed up my sleeve, found a light spell, and activated it. Blinding white light filled the room, illuminating bloodstains on the hardwood, and a solid shadowy outline that shouldn't be there.

Calling my magic, I lashed out at the shrinking shadows. The fury screeched, caught in my trap. I twisted my hands and the whip wrenched off the monster's head. Blood splattered the bare floorboards, and it crumpled into a shrivelled heap. Its head landed at my feet, pit-like eyes still open.

Skin crawling, I lowered my hands. Pain pierced my side, like needles under my ribcage, but Asher needed my healing spell more than I did. I stumbled away from the body, seeing Isabel gaping at me from within the circle. *How can I get her back into her body?* Even a necromancer might not be able to save her, but I had to try.

"Help him first," she said. "I'll be okay."

I removed the healing spell from my wrist with shaking hands. Purple light flared up as I reached Asher, and he groaned. Two more bodies lay beside him, now visible in the light of the spell burning on my wrist. This must be the site of the ritual. Both bodies wore cloaks, indicating they belonged to the necromancer guild. The person who'd summoned that shadowy monster had sacrificed their lives in an instant. I gagged, turned away from the blood pooling on the wooden floor.

Asher stirred, and Isabel sobbed aloud with relief. *Now to save her.*

"Isabel," I croaked. "Hang on."

"Jas, heal yourself!" she said.

I stumbled over to the candles. "I have to get you back into your body."

"I'm fine," she said. "Jas…"

"No…" I whispered. My own voice was fading as well as hers. My vision blurred again, and nothingness embraced me.

———

No. I can't be dying...

Not again.

"Don't you dare," said Evelyn's voice. "If you die, we're both dead. Stay with me, Jas."

Greyness surrounded me. Not five metres away were the towering gates of Death, etched against the grey like exclamation The gates beckoned, calling me through to the realm known as Beyond along with the rest of the dead.

"Hey, I'm not dead." I skidded to a halt, with difficulty. My whole body hurt, which made no sense, because I didn't have one.

Evelyn hovered before me, her eyes narrowed. "Get away from those gates, Jas."

"I didn't come here on purpose." I felt weak, drained, like that vampire had sneaked up on me. Had that shadowy fury's claws done more than injure me?

"We're still alive, Jas," Evelyn said. "And we have a job to do."

———

I gasped, jerking awake on the sofa in Lady Harper's house. My head gave a throb, and so did my side. I groaned, curled in on myself, and looked up into Isabel's concerned eyes.

"You're okay." I squinted at Isabel. "You shouldn't be okay. Your soul was separated from your body. Even most necromancers can't survive that."

"I'm fine," she said. "You, however, are seriously lucky."

"I have nine lives," I said. "I might be the death of Lloyd, though. I have to get back—"

"Not a chance," said Isabel. "The others are fine—even Asher, the fool—but you're not to move until you've recovered. That creature's claw was laced with some kind of poison."

"Poison? Again?" I groaned. "I've officially died so many times I'm stuck on repeat."

"Lloyd told me not to be worried about you not breathing," she said, a note of sternness in her voice. "I'm glad he was right."

She handed me a glass of water and I gratefully drank it, my head resting against the cushions. I still wore my clothes from the day before, and the fury had wrecked all four layers and my only non-necromancer coat.

"I'm sorry I missed your call," I said. "Evelyn decided to jump in a river and wreck my phone."

"Sounds like her," she said. "It's my fault. I heard the ruckus at the market and tried to help out. That vampire drained both of us, and the next thing I knew, I woke up in that circle."

"So who was it who summoned the fury?" I asked. "There were three bodies there… necromancers."

"I didn't see," she said. "Keir killed the vampire and your other friends took care of the wraith and the zombies. They're all fine, Jas. You should be resting."

I pressed a hand to the tender skin over my ribs. "I showed my face at the market. If anyone saw me, they'll know I'm alive."

"I think you have bigger problems." Isabel looked haggard, like she'd been up all night. *I lost over twelve hours in the spirit realm. Again.*

"You're telling me." I sat up, rubbing the back of my head. "I think I went through a joyride through Death without even noticing. But you... you stayed here overnight?"

"I didn't want to risk leaving you here alone," she said. "You were in a bad way. I relit the fire... you're freezing cold, Jas."

"You carried me here?" I blinked. "You should be dead, you know. Since when were you secretly a necromancer?"

"Never," she said, her mouth pinching. Her eyes were tired, haunted. "I'm fine, Jas."

"Your coven magic can't stop you from dying," I said. "Right? Your soul was ripped out of your body."

"Temporarily," she said. "It was the only way they could stop me from using my coven leader's magic. Unlike you, I can't use it as a ghost."

I squinted at her sleeves, which were carefully pulled down. "Isabel, what did you *do?* Did you use blood magic? Is that how you survived?"

She hesitated a second too long. "I did, yes."

"Isabel, you know..." I faltered, not wanting to bring up what the Whisper had done.

"When that evil Ancient used me against my will?" she said. "I wanted to make sure it would never happen again. I knew my coven's magic wasn't a guarantee of survival. An Ancient's magic killed my original coven leader."

"Really?" I hadn't known the circumstances of Isabel's rise to the position of leader of her coven. "I'm sorry."

"I was powerless to stop it." Her eyes glittered with tears. "Besides, Asher told me this type of magic used to be commonplace before the invasion. The mages and everyone who associated with them might have wanted to spread the idea that blood magic has always been dark magic, but it's not true."

"I wouldn't call it evil," I said. "Just dangerous. But that's coming from a Hemlock witch, so…"

"Yeah, you can't talk." She rubbed her wrist in an unconscious movement and gave me a smile. "I know you're worried, Jas, but you can't protect everyone."

"Don't I know it." In her position, I might have done the same. "How did the blood magic bring you back from the dead, though? I didn't know it could do that."

"It didn't," she said. "I got the idea from Ivy. You know she and Vance wore those marks so that if he ended up under the enemy's control, she'd be alerted and the mark would stop him hurting anyone?"

"Yes…"

"I have one that reacts if I'm possessed or otherwise lose control of my body," she said. "It's set on a timer to give me a mild shock, which woke me up. If I ended up under the control of one of those runes again, it would do the same."

"Damn," I said. "I'd never have thought of that. Asher's idea? He's okay, right?"

"Yes, he is." Her mouth tightened. "He got hurt trying to save me from that monster. I'm the one the vampire and his friends targeted."

"Because of me?" I asked.

"No. They… well, they sensed the blood magic."

"What?" I yelped. "Isabel."

"I didn't know that, did I?" Her eyes gleamed with tears. "I'm sorry, Jas, I just… these aren't humans we're up against."

"I'm not blaming you," I said. "Believe me. I'm the walking nuclear weapon here. But if you have a target on your head because of that magic—"

"I'll be fine," she said. "My coven leader magic would have worked in any other scenario. Anyway, I'm not the one who died for twelve hours or more. Jas, I don't know if you actually do have nine lives, but you need to be careful with them."

Not sure that's possible. I'd drifted towards the gates of Death without being aware, and every time I went into the spirit realm, I lost more time. Maybe my nine lives had a limit after all.

If I died for real, what would happen to Evelyn then? And Keir?

"I'll keep that in mind next time a monster from another dimension tries to turn me into wallpaper." I swung my legs over the sofa's side. "I need to clean up. What time is it?"

"Seven in the morning," she said. "You're not going back to Edinburgh, are you?"

"No, I'm going to shower. Want to borrow some of my clothes? They should fit you." Isabel was an inch or two taller than me, but she had a similar build.

"I'll be fine," she said. "I'm staying in a hotel while I'm in Edinburgh. I'll change when we get back."

"If you're sure." I traipsed to the bathroom after picking up a clean outfit from my rapidly shrinking pile of clothes.

Once I'd washed the blood off in the shower, I checked on my wound. The bleeding had stopped, and in an hour or so, I'd be fighting fit. Not that I looked that way. I rubbed steam off the mirror, frowning. How could I have such heavy circles under my eyes when I'd been asleep for so long?

"I'm not dying," I told my reflection. "I have a job to do.

Like Evelyn said." Speaking of whom… "Hey, Evelyn. You there?"

No reply. I tapped the spirit realm and found myself alone. Where was she?

I finished dressing and ran out of the bathroom. "I think Evelyn's gone walkabout again."

Isabel frowned. "Is she in the forest, do you think?"

"Worth checking." Evelyn had saved my life, and yet it disturbed me how off-balance I felt without her snarky presence at my side. She hadn't helped me out during the fight with the shadowy fury, and it wasn't unusual for her to disappear for a while, but after my experience at Death's gates, being without her made a pit of unease open in my stomach.

Once I'd put on my coat—opting for my old necromancer cloak, since my spare coat had been skewered by the fury's claws—Isabel and I left the house. Our footsteps crunched in the frost-covered grass. "A goblin attacked me last time I was here. Cordelia implied something weird is going on in Faerie, too."

"Oh, that's Ivy's area," said Isabel. "Yeah, an uprising of sorts in the borderlands. Shouldn't affect things here, but if they attack the Ley Line, the mages will take the hit."

"I have no idea what they're thinking, trying to claim the place as their own." I shook my head. "The mages barely survived the last war with Faerie. Surely even Lord Sutherland isn't that much of a fool."

Isabel made a small noise. "I'm starting to suspect he might have contacted one of the other gods."

"Question is, which?" I halted on top of the shimmering spirit line, running through the hillside. "All right, no funny business this time, Cordelia."

"She didn't give me any trouble earlier," Isabel said. "Cordelia?"

The hillside vanished, transforming into the dark cave. Green light filtered in from the glyphs snaking along the walls like living spiderwebs, and Evelyn floated in front of Cordelia.

Both of them stopped talking when Isabel and I appeared next to them.

"There you are, Jacinda," said Cordelia.

I turned to Evelyn. "You might have warned me before you ran off. Since you know, we both nearly died last night."

"I was most concerned to hear the news, Jacinda," said Cordelia. "Evelyn has told me of her experiences yesterday."

"*Our* experiences," I corrected. "I was there, too, remember? What was the deal with that shadowy fury?"

"The beasts from the otherworld are awakening," she growled. "Some were banished thousands of years ago, some more recently. Others still may exist in other realms, in liminal spaces… pieces of their power lie scattered around, even in the faerie Courts, as your friend Ivy Lane knows well."

"Oh, that's just bloody perfect," I said. "How are normal people supposed to defend themselves against those monsters? I can't stop them now the mages are marching around the Ley Line like they own it."

"Then you must bring the mages to justice as soon as possible," she said. "It's imperative that you stop Lord Sutherland from waking the gods. Why did you not challenge him when you had the chance?"

"Because Evelyn stopped me." I cast her a disgruntled

look. "Besides, Lord Sutherland is carrying one of those soul-stealing devices—you know, the imitations of the Ether Converter. And he tried to recruit Ilsa, too. Why would he need her on his side?"

"To ensure nobody opposes him, perhaps," she said. "He cannot see the forces of life and death, nor grasp a fraction of the power you have, Jacinda."

"Look, there's only one of me," I said. "Okay, two, technically, but I'm being attacked in multiple directions at once. Cordelia, why in hell did you decide creating symbols that can summon shadowy monsters was necessary? Are you and the furies poker buddies on the weekends?"

Isabel shifted beside me. "That ritual isn't just a summoning," she said. "It's also for communicating. Like necromancy. Isn't it?"

"Communicating?" I whipped around to face Cordelia. "That was a joke, but did you and the furies—?"

Her expression stilled. Silence filled the cave, and words rose to my tongue. Words which, if spoken, would change everything.

"The Ancients weren't always your enemies, were they?"

Cordelia didn't respond.

"You and the Ancients had a falling-out and started a war, didn't you?" I asked. "*That's* why you're being so stingy with information. You used to work together. You and the Ancients."

I should have guessed. Their bitter history went back a thousand years. The last war had led to Cordelia and the others being eternally imprisoned in rock and tree. Yet they were both forces of nature, wild and unrestricted.

My magic reacted with familiarity when faced with another Ancient's power, and hatred that deep-seated didn't spring up out of nowhere.

"The origins of the conflict do not matter," she said. "All that matters is bringing the Ancients' attempt to take over the magical world to an end."

The cave began to fade. *Oh, no you don't.* "Hey!" I shouted. "You're running away again, aren't you? What are you afraid of, Cordelia?"

"Jas," whispered Keir's voice.

I spun on the spot, the forest fading around me. "Keir? Are you okay?"

The cave disappeared, leaving me stranded in Edinburgh. I reached out for Keir, and found nothing, the merest trace of his presence.

No. There must be a mistake.

I tried again, and his spirit appeared, then blinked out. Like he was dying.

"Evelyn—tell Isabel I'll be back!" I didn't wait for her answer, but I broke into a run across Waverley bridge, towards the flickering trace of Keir's presence.

9

I kept running, my feet pounding on the pavement. Keir's presence flickered on the edge of my vision, barely alive.

I reached his flat and hammered on the door, but it didn't open. I called my magic, coaxing the wards to move, and let myself inside. Closing the door behind me, I followed the faint flicker of light and found Keir crouched beside his brother's bed. His eyes were closed, his body still.

I plunged into the spirit realm, following his fading presence. To my alarm, Keir hovered on the brink of Death's gates, the same way I had when Evelyn had woken me up this morning.

"Jas," he said, his voice quiet and echoing.

I caught his hands in mine. "Shit. I'm sorry. I did this somehow… you have to come back with me."

My vision flickered as he drained me, fast. The world turned cold. Ice flooded my veins, and my knees hit the floor, my heartbeat slowing. I'd given too much already.

I was going to die.

No... stop.

Another pair of cold hands shoved me aside. Evelyn took my place, and Keir's vampire touch latched onto her. Gradually, faded back into view in the spirit realm, his features becoming clearer.

In the real world, my eyes flickered open. I'd fallen to my knees beside him. I took his hand, which was still icy cold, and gave it a squeeze. "Keir?"

"He's fine," said Evelyn. "Give him chance to recover before you start shaking him."

"He nearly died." I shivered, horror coursing through my blood. "How—how did that happen?"

"If I had to guess, it might be because you spent most of last night half-dead," she said. "It pulled him close to the edge, too."

"But—it's not the first time I've died since we were bound."

I wrapped both of my arms around him, sharing what little body heat I had to spare. *I can't keep doing this.* Courting death alone was bad enough, but with Keir's life tethered to mine, and Aiden dependent on him... Evelyn was wrong. I couldn't untangle my life from my friends' if I tried.

"Let me guess," I said to Evelyn. "You already knew the Hemlocks and the Ancients used to be friends and not mortal enemies, didn't you? Cordelia told you."

"I guessed, like you," she said. "Also, I had more than twenty years to ruminate in solitude on the relationship between my coven and the gods."

"All right," I said, surprised at her snappish tone. "This is all new to me, you know. I guess they thought I'd be even less likely to embrace my role as the Hemlock heir if I knew the truth. How far back does it go?"

"I've only been around for a few decades, not centuries," she said. "I only know as much as Cordelia told me. The Ancients tried to destroy this realm over thirty years ago, and in preventing that, Cordelia and the others were bound to the forest. As for their prior history, it's irrelevant."

"I wouldn't say that," I said. "Since their history is what *started* this mess. I sure as hell didn't. Nor did you. Why do you think it's your duty to end it, then? What's in it for you? Even if we win, we're still bound together."

Her eyes narrowed. "I have never had the luxury of choice, Jas. My entire life revolved around being the Hemlocks' heir. I never expected the responsibility to rest entirely with me, as I wasn't the only Hemlock witch with magic. I'm just the only one who survived."

Her words dripped with bitterness. I could understand where she was coming from. She'd been alone for a long time, bound to me but unable to interact with the waking world. No wonder she'd lashed out and tried to steal my body not long after she awoke.

Keir groaned, sitting upright. "What in hell just happened?"

"Keir." His name stuck in my throat.

Evelyn gave me a long look, then disappeared. It wasn't the first time he'd fed on her instead of me, but an unpleasant feeling stirred inside me.

"Jas." Keir leaned towards me. "Are you okay? What are you doing here?"

My voice was quiet, my heartbeat quick. "You nearly drifted through the gates of Death. Because of me."

"I wasn't dreaming?" He rubbed the back of his neck. "Last thing I remember, I was sitting here watching Aiden. I must have fallen asleep."

"Doesn't look very comfortable." I indicated the wall he'd been sitting against.

He shrugged. "I sometimes think I hear noises from Aiden's room during the night. Anyway, I prefer to stay close to him in case we have to run."

"Nobody followed me here, don't worry." I drew in a slow breath. "Keir, I don't understand why you were affected, but it's got to be a side effect of being linked. I'm sorry."

He took three steps, closed the distance between us, and wrapped his arms firmly around me. "It's not your fault, Jas. Don't ever think that."

I hugged him back, vowing never to come close to death again. It really shouldn't be that hard, considering most people managed to avoid it. Lloyd was wrong, I didn't have nine lives, I had nine *deaths*. I glanced at Aiden, my chest tightening. If Keir died before seeing his brother wake up… *no*. I would never let that happen.

"I remember killing the vampire, but that's all," he said. "What tried to kill you?"

"A monster that looked like a fury but could blend into the shadows." I released him. "I can draw you a picture."

"No thanks." He smiled. "I take it you didn't come all the way here in the flesh just to save me from certain doom?"

"No…" I trailed off. "Oops. I think I left Isabel in the forest. I'd better make sure she's okay."

If the Hemlocks refused to tell me their real relationship with the gods, maybe Asher could shed some light on the relationship between blood magic and regular magic. I hadn't actually told him about my coven yet, though he must have guessed by now. Perhaps now it was time to bring the Hemlocks out into the open.

"I can't convince you to stay?" Keir wrapped an arm around my shoulder, trailing his lips over mine. "I'll be waiting if you change your mind."

"I wouldn't say no to some company." I wound my hands into his soft hair and kissed him, the warmth of his touch banishing the chill of the spirit realm from both of us.

"I'll be right behind you," he said. "Just warn me next time you run into an unwanted fury."

"I will." I would have said *it won't happen again,* but that would be asking for too much. "I happen to like being alive, even if I'm on the wrong side of the veil too often these days."

"It's where the best of us hang out." He took my cold hands in his warm ones, then let go. "See you later, Jas."

———

I grabbed a sandwich on the way to Asher's place, taking a roundabout route to avoid walking too close to the site of yesterday's attack. I expected to find Isabel there, but when I opened the door, I found Asher sitting alone in his usual spot behind the counter.

"Isabel's not with you?" I asked.

"She went back to her hotel room to grab some spell ingredients," he said. "What do you want, another stealth spell?"

I hadn't even used the first one. It was Ilsa who'd

needed it in the end, not me. "Are you selling those tattoo pens?"

His brows shot up. "No. They aren't for sale."

"You marked Isabel," I said. "I'm guessing it was your idea?"

He pushed to his feet. "You think I'm a bad influence on your friend, do you?"

"That spell saved her life yesterday," I said. "Just name the price and I'll let you mark me, too."

He tilted his head. "Does that mean you're going to come clean about which of the gods you're working with?"

I blinked. "Excuse me?"

"I'm not going to tell tales on you, Jas," he said. "Isabel wouldn't betray your secret, so I'm asking you. That's my price. I'd like to know who it is I'm helping."

"I'm not—I'm not in league with the gods," I said, disarmed that he'd jumped to that conclusion. "My coven hates them, to be honest. The Hemlocks."

He took a step back from the counter, looking me up and down. "Oh. *Them.*"

"You know of them?"

"They disappeared off the radar around the same time as the Bloodroot Coven," he said. "I assumed the League or the invasion destroyed them."

"I'm the last survivor," I said. "It's a little complicated, but my coven is supposed to stop the Ancients from over-running the planet. Problem is, they didn't foresee the mages taking the Ancients' side."

"Some of us did," said Evelyn, but Asher didn't look up, so she must have meant for only me to hear.

"Now I see why Isabel seemed so certain you could

defeat the Whisper single-handedly," he said. "As for the tattoo pen, it's either priceless or worth nothing at all, depending on who holds it."

"Does it work the same now the Whisper is dead?" I asked. "What exactly is their relationship? The gods and the symbols, I mean. She was—*inside* the ink. That can't be the case now she's gone, can it?"

"The Whisper isn't dead." He reached behind the counter, pulling out a drawer. "But the ink in these pens contains the essence of the gods' magic in its purest form."

He tossed a pen onto the desk, which rolled to a halt in front of me. Looked like an ordinary sharpie to me. I picked it up, a shiver running across my shoulder blades. "I thought gods' magic and witch magic didn't mix."

"Says who?" He closed the drawer, turned back to the counter. "It has the same source, does it not?"

"It... does?" I halted, the pen suspended in mid-air. "My coven implied they were the ones who created the symbols used in blood magic. Our ancestors, anyway."

He coughed. "I doubt it. The symbols we use for witchcraft today are nothing more than a shortcut. You could draw a smiley face and it would have the same effect, if you put enough power into it."

He made to take the pen from me, and I yanked back my hand. "Don't you even think about it."

"I'm not going to tattoo a smiley face on you, Jas. I've seen far worse, besides. There was one witch who made a living telling gullible humans that the only way to stave off the pox was to tattoo a naked man on their left buttock."

I choked on an unexpected laugh. "Is that the real reason blood magic was banned?"

"Maybe." He coughed again, his mouth curling up at the side. "I'm not lying, Jas. The ink in that pen is drawn directly from the gods."

I lowered my hand. "My magic doesn't react well to the Ancients. Natural enemies and all."

Yet it had worked just fine when I'd used it to banish the Whisper. Why, then, had my Hemlock magic reacted so violently when I handled the Moonbeam? *It even reacted against Ilsa.* Not that Asher knew she carried the power of an Ancient. Come to think of it, I wasn't sure *how* much Isabel had told him. He hadn't known I was a Hemlock witch, but that didn't explain why he knew so much about the Ancients.

"I told you," he rasped. "It has the same source. All types of magic do, when it comes down to it."

I gaped at him. I'd known witchcraft and necromancy had the same power source, but not the Ancients. And not blood magic.

The rituals were once used to communicate with the gods, Cordelia had said. Yet the gods must have reached out to humans first. Now I knew the Ancients and the Hemlocks hadn't always been enemies, her words took on a whole new dimension.

"How do you know so much?" I placed the pen back on the desk, my palms damp with sweat.

"My coven was a little more adventurous than most," he said. "We knew the true meaning of blood magic. In essence, it's simply the same as creating a regular spell, except the effect is attached directly to you. You can ward yourself or use an amplifying rune to enhance the effects of another spell you're already using."

"And mage marks," I put in. "That's what they are,

right? A variation on the same spell. Creating a two-way link between two people."

Which wasn't all that different to the spell binding Evelyn and me. Except one of us was dead, and it didn't appear as a physical mark.

He scoffed. "Hypocrites. They might not use the same pens my coven did, but it's still blood magic. They slide by the law by pretending it doesn't count as witchcraft because they aren't witches."

"Figures," I said. "So how *did* blood magic gain the reputation of being the most evil form of magic imaginable? Because people used it in ritual summonings?"

"Essentially," Asher said. "Those rituals give regular blood practise a bad name."

"Who taught you all this?" I asked him. "I guess you didn't get this pen from a market stall."

His jaw tightened. "No. This particular marker was taken from the Orion League after they fell, which they in turn stole from the Bloodroot Coven. Maybe the gods would frown upon us for using their power, but they aren't all like the Whisper. The pen contains a fragment of their magic, nothing more."

The door clacked open and I tensed, but it was only Isabel.

"Oh—Jas," she said, with some surprise. "What're you doing with that pen?"

"Experimenting," I said. "I might need a hand."

"Are you sure?" Isabel said. "I wouldn't say I'm an expert yet. I don't think you need any help returning to your body from the spirit realm, either."

Actually, I think I do. "I wouldn't mind being able to

stop myself from being controlled against my will, though."

"I thought you trusted me," Evelyn said.

I cast her a sideways look, but neither of the others acted like she'd spoken. Either she didn't want Asher to see her, or she was in one of her moods. It was hard to tell with Evelyn.

"And sometimes my body gets attacked when I'm in the spirit realm," I added. "Can I see your mark?"

"Sure." Isabel pushed up her sleeve, revealing a faint tattoo mark on her warm brown skin. "It's like the mages' marks."

"We were just talking about that," I said. "Can you teach me?"

"Go right ahead," said Asher. "But if you're going to use your experimental powers under an amplifying rune, please don't do it in my shop."

"We'll behave," said Isabel, holding up her arm so I could see the mark. "Can you copy that?"

"Sure." I pressed the point of the pen to my skin. Keeping an eye on Isabel's arm, I copied the symbol onto my own wrist. The skin tingled a little, but the pen glided smoothly, finishing the symbol.

"I expected something more dramatic," I admitted. "Okay, I'll use the amplifier, too."

I pushed up my other sleeve and drew the amplifying symbol from memory. My skin tingled, but my Hemlock magic didn't react. As Asher had said, it was a low dose of the gods' magic, hardly noticeable.

"Now are you going to tell me your plan?" Asher asked.

"Nope, because I don't have one," I said. "I wanted to

prove Lord Sutherland's guilt, but he's carrying around a device that can suck out people's souls and has spies planted inside the necromancer guild."

Asher's eyes grew round. "He's carrying *what?*"

"He stole the device from the necromancers," I said. "How many people attacked you at the market yesterday? Might some of them have got away?"

Someone had conducted the ritual that had nearly killed Asher and Isabel. We'd found three bodies, but unless they'd turned their weapons on themselves, there was at least one missing perpetrator.

"It's worth checking," Isabel said. "Would it help if we returned to the scene of the crime?"

"All right." I gave a grim nod. "I think I have an idea."

10

The abandoned shop where the ritual had taken place was deserted, which came as no surprise since we hadn't reported the crime. Who were we supposed to tell, the mages? They'd sent the necromancers to their deaths themselves.

I stepped over the bloodstained hardwood where Asher had lain, tasting bile at the back of my throat. Isabel moved in behind me, her hands clenched at her sides.

"I'm glad he survived," I said. "He was lucky."

"He has almost as many lives as you do, Jas," she said. "Uh, not in the same way, though."

"No…" Asher wasn't a shade, and however he'd injured himself, it hadn't even been reversed when Evelyn had used her healing magic on him. "You like him. Don't you? Just how often have you come back here since my exile?"

An embarrassed smile came over her. "I have enough responsibilities with my own coven. I'm not naïve enough to think anything can come of this."

"You deserve to be happy, too." Until this morning, I hadn't known that she'd been forced into the role of coven leader early because her mentor had died due to the Ancients' magic. Now did not seem the time to broach the subject, not on top of a site of ritual magic which had spawned a shadowy monster.

I pulled out my phone to act as a torch, scanning the blood splatter on the floor where necromancers had died. Someone had removed their bodies, but the blood remained, along with the faded lines of the chalk circle.

I knelt down beside it, reaching for a spell. "Isabel, can you stay here and keep an eye out in case something else comes crawling out of the ashes?"

"Sure." She stepped back, shining her phone's torchlight into the room's corners.

I pulled a tracking spell off my wrist and laid it carefully down on top of the blood-splattered floorboards. Then I pushed my Hemlock magic into it, tapping on the amplifying mark as I did so.

For a heartbeat, nothing happened. Then I plunged forwards, headfirst, into a vision of the same room I was already in. At least five or six individuals stood on the bare wooden floor, wearing long cloaks with their hoods pulled up to hide their faces. Necromancer cloaks.

"What are you doing?" asked the smallest of the cloaked figures. His voice was high, scared.

"What nature intended for us," said a female voice. The speaker was tall and thin, and her hood moved as she approached the area I'd appeared in, revealing pale features and blond hair. *I know her. She's at the guild.* She also hadn't been among the dead, that I'd seen.

The blond woman moved forwards, a knife in her hands. One of the other necromancers gasped. "What are you going to do to us?"

She grabbed the closest necromancer by the scruff of his neck, slicing the knife across his throat. His body hit the ground next to me, blood spilling across the wooden floor.

I'd seen enough. Letting the spell fade out, I lurched to my feet, squeezing my eyes shut in the hope that the room would stop spinning.

"Jas, what did you see?" asked Isabel.

"The ritual." I swallowed down the taste of sour bile. "There are still spies at the guild and they didn't all die in the sacrifice. I have to warn the others."

"You saw their faces?"

"One of them." I dug in my pocket for my notebook and pen and sketched out the blond woman's face from memory. "I've definitely seen her at the guild before, but I'm not sure she'll be there now. She might be lying low if she suspects we might have tried a tracking spell."

"Did she leave any traces behind that we can use to track her?" Isabel paced around the ritual site. "I guess not, if she's still alive."

"I can try anyway." I reached into the ashes of my collapsed tracking spell, feeling for the spark of magic that remained beneath the surface. The blond necromancer had stood right here. I pulled her image into my mind's eye and focused as hard as possible.

I'd used magic without props beforehand. Asher himself had said the actual symbols didn't matter as much as the intent, as I'd known applied in necromancy for years. In its purest, rawest form, magic came direct from nature, and held no limits.

Especially for a Hemlock witch.

If Evelyn was confident that I had power enough to kill the leader of the Mage Lords, then I should be able to use a simple tracking spell without an anchor.

Magic flowed to my hands, lighting them up in green iridescence. Isabel exclaimed aloud. "Jas—what are you doing?"

"Testing a theory." The glow brightened, and a tugging sensation propelled me towards the door. "Whoa. I think it's working."

"You're tracking her?" Isabel's dubious tone faded as she saw my hands glowing, a thin thread of light running from me through the closed door.

"I think she's close." I nodded to Isabel. "Let's go."

———

I strode down the street, following the tugging sensation of the tracking spell. It grew stronger the further we got from the market but didn't appear to be leading us towards the guild, either. Keir hovered behind me, occasionally grabbing a vessel to have a look around. He didn't seem surprised by my display of magic, but my conversation with Asher had reminded me that I'd neglected my witch magic lately, forgetting how useful it could be for tracking people I hadn't seen face to face yet. The amplifying mark on my arm tingled as I walked, and I suppressed the urge to scratch it.

Finally, the tracking spell gave a firm tug, like a piece of elastic growing taut. Spotting a necromancer patrol coming the other way, I ducked into an alley, pulling Isabel along with me.

"I think she's with them," I whispered.

"Are the others her allies?" she whispered back.

"Not sure." If not, then it meant they were her next sacrifices. *You won't get past me.*

As I'd suspected, the blond necromancer slowed her pace when she drew near to our hiding place, sensing the presence of another necromancer.

The instant she looked our way, I pounced. Two knockout spells flew from my hands, hitting her companions. They dropped like stones on either side of her.

"Nice try." I strode out to meet her. "But you won't be making any more sacrifices."

She snapped out a hand and a blast of power rushed towards me. I conjured a shield to deflect it, feeling the sizzle of magic against my skin. *Witch* magic.

"Who are you?" I raised my shield, pushing back until her attack dissipated. "You're not a witch."

A thin-lipped smile crossed her face. "I was, once, dear, but this young thing is much more adaptable, wouldn't you say?"

Her voice sounded much older than it should have. I tapped on my spirit sight, and my blood chilled. The soul inside her body didn't match her outside appearance. She wasn't a necromancer, but a witch, wearing the body of a guild member.

A shade, like me.

Isabel tensed at my side. "What *are* you?"

"I think you know, little witch," she said. "I have a long and happy life ahead of me, and I won't let either of you take that from me."

"You're wearing someone else's skin." *That* was how the mages had infiltrated the guild—by snatching necromancers off the streets and replacing their souls with their witch allies to avoid detection. "Did you offer to help the mages gain power in exchange for a new life in the body of an innocent person?"

"It seemed a fair trade," said the witch. "My master gave me new life, and I intend to use it well."

Bile rose in my throat. "He used a blood sacrifice. Now he has you doing the same in turn."

Not only that—he'd bound her to her new body using the exact same ritual my coven had used to save my life. Why?

The truth slammed into me. Since he'd found out Evelyn and I had been bound using a ritual, he must have wanted a piece of it himself. For someone who seemed determined to extend his youth, binding his soul to a younger person's body was just the sort of thing he'd do.

"You're nothing but a lab rat," Isabel said. "And I don't like people who use magic for evil ends."

A flash of light enveloped the blond woman at a snap of Isabel's fingers. As she stumbled, I conjured a whip of energy to my hands and lashed her legs together. She squirmed, fighting, and I hesitated. If I killed her, I'd never be able to prove the wrong soul had been trapped in her body. Handing her over to the authorities and wringing a confession from her would have to do.

The witch raised a hand. "May the power of the grave take you."

Necromantic power slammed into me, knocking me out of my body. Alarmed, I caught my balance, flipping over in mid-air. The witch's true form glowed through the fog of Death, her mouth twisted in a snarl.

Shit. She knows how to use her shade powers. Where in hell had she learned that? Surely not from the Mage Lord.

"Begone, shade," she hissed. "I banish you."

To my horror, I felt myself slipping away. My body remained inert as my spirit floated backwards, towards the gates of Death.

I won't die. I can't die.

I held onto my Hemlock magic, let it flow through every inch of me. Calling me back to life. *As long as it runs in my veins, I can't die.*

The gates of Death faded as Keir caught me by the arm, steadying me. "Jas, what in hell just happened?"

"She tried to banish me. Like a ghost." And she'd almost succeeded. I scanned the spirit realm, but the blond witch's real form had vanished. I swore loudly at the haze of ghosts surrounding me. *Damn her.*

Focusing on the waking world, I blinked back into my body to find Isabel shaking my shoulder.

"She ran off. I didn't want to leave you." Her brown eyes were wide, concerned. "Are you okay?"

I jerked my head in a nod. "Which way?"

"That way." She pointed, and we both broke into a swift walk. My legs weren't happy about that, but I pushed ahead through sheer stubbornness. "I reckon she's off to fetch backup. Are you okay to fight?"

"Yes," I said, cursing my trembling limbs. "I have to warn the necromancers in case she's heading back there." I gave the spirit realm a quick scan, searching for anyone familiar. "Keir, is Ilsa at the guild? She's the easiest to reach."

"No…" He fell silent. Then: "She's patrolling. Also, that witch is heading her way."

"What?" *Damn her. She's after my friends now.*

"I'm on it," Keir's voice said in my ear. "I'll send a vessel after her and give her a nice surprise."

"Thanks." I quickened my pace, my breath coming out in gasps.

"Hey," Isabel said, at my shoulder. "You're forgetting I can only hear half of what you say to people in the spirit realm. Are you going after Ilsa?"

"Keir told me the witch has her sights set on Ilsa next," I said. "She's a shade. I'm not sure she can even be banished beyond Death's gates. She's like…"

"Like you?"

Like I was. Before I burned out my shade powers. "Yeah. And Evelyn. That means she can use both necromancy and witchcraft."

Speaking of Evelyn, it would have been nice if she'd helped me out back there. *That was too close.* I had to be more careful next time.

Ilsa's presence pinged on my radar, drawing me closer. Lloyd, Mackie and Morgan were with her. They'd taken the idea of sticking together to heart, but none of them would see another necromancer as a threat. They wouldn't know she was a witch until she attacked.

A single street lamp marked the end of the road. "Hang on. I know this place."

This street was where the deceased vampire king had once lived. Most of the houses were empty now, thanks to the pack of furies which had escaped through the spirit line and swarmed through the tunnels connecting the basements of every house on the street. A semi-transparent silver line threaded down the middle of the row of houses on one side of the street, humming with energy.

Oh, crap. Not only was the entire street sitting on a spirit line, it was also the spirit line the Soul Collector had tried to break. Oh, and the one which Evelyn had awakened and let a dragon through.

I stopped walking, detecting a spark of life beneath the house where the vampire king had once lived. "She's in there. Why the hell did Ilsa go into the basement?"

"This place feels… wrong," Isabel said. Even she could pick up on the humming energy of the spirit line.

I stepped towards the house. "That'd be because the entire street is on a spirit line. Ilsa and the others are in the vampire king's old tunnels."

"Get fucked, shade." Keir's harsh voice beside me made me jump, and I switched on my spirit sight in time to see him crash headlong into the witch, nearly knocking her out of the necromancer's body. *And that's my cue to jump in.*

Leaping down the stone steps, I kicked the basement door inwards and sprinted into the dark tunnel, Isabel on my heels. The cloaked witch-shade wheeled around to face me, looking decidedly paler. *Nice going, Keir.*

"You again?" said the witch-shade. "Don't you know when to quit?"

"No," I said. "The thing about being a shade is that we're pretty tough to kill. But that doesn't mean I can't bring on the pain."

Hemlock magic lashed from my hands, hurling her sideways into the wide cave at the mouth of the tunnel. Behind her, Ilsa crouched down, gripping the book that contained her Gatekeeper's magic. The body of a fury lay crumpled between her and Lloyd, while Morgan and

Mackie dodged the swiping claws of another beast. *Damn. Not more of them.*

As the fury lunged at Mackie, I steered my magic in that direction, latching onto the beast's ankle. Isabel threw a spell into the fury's face, sending him crashing sideways into the witch-shade. Both collapsed into a heap.

"Nice going." I let the whip dissipate into flickering ashes, reforming in my hand.

The fury recovered first, its claws digging into the witch-shade's back. She let out a hoarse cry of rage, struggling like a fish caught in a net.

"That's what happens when you make deals with monsters," Keir said, grabbing the witch-shade's hand through the spirit realm. Her eyes widened as his vampire's touch drained her energy away. "The monsters sometimes bite back."

Morgan threw a knife at the fury from behind, which wedged itself into the beast's spine. As it turned on him, Isabel threw an explosive spell into the fury's face. With a shriek, the witch-shade pulled herself free, staggering in my direction.

"You won't survive this," she croaked. Her hands glowed green-blue, and an explosion sent both Isabel and me flying off our feet. Isabel's arms lit up with a silver glow and she caught her balance, her mouth set in a grim line.

I wasn't so lucky. My back slammed into the wall, the wind exiting my lungs in a rush. As she closed in, the banishing words on her tongue, I lunged out of my body and punched her.

The witch-shade staggered back, visibly surprised that

I'd managed to do some damage to her from within the spirit realm.

"Guess what?" I said, my hands glowing blue. "You can't master necromancy by stealing the magic from its original owner."

I lunged forward, grabbing her—not her body, but her spirit. Snarling, she fought back, but I tightened my grip on her in the spirit realm. Drained from Keir's vampire attack, she struggled, her spirit slipping loose from her stolen body.

I bared my teeth. "I bet whoever performed that ritual on you didn't warn you that being bound to another person's body doesn't mean you can't be ripped out of it again."

"I could say the same of you," she growled. "I heard what you did. That magic you stole isn't yours, and now the realm of Death will take you back."

Her form became indistinct, turning dark. An empty hole shaped like a person. A shade, with pitch-dark eyes. Dragging me into oblivion along with her.

Mackie's scream hit both of us, sending me reeling back into my body. The others had successfully killed the fury, leaving only the witch-shade. Turning on Mackie, she attempted to grab the psychic, but Mackie danced out of the way with another precise scream. She really had got much better at control. At first, when she'd used the screaming power of hers, it tended to hit everyone in her path and shook up the whole spirit line. This time, the witch-shade took the brunt of the attack, flying backwards out of her body.

"I will not die!" she screamed.

"I beg to differ." Ilsa kicked the dead form of the fury

aside. "Whatever you are, I'll send you to a place you can't return from."

"Not before she stands trial." Red light suffused my hands, mingling with the trapping spell on my wrist. "Isabel?"

She gave me a nod. "Ready."

The two of us directed our magic at the witch-shade's body, the combined force of our trapping spell pinning her to the wall. Her spirit turned on the spot, but Keir got there first, pinning her ghostly hands behind her back.

"Well, well," she said. "A shade-touched vampire. It's an honour to meet you."

"The feeling's not mutual, believe me." Gripping her arms, Keir began to drain her.

"Someone set up a circle!" I yelled. "Please tell me one of you has candles."

"Yeah, got it," said Morgan, and there came the sound of swearing and dropping candles. "Lloyd, help me out here."

"I'm on it!" Lloyd moved to help, followed by Mackie and Ilsa.

I joined Keir in restraining the witch-shade's struggling ghost, yanking her towards the crooked circle of candles. The realm of Death tugged at me, the spirit line threatening to drag me in like the current of a river, but Keir kept me grounded, draining more of her spirit with each step.

When the lights of twelve candles surrounded her, she finally fell still. Her eyes narrowed in malevolence.

Isabel stood over her body, restrained in the trapping spell. "There's no life left in her, right?"

I tapped the spirit realm. "None."

That meant the girl was dead. Murdered.

Silence filled the cave, thick as paste. The witch-shade hovered on the spot, trapped in the circle of lights. Dead furies lay sprawled around the cave where the vampires had once held their council.

I licked my lips, my throat dry. "Someone call Lady Montgomery. She can handle the interrogation."

11

Lloyd went outside to call the boss. Mackie followed, saying the tunnels gave her the creeps. That left Isabel, Ilsa, Morgan and me to clean up the mess their fight had left behind.

"Why did you come here?" I threw a dissolving spell at the nearest fury's corpse. "You know, an empty house with a bunch of creepy tunnels underneath—where the vampires' king died in a few months ago—and right on top of a spirit line. It couldn't be a more obvious trap if it had a sign in the window telling you to surrender your souls."

"The vampire king died here?" Ilsa wiped her bloody knife on her necromancer coat. The pocket was still glowing, indicating the presence of her talisman. "I didn't know it happened on a spirit line."

"It was when all those furies got loose in the city back in December," I said. "Right, Keir?"

"It's one of my fondest memories." Keir hovered at the back of the cave, peering into the tunnel entrance.

"Wait, is the vampire here?" Morgan turned to the spot where Keir's voice came from.

"Surprise." Keir appeared, flickering around the edges. "I can't kill furies in this form, but I can make sure there aren't any other shades around."

"I bloody hope not." I moved to the circle, where the witch-shade lay sprawled in mid-air. "The enemy killed a guild member to do this."

"The *mages* did," said Ilsa, looking vaguely nauseated. "I'm—I'm getting out."

I didn't blame her, but if I let that witch-shade out of my sight, she might break the circle and return to her stolen body. Isabel stood guard over the trapping spell as though she'd had the same thought, so I walked into the tunnel to destroy the furies' other corpses.

"Evil fuckers." Morgan slammed the heel of his shoe into the cave wall.

"I thought your sister was the voice of reason," I said. "Why'd she let you guys throw yourselves into harm's way?"

"Mackie and I heard the furies first," he said. "We didn't know there wasn't anyone living in the houses. Didn't know that necromancer girl wasn't an ally either."

"Nobody would have, not if they didn't know her personally," I said. "Anyone else at the guild might be a target. Our esteemed Mage Lord strikes again. He's taking witches under his wing and offering them a new life in exchange for their knowledge."

And sacrifice, I didn't doubt. My skin crawled.

"All that because the boss won't support him," Morgan said sourly. "She'd rather sell her own soul, and he knows it."

"She's ten times the person he is," I said, surprised to find Morgan and I actually agreed on something. "And to think necromancers are supposed to be the evil ones."

He grunted. "I've met vampires living on the streets with more sense than he has. Sooner or later he's going to push too far."

On the streets... "Uh, Morgan, you met other vampires before you came to Edinburgh, right?"

He tensed. "Yes…"

"There was a vampire working with those necromancers last night who Keir didn't recognise," I said. "Know where he might have come from?"

Morgan shook his head. "Not if he was into sacrificial magic. That's not my thing." He cast a self-conscious look over his shoulder and carried on dragging the fury's mangled head out of the tunnel. It looked like someone—probably Mackie—had hacked it to pieces with a blunt knife.

I threw a charm over the fury's head and it dissolved into ashes. "Hey, I'm the last person who'd judge anyone for turning to dark magic to survive." The proof of that was branded into my arm, in the blood magic I'd accepted, used to my advantage.

"It's not you I'm worried about," he said, almost too quietly for me to hear.

"What, your sister?" I dragged the rest of the fury's mangled body out of the tunnel and fumbled for another spell. "I don't have siblings, so I can't really comment."

"You're his friend."

I stopped short. "You mean, Lloyd?"

I'd known about Lloyd's crush on him for a while, but I hadn't known it was in any way reciprocated. Morgan wasn't the most observant person and generally seemed more interested in the spirit world than the real one.

"Lloyd isn't that complicated," I said. "He likes zombie movies and comic books. He has a younger sister at uni. You have two younger sisters, don't you? Same thing."

"Yeah, right," he said. "His sister's human. One of *my* sisters is the ambassador between the mortal realm and the Summer Court, the other guards the gates of Death, and my only shining achievement is being the second-best psychic at the guild. And there are two of us."

"Do you really think Lloyd gives a shit?" I said. "If anything, he's glad not to have half the problems I do. Being the supposed saviour of the universe is overrated."

"Huh." He looked me over. "Yeah, you look like shit, and you're fading. Where's that second soul of yours?"

"Probably napping." Considering I'd nearly been dragged over the veil and into Death, you'd have thought she'd want to check up on me. But when I tapped into the spirit realm, all I could sense were Isabel, the unconscious witch-shade... and no Evelyn.

I looked down and found I'd somehow drifted out of my body, almost through the ceiling. *What in hell?* Gritting my teeth, I slammed back into my body with such force that I tripped over.

Morgan took a step back. "Whoa. Don't strangle me again."

"I'm not."

The realm of Death will take you back, the witch-shade had said. Was she right? Maybe the price to pay for leaving the world behind too many times was that eventually, Death and I would become one.

But didn't that mean the same would happen to Evelyn?

"I am so fucked." I rested my head against the wall. "Be glad you only have to worry about Lloyd."

"What about me?" Lloyd said from behind us. "The boss is on her way, but we have to get the witch's body aboveground first."

"He thought you might have run into another fury," I said vaguely, not wanting to worry him by mentioning my latest out-of-body experience.

I couldn't be dying. I was a shade, with two souls to boot. If it was easy to kill me, the Hemlocks would never have bothered to bind us.

"Nah, but you might wanna disappear when the boss shows up." Lloyd nodded to Isabel. "You, too."

"Sure." Isabel gave the spell trapping the witch's body a last cursory look. "What does Lady Montgomery have to say about the shade? Does she believe you?"

"She does," said Ilsa, who'd entered the cave behind Lloyd. "She's ordered an examination of every guild member to make sure nobody else is harbouring the wrong soul."

Yeah, definitely time to go.

The witch jerked awake when I walked past the circle of candles, her blue-grey eyes following me. "You're going to die, Jas," she said softly.

A chill ran up my arms, but I stared her out. "Good, because if we didn't all die, I'd be out of a job. Meanwhile, there's a first-class ticket to hell waiting for you. So long."

I turned heel, leaving the tunnel and the witch-shade behind.

———

"Wish I could eavesdrop on the trial," I said to Isabel as we walked down a deserted side street. "I want to hear the witch-shade confess that it was the Mage Lord who bound her soul to the wrong body and murdered its original owner."

"I just hope a dead person's word is enough," Isabel said.

"To your guild, it is." A dead man wearing a hoodie closed in behind us, speaking with Keir's voice. "There are more furies on the loose elsewhere. Looks like it's a problem up and down the whole spirit line."

"Ugh." I turned to Isabel. "What do you reckon? They were summoned?"

"Not on that spirit line," she said, her mouth pulled in a frown. "Jas… what happened to you during that fight? You kind of spaced out."

"The witch-shade tried to drag me out of my body and banish me," I said. "Like I was a ghost. Bloody cheek."

Also, I fell out of my body afterwards. Maybe I was just shaky from the aftereffects of the witch-shade's magic, but I still hadn't heard from Evelyn.

"Damn." Isabel glanced at Keir. "When the mages bound the witch's soul to the necromancer's body, did they use the same ritual…?"

"As the one the Hemlocks used to bind Evelyn and me?" I finished. "Yes, they did. And yes, the mages must have started researching as soon as Evelyn told them she wasn't really me."

Which meant there might be resources on the ritual inside the mages' headquarters right now.

Isabel's eyes grew round. "Research? So they might know how to undo it?"

"I guess they might." I glanced over my shoulder at Keir's vessel. "I don't know what's best for Evelyn and me in the long-term, but I want the option."

Isabel bit her lip. "Uh, Jas. I was going to mention it to you, but I wasn't sure... I mean, Asher wasn't. But they kind of stole it from him."

"Who stole what?" I frowned.

"The mages stole the book of ritual magic from Asher," she said. "It belonged to—the Bloodroot Coven, so it wasn't his to begin with, but they barged into his shop a few years ago demanding he hand over anything connected to the Orion League. He kept the pens hidden, but he told me he's convinced that Lord Sutherland must have learned all the ritualistic symbols from that book. Including the binding."

I stopped walking. "Lord Sutherland stole a book with the Hemlocks' ritual inside it from *Asher*?"

I'd suspected the Hemlocks weren't the only people to use that ritual—in order for it to have ended up being banned, someone must have tried the ritual at home, with violent results. Asher, though, didn't know I'd had the ritual used on me as a baby, so he wouldn't have thought to mention it to me.

"Yeah," said Isabel. "Sorry I didn't tell you sooner. I didn't know the book had *that* ritual in it, and it probably wasn't the only book they stole."

No kidding. But if the book contained a ritual designed to bind a soul into a new body, then maybe I'd be able to disentangle myself from Keir as well as Evelyn. Our bond had come close to pushing him through Death's gates. The sooner I disconnected us, the better.

Evelyn, though? She had no body of her own, and she wouldn't thank me for exorcising her without one. We'd have to find a soulless body lying around which was suitable for a new host to even consider the possibility. But choice… choice was something I'd lacked for a long time. Evelyn, too.

I turned to Keir—or the zombie he piloted. "I don't need to get up close to Lord Sutherland to get my hands on a book. I bet he left it in his library. I can't see him carrying it on him."

And if it frees me from Evelyn…

Did I want that? What if I lost her magic along with her?

What if it was too late to stop the side-effects from claiming my soul?

"I don't disagree, Jas," he said. "But the mages will doubtless have made a copy of that information now they have it. They'll keep using the binding spell on their own people."

"Maybe, but it's worth a shot," I said. "Also, if we're looking for proof the mages are crooks, bringing that book to the boss's attention might be the edge we need. Add that to the witch-shade's confession and they won't be able to accuse her of lying."

And after that? We were one step closer to displacing the mages from the power they'd stolen and gifting Lord Sutherland with a one-way trip to jail. Better yet, if I reversed the ritual, then Evelyn and I would be separate entities. Publicly, at least, neither of us would be a product of illegal magic. The mages would have to remove the price on my head, and the guild would be allowed to let me back in without fear of repercussions.

It was too easy to come without a hitch, yet for a single giddying moment, I let myself dream of handing the book over to Lady Montgomery and claiming my old job back —and breaking free from the Hemlock Coven forever.

Keir cleared his throat. "Not to burst your bubble, Jas, but breaking the link with Evelyn won't stop the war from coming."

"I know." I forced the tantalising images down, to examine later when I had time. I knew the book wouldn't bring back Keir's brother's soul or break the mages' link with the Ancients… and we never did find out if they'd stolen the mirror.

"I think we should head over to the mages' place now," I said. "Once the witch-shade makes the accusation, the guild will send a search patrol to look for more proof. Not just the book, but if they're hiding that mirror somewhere as well, the guild will be able to get it back."

"And if they have other witch-shades waiting to ambush us?" asked Isabel.

"So much the better," said Evelyn, startling me.

"Jesus, you've been quiet," I told her.

"Just because you talk all the time, doesn't mean we all have to," she said snippily.

"Evelyn's speaking to you again?" asked Isabel. "Why can I hear Keir and not her?"

"Both of them can be selective about who can hear them," I explained. "One is slightly less antisocial than the other."

Evelyn sighed. "Get on with it, then. It won't be long

before the witch-shade's trial starts, and I doubt it'll take long."

"I know how to get into the mages' place the back way," I said. "That smarmy twat Neil won't be guarding *that* gate."

Reckless exhilaration flooded me, and I twisted the band on my wrist—the illusion spell Asher had given me, which I hadn't used yet. "Asher mentioned four different stealth options," I said to Isabel. "Can you fill me in?"

"The first one's for invisibility." She indicated a notch on the bracelet-shaped spell. "That one makes it so nobody can hear you—the downside is that I won't know where you are, either. The third causes a diversion, and the fourth makes you impervious to most tracking wards."

"I'll use that one to get in." I walked quicker, my heart racing. "Keir, has the witch-shade woken up yet?"

"Let me see." The zombie stopped walking for an instant, the blue-grey sheen disappearing from his eyes. "Ah... there's a slight issue. Lady Montgomery isn't there. She's standing in front of the mages' place, talking to Lord Sutherland."

"What?" I halted. "Seriously?"

"She went directly there?" Isabel guessed. "We can still go in the back way. I doubt anyone will be paying close attention."

"Yes, but why is she speaking to him now? Is she making a direct challenge?"

Alone? Lady Montgomery was a force to be reckoned with, but Lord Sutherland had made a deal with one of the gods and wouldn't hesitate to twist the laws to get what he wanted. That made him more dangerous than anyone I'd ever gone up against before. Sure, Lady Montgomery had fought against the Sidhe of Faerie in the invasion, but Lord Sutherland frightened me more than the idea of invincible faeries striding out of nowhere. Maybe because he still seemed so human, despite his depraved actions.

The three of us neared the mages' guild, heading for the back gates. My instincts screamed at me to go to the front instead and eavesdrop on Lady Montgomery's conversation, but if I did, she'd see me for sure. A quick scan told me there were no other necromancers on the ground floor. Nobody stood in my way.

I'll find that ritual magic book first.

"I'll snoop in on their conversation," Keir whispered. "And I'll warn you if they're coming."

"Thanks." I turned on the stealth spell, switching to the ward-proof option. Isabel vanished, too, employing an identical spell.

Two mages stood guard outside the back door, but a couple of simple knockout charms took care of them. I had to admire Asher's technical skill. He could break into the mages' place every week if he wanted to.

Granted, it helped that I had an extra way to sense obstacles. I gave the spirit realm a quick scan for potential traps, finding none. Lady Montgomery's presence was so close, I felt sure she would turn around and spot me, but she remained focused on Lord Sutherland.

The back door opened with a click, courtesy of Isabel. Then we were in.

I knew the route into the dungeon by heart, but I suspected the book was in Lord Sutherland's office or in the library, somewhere easily accessible. Betting on the latter, I crossed the lobby with silent steps. The library door was unlocked, which came as no surprise. He hadn't expected visitors.

There were no books left discarded on the table. I gave the shelves a cursory scan, but if he'd used the ritual recently, he'd have the book somewhere closer to him. Then again, he wouldn't have actually performed the ritual himself. Maybe the book was in the hands of one of his witches instead.

I made for his office, sensing a flash of blue-white light in the spirit realm. *Hang on a minute.* The spirit device. He'd left it out on his desk. Speaking of incriminating evidence…

Sure enough, the small remote-shaped device lay out on the table. I reached for it, then hesitated as the hum of protective spells buzzed against my palm. I pushed a little of my Hemlock power at them, undoing each spell until the device lay bare and gleaming, looking deceptively innocent. A smile tugged at my mouth and I picked it up. Never mind getting him arrested. It would take mere seconds to sneak up on him from behind using the stealth spell to cushion my steps. One click of a button and he'd never hurt anyone again.

"Jas, what are you doing?" Isabel hissed from behind me.

"Do you reckon he has the book on him?" I asked. "I can't see it."

"Me neither, but if you use that device and get caught, you'll be the one arrested."

I gritted my teeth. It would almost be worth it. Cordelia and Evelyn would do it without hesitation—which was reason enough to give me pause. I didn't want my boss to take the blame, in the absence of any other target.

I tapped into the spirit realm, floating out of my body to listen to his conversation with Lady Montgomery.

"A shade?" asked Lord Sutherland. "I believe that's your area, not mine."

"Not in the slightest," she said. "Your laws forbid it, as you frequently remind me."

"Yes, but there are some individuals who work for you who are known for flaunting the laws when it suits them," said Lord Sutherland. "For instance, the Gatekeeper, the person who supposedly guards the gates between life and death. Who was it who chose Ilsa Lynn for that role? Not you."

"It's not my place to say," said Lady Montgomery. "But I trust her."

"Her brother is a psychic," he went on. "And you've taken in another rogue psychic within the last few months, too, who is known to have committed a number of crimes."

Oh, damn. I should have expected this. Now the mages had failed to recruit Ilsa, they planned to add her name to the wanted list right next to mine. And I'd bet whatever remained of my nine lives that the rest of my friends would be next. Starting with Mackie or Morgan, by the sound of things.

"If you define me by the company I keep, you might call yourself a hypocrite," she said. "The shade confessed that it was you who raised her and bound her to her new body. I would say that's grounds enough for an inquiry, wouldn't you?"

A glow caught my eyes, from his pocket. *Bugger. He has more than one device.*

As his hand moved to his pocket, I slid back into my body and shoved the doors open, staggering down the steps to the front entrance. Magic flowed from my hands, forming a shield between Lady Montgomery and Lord Sutherland.

I marched up behind him, the spirit device in hand. "If you attack her, you'll have to answer to me."

"Hemlock," he snarled. "Put that down."

"I don't think so," said Evelyn, and hit the button.

12

Kinetic power burst from the device as it exploded. Before it made contact with Lord Sutherland, a rippling current of energy deflected it, shimmering around the Mage Lord. He wore a shield charm—and a powerful one, too. Should have seen that one coming.

I poured more power into my own shield, drawing it around both Lady Montgomery and me. *You won't hurt her. Not on my watch.*

"Jas," she hissed out of the corner of her mouth. "Go. He'll kill you—"

"No, he won't." Evelyn took the wheel, throwing the splintered remains of the device at Lord Sutherland. His shield clicked on again, and the device rebounded, clattering onto the path.

"Father!" Neil Sutherland ran through the front gates, ducking the erratic currents of energy still pouring from the obliterated spirit device.

"How many times do I have to drain you before you

stay down?" Keir tackled Neil through the spirit realm, grabbing his arms.

"Ghosts are attacking me again!" he yelled. "Father—"

"It's not a ghost," snarled Lord Sutherland. "It's a cursed vampire who's going to be sorry he crossed me—and his brother, too."

"What do you know about my brother?" Keir's grip on Neil faltered. "Answer me."

The hesitation cost him—cost both of us.

Lord Sutherland pulled out the second spirit device, pointing it directly at Keir. "I know enough to be certain that your soul doesn't have to be attached to your body for me to use it."

"Don't," I said.

A smile formed. He hit the button.

Keir disappeared in a flash.

"Keir!"

No. He can't be gone. He can't be.

Lord Sutherland spun to face me, and Evelyn took over, diving to the ground. Hemlock magic burst from her hands, crashing into his shield. His hands glowed, indicating that he was using an active charm to shield himself from damage.

Two could play at that game. Drawing on my amplifying rune, I twisted the stealth charm and turned on the option to silence my steps. Not only could he not see me, now he wouldn't be able to hear me either. Nor would Isabel, but she'd gone quiet. *Hope she has a plan.*

Silently, I trod around Lord Sutherland from behind, inching closer. Then I struck.

A shield slammed into me, and I pushed back, my Hemlock magic reacting to whatever spell he wore. My teeth chattered, my entire body humming with energy, but I kept pushing. He might have a witch on his side, but my Hemlock magic was stronger. "Break," I hissed, unsure whether it was my voice or Evelyn's.

Lightning flashed inches from my feet, making me freeze. Neil spat out blood, his hands crackling with mage power.

Before he could attack again, Evelyn punched him in the face. He fell backwards into his father—and the shield spell cracked.

My next attack hit the spirit device, knocking it out of Lord Sutherland's hand. I caught it, gritting my teeth against the tremble of restless energy beneath the surface. *Shit. It's going to explode.*

Pushing as much of my own magic as I could into it, I threw the device at Lord Sutherland.

Neil threw himself in front, his own wrists glowing. That was no ordinary witch charm—both of them were using blood magic.

The device exploded in a torrent of blue light. Neil and Lord Sutherland ducked for cover, as did Lady Montgomery. Isabel screamed my name, and I steadied myself, flipping head over heels, knocked loose from my body again.

The spirit realm trembled as a gale-force wind tore through the grey fog. Ghosts floated past, fighting the current, and I fought along with them.

Beneath me, the spirit line through the heart of the city was fracturing, torrents of energy diverging and colliding in mid-air. The line had split in two, and as I watched, a fury pulled itself out of the gap, its jagged wings beating as it flew over the city. The line passing through the abandoned train station had also split in two, leaving a gaping hole filled with emptiness.

My magic did that. I pressed a hand to my mouth, horror-struck. The Hemlock spirit line... had cracked open.

"No," I whispered.

If the mages found the Hemlocks' forest, the war would end before it could even begin.

Concentrating fiercely, I pushed my way back into my body, pressing my hand against a brick wall to keep from falling over.

"Nice for you to join us again, Jas," said Evelyn. She must have taken off as soon as the blast struck because she'd managed to make me run halfway to the disused train station.

"Can you close the line?" I looked down, disorientated by the sudden change of scenery.

"With you?" she said. "Yes, I can."

"All right." I broke into a run, towards Waverley Bridge, and deep into the heart of the breaking spirit line. Hemlock power seared my hands, mingling with the currents of energy rippling overhead.

"Ready?" Evelyn asked.

"Ready."

Together, we directed our magic at the spirit line, twin currents of white light. From a crack in the line, a fury sprang into being, diving over the city with an ear-splitting screech. *It's not working. We're too late.*

"Try harder!" she yelled. "Give it everything you have, Jas."

I called on the amplifying rune, demanding it turn my

magic up to max. My blood hummed with power, igniting, reacting.

The enemy wanted to destroy the spirit line and my coven along with it. This time, permanently.

I won't let them do it.

Evelyn and I combined our power, fusing two currents of energy together. Then the line began to fuse, too. I swayed on the spot, my vision flickering, but somehow, I kept going, the same way I'd sealed the Soul Collector outside of this world. Gritting my teeth, I gave one final tug, and the currents of power became a single rippling line once again.

"Now the other one," said Evelyn.

"Right." I took a step forwards, alarmed when a rush of dizziness nearly brought me to my knees. "I thought you wanted to open the spirit lines yourself. Why close them now?"

"Not as long as that Mage Lord is working with the Ancients," Evelyn said. "He has no place in this conflict, and we will vanquish him before we take on the betrayers."

"I'll take your word for it." Ignoring the screaming pain in my legs, I broke into a sprint. "Did you leave Isabel and Lady Montgomery behind with the Mage Lord?"

"Your friend will be fine," she said dismissively. "I think Lord Sutherland was a little stunned by that blast."

I hope they got out. The necromancer guild didn't need to lose their leader at a time like this, however little Evelyn cared. Still, I didn't like to think what might have happened if Evelyn hadn't added her strength to mine to seal the broken spirit line.

Now the question remained... could we pull it off a second time?

Above, the flickering hint of red in the sky indicated the crack between worlds was widening. The last time it had looked like that, a dragon had got loose, and only Ivy had been able to convince it to leave. Now it was down to Evelyn and me, and it was probably a bad sign when my dead relative who'd been a ghost for twenty-something years was in better shape than I was.

The spirit line drew closer, and so did the furies circling above the threads of energy unravelling in mid-air and forming rifts above the peaked roofs. Pitying the poor people living below, I careened around a corner— and stopped.

A line of mages greeted me, standing below the spirit line as though to welcome the flood of monsters into the street.

"Get her," snarled Lord Sutherland.

The cloaked mages advanced on me. I called my magic, but it'd died to a flicker. I'd given everything I had to close the first spirit line and had nothing left to fight with.

No. I can't let it end here.

"I wouldn't," I warned him. "If you kill me, that line is going to stay open, and people will die."

"People die every day," he said. "The world is in ruins. If someone doesn't take control, all will crumble to ashes."

"Is that how you're spinning it?" I recalled what Asher had said. "You're terrified, aren't you? You're so scared that you'll burn half the world down to gain the other half's favour rather than admitting you're going to die and be forgotten."

His eyes darkened with anger. Three mages closed in, trapping me between them.

"Hold her still," he said. "Give her to the monsters."

A fury descended, claws outstretched. Above my head, currents of energy tore through the sky. If I used my magic to save my life, it would tear open the gap wider, and the world would pay the price.

The fury's claws dug into my back. I cried out as it lifted me off the ground, into the air. The world rapidly fell away, and the roaring wind battered at me.

Then my spirit came loose from my body.

No. Not now. Please...

Evelyn's hand caught mine, steadying me. Her magic and mine intermingled, directed towards the gap in the sky. A gap that was suddenly all around us, cutting off all my senses, even the spirit sight.

But not my magic.

I called the energy of the line itself to fuel my spell. Magic spiralled from my hands, repairing the spirit line. The roaring wind stopped, the raging currents died to a flicker. A burning sensation on my wrist jolted me back into my body in time for the fury's grip on my coat to slip.

I'd done it. I'd sealed the spirit line... but I was on the wrong side. Below, emptiness beckoned. Above, the same empty grey fog.

My cloak tore. I grabbed for a hand-hold, but nothing remained but cloud and fog.

Emptiness swallowed me up, sending me cascading down into endless space.

———

I kept falling, the wind buffeting me on either side. This wasn't Death, and for all I knew, it had no end at all. Would I pop out of existence, or keep falling into nothingness for an eternity?

The air rushed past, getting colder by the second. Then suddenly there was solid ground, coming at my face at an alarming speed.

Shit.

Magic flooded me, surrounded me. Numb terror took hold, then true darkness carried me away me on its wing.

———

My head throbbed with pain. Softness brushed against my cheek, and when I opened my eyes, the world turned itself the right way up. It also felt solid. Definitely not Death, or even the realm beyond the gates. A firm, grassy surface lay beneath me, soft enough not to hurt, hard enough to be real. I lay on the edge of a hillside wreathed in thick fog. I grabbed a handful of grass, tugging it loose from the mud. Real, solid—and familiar.

I'd been here before, or somewhere very similar, when I'd stepped through the mirror into the mages' secret bolt hole.

The hillside stretched in all directions, covered in so much fog that it was impossible to make out any landmarks. I sat up, eyeing the rolling hills. Unless I'd somehow teleported to the Highlands, this place couldn't be our realm. It was way too quiet. And there were too few rogue fae, come to that. No signs of life. A jagged hillside ran parallel to where I stood, almost close enough to reach out and touch it.

Wait. That wasn't a hill. The jaggedness moved, opening an eye. Wings extended, revealing that it was not, in fact, a small hill, but a dragon, covered in blue-white scales.

Oh... my god.

I half-fell backwards down the hill. The dragon's eye blinked. Then he turned his head around, eyeing me like I was a tasty snack.

I stiffened. "Nice dragon..."

The dragon stretched out, revealing that he was at least seven feet long, not counting his wings, which were bunched up against his long, scaled back. How I knew he was a *he*, I wasn't quite sure, but he looked bigger than the dragon Evelyn had let out to take down the zombie army.

Speaking of whom... Evelyn had gone quiet again. I'd bet she didn't fancy her chances against a dragon, shifter or not. *Thanks a lot.*

"Hi." I gave a weak smile. "I'm not that tasty, you know. I'm covered in the smell of dead bodies and fury blood, and this cloak will probably choke you to death. So, uh, please don't eat me."

Not my best line, but they didn't teach 'negotiating with bloodthirsty giant reptiles' in necromancer training. I couldn't stand here having a staring contest with the big scaly monster forever, so I tentatively rose to my feet. The dragon's eye followed the movement, but he didn't attack.

Okay. The dragon wasn't going to eat me. Now all I had to do was find a way out.

"I don't suppose you know how I can get back to Earth from here? I assume you know the dragon shifter who came to Edinburgh before?" My words rang out into the silence. Even in the spirit realm, there was the constant background hum of spirits moving on to the afterlife. This place was a dead zone.

The dragon didn't respond.

"Not a talker, then," I said. "I'm not from around here. I'm a necromancer. I deal with dead people. What do you do? Do you have a spirit realm here?"

The dragon remained silent. Okay, then. Looked like I was on my own.

The spirit lines connected this realm with Edinburgh, so all I had to do was find a spirit line, and then…

Then what? Tear it open? Who knew where I'd end up if I did? I couldn't be *that* far from the line I'd fallen through, so if I found a point where I could cross over, I should end up back where I came from. If it was possible to do that without ripping open the spirit lines and undoing all the magic I'd used to fix it. Considering the power I'd expended, I might not have the energy to so much as touch the spirit lines for a long while.

I walked down the hillside, and the dragon's gaze followed me. It was a little unnerving, to say the least. If I got too close, maybe he'd change his mind about not attacking me.

"Have you seen a giant stone construction anywhere around here?" I asked the dragon. "Or—some pieces of shattered white stone? They're pretty noticeable."

Did dragons know what the Moonbeam was? Perhaps. One of them might have broken it to begin with. Given how even my Hemlock magic had been unable to break through the stone surface, that made the dragon someone I did not want to make an enemy of.

The dragon's wings bunched. Then it leapt, claws

outstretched. I cringed as a claw wrapped around my body, lifting me into the air.

For the second time that day, I flew upwards into the foggy sky. Swallowing a scream, I gritted my teeth and released a breath when the dragon put me down on the hillside. "Thanks."

For all I knew, the dragon couldn't understand English. But he'd got my message, and he'd brought me right where I wanted to be. Limbs trembling, I walked towards the towering construction. It *was* the same place where I'd found Wanda and Keir's brother held hostage. The dragon had put me on the hall's opposite side, so I had to climb over a heap of jagged stones to get to the front of the hall. This place seemed quieter, too, but of course, the Whisper had gone.

Was his realm where the mages were trying to get to? Perhaps the dragon was their ally, but the one who'd come into Edinburgh before hadn't seemed to be on Lord Sutherland's side. And I would have thought the mages liked their home comforts too much to set up a base on a desolate realm like this one.

I skirted the hall, peering through the entrance. Last time, there'd been barrier spells blocking the way in, but there was no such resistance now. I trod over the cracked stones, approaching the pillars where I'd found Wanda and Keir's brother tied up as hostages. Maybe I should have asked the dragon if he'd seen a vampire's soul floating around, but I doubted I'd be that lucky.

The pillars were bare, but lines of text were carved into them. It didn't look like any language I'd ever seen before, and the text had an odd shimmering effect. I tried turning on my spirit sight, but not a soul was within reach, despite the thick fog surrounding the cathedral-like space.

I left the empty hall and picked my way down to the heap of shattered pieces of broken white stone. A dazzling stream of light reflected off every fragment. Maybe sunlight, though the clouds made it hard to tell if a sun existed in this realm.

It's been a nice trip, but I think I've overstayed my welcome.

I trod closer to the Moonbeam pieces, my heart beating faster. I didn't know *where* the mirror was, but I had to trust that it was in the hands of my allies.

Crossing my fingers that I wasn't about to fall into another trap, I walked onto the pieces of Moonbeam.

A dazzling white flash swallowed up my body, and once again, I fell into emptiness.

Then I tumbled out of the mirror, and a blast of air hit me in the face, pinning me in a web of red lines.

A trapping spell… a *witch* trapping spell. My knees buckled in mid-air, suspended inside a room filled with expensive furniture.

I knew this place. It was a hotel room Vance and the mages had rented out as a bolt hole. I'd never seen what it looked like on the outside, so I wouldn't have been able to find it in the real world.

Carefully, I used my Hemlock magic to find the strands of the trapping spell and pulled them undone. The spell released me, and I wriggled free.

As my feet hit the carpet, someone ran into the room. "Stop right there!" boomed a voice, and fire exploded overhead.

13

I ducked the stream of fire, which dissipated as it hit the mirror head-on. My attacker summoned another flame to his hand. He was tall, thin, and wore a knee-length cloak. He lowered his hood, revealing coppery hair and a long, thin scar on one side of his face.

"Ow," I said. "Hey—Drake, it's me!"

Drake's hand stilled, a flame dancing on his palm. "Jas? You're supposed to be dead."

"Takes more than a hole in the sky to bring me down." I turned back to the mirror, which glittered with faint white light rather than showing my reflection. "I didn't know the mirror was here."

"I didn't know you knew how to dimension-hop," he said. "Wanda's going to throw a fit. And Isabel."

"Sorry I worried everyone," I said. "I found my way back, after a fashion."

"No shit," he said. "You've been gone two weeks. Everyone thinks you died."

"Two *weeks?*" I stared at him. "That can't be right."

"It is," he said. "You disappeared fifteen days ago. You've been gone so long that even the mages have stopped looking for you."

I sank into an armchair. "It's been less than an hour for me. How is that even possible?"

"Did you go to Faerie?" he said. "Time passes weirdly there. That's what Ivy says, anyway."

"Not Faerie." For all the weird things I'd seen in that realm, faerie magic hadn't been one of them. "How are the others? Isabel?"

"She's fine," he said. "At least, she was when I saw her yesterday. I don't know about your other friends, though, sorry."

"Don't be. I'm the one who took an unintended holiday." I rubbed my forehead. "I guess Lord Sutherland and his people think I'm gone for good, right?"

"Yeah," he said. "They do. But they haven't dropped the charges against you."

"At this point it's easier for them to assume I'm still alive, given the number of times I've walked back from the other side." Not that I'd died this time, but still.

Drake tapped his phone. "Vance and Wanda will be here in five minutes. Are you sure it wasn't Faerie? I've been to the weird part of it and it doesn't all look shiny and new."

"Are there dragons in Faerie?"

A rush of air blew through the room, and a tall dark-haired man wearing a knee-length coat appeared from thin air. At his side stood a woman my age, tall and willowy with long brown hair.

"Hey, Wanda." I waved at her. "And you too, Vance."

"Jas?" Vance's eyes widened. "It really is you."

"Do you think I'd lie about something like that, Vance?" Drake said, putting on a mock-hurt tone. "You know Jas is special."

"That's one way of putting it." I stifled a yawn, exhaustion tugging at my bones. It seemed surreal that days had passed here in the blink of an eye and I hadn't even known it.

"Jas!" Wanda ran to me and hugged me. "I'm so glad you're okay."

"Me too, believe me." I hugged her back, surprised to find tears stinging my eyes. Wanda and I had been best friends as teenagers before the universe had sent us lurching on entirely separate paths. I'd nearly lost her. Nearly lost everyone I knew.

"Tell me everything," said Vance, when she released me.

"Don't pressure her, Vance," said Drake. "Jas just came back from the dead—granted, it seems to be a hobby of hers, but you might want to offer her a drink first."

"Got any liquor?" I asked. "I'm joking. I need a caffeine hit, if anything. I'll start on the wine later."

The hotel room appeared unreal to my tired eyes, as though the fog of the dimension I'd come out of was about to smother the place and reveal it for the illusion it really was. I accepted Vance's offer of coffee, while Wanda pulled out a bag of Isabel's cookies. I munched one gratefully as I told them about my experiences on the other side of the mirror.

Vance wore a calm expression, but I could see his mind ticking as he took in every word. He was descended from the Ancients himself, through his shifter bloodline, and had come close to falling under the Moonbeam's influence. Now I knew the link between the mirror and the Moonbeam pieces remained open, it seemed doubly important that Lord Sutherland never learn that the mages had kept the mirror hidden within the city.

"Did the spirit lines definitely close?" I asked the others. "Because I saw furies spawning everywhere."

"We're still hunting the bastards down," Drake said. "That's why we're up here. They appeared all over England, too, but Edinburgh got hit the worst because it's on top of where both spirit lines broke open. The local mages weren't thrilled that we showed up, but they were too polite to turn us away."

"Guess they hoped the former Council of Twelve would leave them alone, huh," I said.

"There's still a Council of Twelve," said Vance. "The cooperation of Lord Sutherland isn't necessary for us to continue doing our jobs. What concerns me is his treatment of the other supernatural leaders."

"He doesn't care about burning bridges," I said. "What do the rest of your people think about him claiming the Ley Line? Have the faeries thrown a tantrum yet?"

"No, because he seems to have pulled back on patrolling," Vance said. "Perhaps as a result of the explosion which hit the other spirit lines."

Weird. I thought he wanted to open the spirit lines. No... that was what Evelyn wanted. Lord Sutherland just wanted power, and he'd mow down anyone who stood in his way. He hadn't even given me a fair fight. Dickhead.

"Now you're here, can't you march into his office and displace him?" I picked out another cookie.

"That's not how it works," Vance said. "Besides, I've no desire to rule two mage councils. I've been reaching out to my contacts across Scotland to see if I can find a suitable replacement. In the meantime, I'll meet with him alone—"

Wanda shook her head. "I wouldn't."

"No way," Drake said firmly. "We've been through this. You ask for a solo meeting, he kills you and makes it look like an accident."

"I'd like to see him try." Vance's grey eyes simmered with the hint of a threat, and the temperature of the room dropped a little. "Was anyone you met in that other realm in contact with the Mage Lord, Jas?"

"I don't think the dragon was," I said. "He did carry me over to the Moonbeam pieces when I asked."

"Probably thought you were threatening his hoard," Drake said, snickering. "This is fucking wild. And Lord Sutherland had this mirror in his back room for ages and never knew?"

"Of course he knew," Vance said. "As for the mirror, as far as I can work out, it's been here at least a decade, if not longer. Lord Sutherland claims it was the mages' possession from the start, but I have my doubts."

"I heard it links to a place called Foxwood, too," I said. "Is that true?"

"Ilsa Lynn told you that?" he guessed. "Lord Sutherland kept the mirror's existence under wraps, and every time any of us has used the mirror, we've ended up in that other realm. Why do you need to get to Foxwood?"

"Lady Harper was in contact with a coven of witches who lived there," I explained. "The Briar Coven. They saved my life. I found a letter in her house addressed to them, so I figured they might know... something."

Like how to translate the coded journal, for instance. Or what the deal was with the inexplicable map she'd left behind. Both were problems I hadn't thought about for a while, but with the mirror so close, the memories came flooding back.

Does it matter? Everyone thinks you're dead, for god's sake. Exhaustion dragged at my bones, and while fifteen days had passed here, it'd barely been an hour since I'd almost killed myself trying to close the spirit lines.

Vance gave a nod. "If that's the case, you're free to use the mirror if you deem it important."

Do I? "Not as important as proving Lord Sutherland's guilt," I relented. "Didn't the necromancers run a search of their headquarters… fifteen days ago? My boss was in the middle of interrogating him when the spirit lines exploded."

You'd think the soul-stealing spirit devices would be proof enough, but only Lady Montgomery and I had witnessed him try to use them on us.

"Uh…" Drake frowned. "Jas, there was a search of the mages' headquarters soon after you disappeared. They didn't find anything incriminating."

Nothing? That can't be right. "But—the witch-shade," I said. "Did you hear about that?"

Drake and Vance exchanged glances, while Wanda looked concerned.

"Isabel told us about the shade," Vance said. "She died by suicide right there in the guild around the same time you disappeared. Lady Montgomery didn't get back in time to begin the questioning."

Anger drove me to my feet. "Suicide? Seriously?"

"That's… not what Lady Montgomery really thinks," Drake said, his tone unusually serious. "Vance managed to talk his way in, and…"

"And?" I raised an eyebrow.

Vance turned to me. "Ilsa Lynn told me she was certain someone else killed the witch-shade, but it happened too fast to prove anything."

Someone else. Like a vampire. Or...

A chill settled around the base of my spine. I glanced towards the glittering mirror, then back to the others. "That place... it lies between the spirit lines. I thought when someone falls through the spirit lines, it's impossible to get back."

"I dunno, you're the one who fell into it," Drake said. "And you got back okay."

"Exactly." I swallowed. "I think I might know who we're dealing with."

"Who?" asked Wanda, a quizzical look on her face.

"I didn't kill the Soul Collector." I dropped my gaze to the carpet. "I shoved him into a tear in the spirit line. I thought I got rid of him for good, but if he survived..."

He could be summoned using a ritual by anyone who knew his real name.

Vance leaned forward in his seat. "Nobody else came through the rift with you, did they?"

"Not that I saw. The only person I ran into over there was the dragon." My head throbbed. "Maybe I should have asked him to take me to meet his friends, but I was scared of being someone's lunch."

"I don't blame you," Wanda said. "I didn't see any dragons when I was there, for the record."

"Do you remember anything else?" I asked. "From your time in the other world?"

"Not much," she said. "Two of those zombies dragged

me into the hall and tied me to a pillar. I tried to fight them off, but there were too many of them."

"And you didn't see any... gods." Of course not. The Whisper hadn't been there, not in person.

"Do you think I'd have lived to tell the tale if I had?" She shook her head. "I don't know why they spared me as it is. I never saw who was pulling the strings."

Drake rested a comforting arm on her shoulder. "Relax, we won't let them take you again. Just stay away from that mirror. Does it have an off switch?"

I shook my head, but Vance moved towards it. "It's worth checking."

"I doubt mysterious otherworldly artefacts can easily be turned off," I said to Wanda.

She gave a slight smile. "I'm glad you made it out. I knew you would."

A rush of emotion hit me, and I blinked hard. If I didn't get control of myself, I'd be in floods of tears by the time I showed my face in front of Lloyd and Keir. "I almost became a dragon's snack. I don't have much of my power left in me."

If anything, my Hemlock magic seemed to be draining away by the day.

Wanda hugged me. For a moment, I let myself pretend we were two failing apprentices suffering under Lady Harper's wrath again like we'd been as teenagers. Before her magic had manifested and mine hadn't, and Lady Harper had separated us.

Speaking of Lady Harper...

The image of the glowing, oddly familiar text on the pillars came back to mind, and I stifled a gasp. Now I knew where I'd seen it before.

Lady Harper's journal.

That... that must mean she's been there before. She spent time in the other realm. But when, and why?

"I need to tell my friends I'm alive." I pushed to my feet. "Is Isabel still in Edinburgh?"

"Last I heard, she was," said Drake. "She's been helping guard this place when we're busy."

"I knew it was one of her trapping spells I fell into." I wondered if Isabel had told the others about her experiments with blood magic. Most likely not. Though without that amplifying rune, I might not have survived closing the spirit lines. "I wrecked my phone. That's why I haven't been in touch. Aside from, you know, that." I gestured to the mirror, which glimmered back, deceptively innocent.

Answers might well lie on the other side, but that could wait until after my friends knew I'd survived.

Time for my official resurrection.

14

"You're supposed to be undercover," Evelyn said to me as we left the hotel.

"I'm supposed to be MIA," I corrected. "Everyone will expect me to lie low. Why not subvert expectations? It's not like I can hide from the guild. Hell, it wouldn't surprise me if Lady Montgomery knew I was alive all along. River will have, too, even if Ilsa didn't tell him. I don't know about the other senior guild members, but they don't have a high opinion of the current mage leadership."

"You'd better be right," she said. "After all, Lord Sutherland will doubtless know the mages hid the mirror. It's only a matter of time before he finds it."

"And we're not even a consideration," I said, with an eye-roll. "He let the furies carry me off like I wasn't worth bothering with. I'd be tempted to say he doesn't think we're a threat to him at all."

A dangerous assumption to make, but I'd seen that shield of his. He and his son were both using blood magic. I just hoped I'd destroyed the last of those spirit devices.

As for the witch-shade? A vampire could have disposed of her with little effort if they'd been strong enough, but the idea of any vampires willingly working with the Mage Lord didn't sit right with me. Let alone sneaking into the guild to commit murder.

The alternative was far worse. If the Soul Collector had made it back into this realm, I'd assume the psychics would have noticed, but both Mackie and Morgan wore iron bands everywhere they went now, and without his weapon, the Soul Collector was fairly weak. Call me paranoid, but if someone had tricked me into falling into a rift between worlds, you'd better believe I'd have done my level best to come back.

"Evelyn?" I said.

"What?"

"Do you think he's back? The Soul Collector?"

She was silent for a long moment. "He's not dead."

"I'm aware of that," I said. "Lord Sutherland has at least one Ancient on his side. Who else hates us enough to ally with humans against us?"

"You'd be surprised," Evelyn said. "Where are you going, anyway? Ilsa and your other friends are at the guild, along with Lady Montgomery. The instant you reveal yourself to her, you'll draw the mages' attention. I don't doubt they still have spies there."

"They'd better not." I ducked into an alley to turn on my spirit sight in search of my allies. Sure enough, Ilsa was at the guild, along with Lloyd and the psychics. And— wait, where was Keir?

Shit. Not again.

"Keir?" I conjured up a mental image of him and reached out, relief sweeping through me when I zeroed in on him. He hovered there, a shadowy form, his gaze fixed somewhere ahead.

"Hey." I waved a hand. "It's me."

"Little busy here," he said, his shadowy outline flickering around the edges.

"What are you doing, fighting a fury?" I asked. "It's me, Jas."

"A hellhound." He stopped, looked directly at me. "You… you can't be Jas. She's gone."

"I *am* Jas." From the distant expression on his face, he was too occupied in both physical and spirit worlds to pay proper attention. "I'm alive, Keir. Where are you?"

"Fuck—ow. Jas, is that really you?"

"Don't talk to me when a hellhound's trying to eat you," I said. "I'm on the way to Asher's, but if you need help—"

"I'll be there." He vanished in a blur of shadow.

Honestly. I tapped out of the spirit realm and found myself floating in mid-air. It took three firm blinks to get back into my body, and at that point, Evelyn had almost walked me all the way to the market. The smell of fresh herbs for spell ingredients tickled my nostrils. The witches' market went on the same as usual, with no signs remaining from the attack two weeks ago.

Two weeks. Keir must have thought I was never coming back. How had he survived, considering our connection? It wasn't the first time he'd gone without feeding on me for weeks, but he must be in a bad way. Not bad enough to avoid fights with hellhounds, though, apparently.

I climbed down the cobbled path to Asher's shop and pushed the door inwards.

Isabel gasped and dropped the spell she'd been holding. "Holy shit. Drake wasn't messing with me."

"Of course not." I walked to her and wrapped her in a firm hug. "It's good to be back. Keir is on the way, if that's okay."

"The vampire?" Asher said from behind the desk. "All right, but only if he doesn't bring any zombies. This place still smells like the dead."

"He's fighting a hellhound," I said. "They're not overrunning the city, are they?"

"No, but those furies keep spawning where you opened the spirit lines," said Asher. "The mages had to call in support teams from outside the city. Meanwhile, the humans are panicking, and so are most supernaturals, considering a lot of them didn't even know furies existed until they started materialising all over the place."

"I didn't open the spirit lines," I said. "I closed them. With me on the other side."

"I know," said Isabel. "I thought you must have survived, but I didn't know you'd landed in the same realm the mirror led to. Lucky."

Or not so lucky, considering who might have followed me back. "I didn't know two weeks would pass in the space of a few minutes."

"I get it, believe me," Isabel said. "Did Ivy tell you about the time she got stuck in Faerie for three years and came back and found it'd been a decade?"

The door swung open behind me, and Keir walked in. Blood matted one side of his head, and he had a knife in his hand. Pushing the knife into the pocket of the thick coat I'd bought him at Christmas, he strode over to me and wrapped both arms around me.

"You're alive," he murmured into my hair. "I know the spirit realm doesn't lie, but I thought—I thought you were gone."

"How are *you* alive?" I hugged him back, and he gave a stifled gasp of pain. "You okay?"

"I'm fine," he said, waving a hand and wincing a little. "Wouldn't say no to a healing spell, though."

"On it." I released him. "What did you do, single-handedly take on two hellhounds?"

"Five." He rubbed the side of his head, smearing the blood even further into his hair. "They've kept me busy while you've been gone."

"What're you like?" I passed him a healing spell, my last one. "Seriously, how are you alive? I thought you had to feed on me or die." True, he'd lasted a month without contact with me once before, but his vampire powers had nearly been wiped out in the process.

Unless...

A cold pit formed in my stomach. "She... stayed behind, didn't she? Evelyn."

"She didn't mean to," he said, activating the healing spell. "From where I was standing, it looked like both of you were dragged out of your body at the same time. If you hadn't reconnected before the rift closed, you'd have been stuck on this side with your body lost in limbo."

Then how—?

I looked up, but Keir had averted his gaze. Over his shoulder, Asher caught my eye for a brief moment and a jolt of understanding hit me. The blood magic rune on my arm was set to activate whenever something happened to my body when I wasn't at the wheel. It must have pulled me back into my body just before the rift closed—but not Evelyn.

"I didn't know that was possible." I'd thought Evelyn and I were one entity—or at least, that's what she'd once told me. How could we be literally worlds apart and survive it?

"Apparently." Keir lifted his head. "She kept me alive. That's all."

"I know." I didn't want to say more in front of the others, so I eased a cleansing spell off my arm and handed it to him. "Did you walk through the market covered in blood?"

"I had to." He spoke quietly. "When you disappeared—I even tried a summoning."

"Whoa, really?" I raised an eyebrow. "That might have worked if I hadn't been in my body, but I don't think you can summon anyone who isn't a ghost."

"Ilsa tried it, too, when Lloyd begged her to," he said. "Your friends didn't give up on you."

My heart squeezed, and I forgot all about the mental image of Evelyn helping to keep Keir alive. *They didn't give up on me.*

"I need to see them," I said. "But my phone's still dead and I can't go to the guild. Besides, I need to tell a certain relative of mine I survived."

Evelyn had made me believe she'd been at my side all along. Perhaps she figured I'd be jealous of her helping Keir, but I doubted it. Our extended separation proved our spirits weren't as closely linked as the Hemlocks claimed—but where did that leave the binding spell?

Isabel's eyes widened with understanding. "Uh, I

haven't been into the forest since you disappeared. To be honest, I didn't dare."

I winced. "Cordelia is going to kill me."

"She won't," Keir said. "I'll go with you for moral support."

"I'll tell your friends you're okay if I see them," Isabel said. "I don't blame you for wanting to avoid the guild. Your boss was furious when you vanished, too."

"I can't believe the mages wriggled out of paying for killing guild members to host their witch allies." A spark of anger formed, but I pushed it down. Lord Sutherland thought I was gone, and as long as he did, he'd never see me coming next time.

"We'll get them." Keir took my hand, giving it a squeeze. "Let's go and tell your extended family the good news."

I walked out hand in hand with him. "I wonder if Cordelia's ever been to that other realm? She must know about it."

Keir halted. "Wait, *that's* where you ended up? The place behind the mirror?"

We turned away from the market and began to walk through Edinburgh's Old Town. "Yep. That's how I got out. I landed in the mages' bolt hole."

Keir gave a low whistle. "Lucky, that."

"Maybe not so lucky." I gave a rundown of what I'd told the mages… along with my realisation about which Ancient might be roaming free in this realm again.

Keir was silent for a long moment. "I haven't heard any rumours about the Soul Collector," he said. "Not a word from the guild, either. I assumed a vampire killed that witch-shade, but honestly, everything in the first few days after you disappeared was a mess. Rumours all over the place… I had to lie low, but I kept searching for you."

My throat tightened. "Keir."

"I knew you were alive," he said. "Evelyn would have disappeared if you weren't, for one, and she seems fine."

"I bet she had a party in my absence," I said. "Invited all her ghostly friends."

"Actually, she just showed up at my flat every morning and then left immediately afterwards. Not much of a conversationalist, is she?"

"You'd be surprised," I said. "You just have to get her on the right subject. Like the superiority of the Hemlock magic and our how we're going to destroy the Ancients and save the world.

I expected her to interrupt then, but she remained quiet. Guilty conscience, maybe. *Why* she hadn't just told me she'd been left behind and had been floating around as a ghost for the last two weeks—who knew, maybe she'd enjoyed the freedom. I might have done the same in her position.

"She isn't you." His voice was a soft murmur. "In case there's any doubt on the subject. Every morning I hoped you'd show up instead."

I caught his shoulder, and his head whipped around, his lips on mine, hands digging into my upper arms through my coat. I felt his vampire's spirit brush against mine and deepened the kiss, inviting him in. He shivered, then broke the kiss. His stubble grazed my cheek as he hugged me instead, his arms warm and reassuringly solid.

"I won't do that to you now," he said. "You're fading. Badly."

"That's because it's only been a few hours since I had

to seal two spirit lines shut using all the magic I had," I said.

"And you lecture *me* about risk-taking." A smile caught his mouth. "Okay. I'll buy you lunch and then we'll deal with your creepy relatives. Then we'll make up for lost time. Deal?"

"Deal."

We picked up sandwiches from a street vendor Keir deemed safe and ate them on the way to the abandoned train station. Evelyn remained stubbornly silent, but Keir took in every word I told him about my experiences on the other side of the mirror—and my expectation that the same mirror might lead directly to Foxwood, home of the Briar witches.

"That should be our next stop after this." He finished his sandwich in two quick bites. "Seems these Briars might know what's up with the mirrors and that other realm."

"I'll pick up Lady Harper's journal first." I licked mayonnaise off my fingers, wiping them on the sandwich wrapper before tossing it into a bin. "Whatever code she wrote in, she's not the only one. There were markings on the pillars in the other realm which looked the same. Inside that weird hall where I found your brother."

"Did you find… anything else there?" The catch in his voice told me he meant, *any sign of Aiden's soul.*

"Just the dragon. Sorry."

He crumpled his own sandwich wrapper, his mouth tightening at the corners. "I guess the odds were always against us."

"I beat the odds when I came back." I gave his hand a squeeze. "C'mon. Lloyd will skewer me for not coming to see him first, but the longer I leave the mirror, the more likely it is that Lord Sutherland finds out where it's hidden." I didn't *think* he'd put tabs on me considering he thought I was permanently stuck on the other side of the spirit line, but he doubtless had people watching Drake, Vance and the others.

We reached Waverley Bridge, halting on top of the spirit line. No signs remained of the damage the blast from the spirit device had caused. The line was intact, a flowing current of energy, rippling with achingly familiar magic.

In a blink, we appeared in the forest, on a path I didn't recognise. "That was fast."

Keir ran his hand up my shoulder. "I kept thinking I sensed you in the spirit realm. I knew you couldn't have just disappeared for good, otherwise there'd have been more of an outcry from... this direction."

"You may be underestimating the Hemlocks' ability to give a shit about me." I scanned the thickly crowding oak trees. "Hey Cordelia. I'm still alive."

"She doesn't care," said Evelyn. "It might have been five minutes in this realm for all we know."

"I thought you were the expert." Considering the forest had an odd relationship with time, too, they might not even have noticed I was gone. That they'd been annoyed with Isabel suggested they had, but 'annoyed' described Cordelia's default state. "And on that note, why not tell me you've been roaming around the city alone the last two weeks while I was making friends with one of the dragons?"

"You never asked."

I opened my mouth to respond, and the trees disappeared, to be replaced by the cave and Cordelia's stern face.

"Oh, good," she said. "You're alive."

"You noticed?" I gave a mock gasp. "Yes, I'm alive. Have you ever been to a realm inhabited by dragon shifters, which may or may not belong to the Ancients? Did *you* know that realm was on the other side of the spirit lines?"

Cordelia didn't answer for a long moment. Then she said, "I thought I told you to kill the mage."

"He's the one who ordered a fury to throw me in there." I folded my arms across my chest. "Come on, you can admit you missed me. It won't kill you."

The wall of the cave folded open, revealing the hunched shape of the beast sleeping within the void. Fear crawled up my throat and even Keir took a step backwards, swearing.

"You can't throw that thing in my face, Cordelia." I gestured at the giant eye. "Yes, it's my job to defend the world from the Ancients, which is exactly what I was doing when a fury yanked me through the spirit line. A spirit line that cracked open as a result of the magic *you* gave me." My breath heaved out. The aura of raw fear surrounding the hole in the cave wall didn't help, but I'd passed the point of fear and gone straight into white-hot rage.

"What would you have me do, Jas?" she croaked. "Trap you in the forest prematurely?"

"If you even think about trapping Jas in here, I'll see if you have a soul worth feeding on, Hemlock," said Keir. Fury that almost matched my own was etched on his face. *He* blamed them, too, in the absence of any other target.

"Vampire." Cordelia spat the word out. "This is none of your business."

"I'd say it is." He jerked his head at the giant furred head of the sleeping beast. "Is he related to the dragon Jas met over in the other realm?"

"Yeah, that guy didn't attack me," I added. "He helped me, actually. I thought the shifters were direct descendants of the Ancients, aka our 'natural enemies'." I made quote marks with my fingers.

"The modern dragon shifters, if they still survive, are not our enemies any longer," she said. "But they did fight on the wrong side in the war."

The dragons had opposed the Hemlocks and fought on the side of the Ancients? Was that how they'd ended up stuck in that world?

That is, assuming Cordelia told the truth… which was debatable, given my recent discoveries about my coven's former relationship with the Ancients.

"And the mages?" I asked. "Were they involved?"

"The mages did not fight in that war, child," she said. "The Ancients see them as the enemy, but they say the same of most humans. Kill the traitor and be done with it."

"I think he's working with the Soul Collector." Speaking the name aloud, even in the forest, brought a chill to my skin which went beyond the gaping hole in the cave wall. The Soul Collector had nearly torn apart this very forest. "Did… did you know he survived?"

"Of course he did," said the Cordelia. "The Ancients are immortal. They can be defeated, yes, but not killed."

"So why bother fighting a war against them?" Keir put in. "There can only be one victor in the end. You're not immortal, and if you die out, it's over."

And I'm the last of the line. I gave the sleeping monster another glance, then regretted it. The magic sealing the hole shut was woven into the cave walls in shimmering lines that made me dizzy to watch.

"Don't you judge us, vampire," said Cordelia quietly.

She'd claimed not to even know vampires existed when I'd first told her about Keir, but the longer I spent around him, the more I became certain that vampires were also linked to the Ancients in some way. Keir's own brother had made that connection, and that might have cost him his soul.

"Tell me the truth, Cordelia," I said. "You know what's happening to me at the moment? I'm disconnecting from my body when I don't mean to. Evelyn keeps taking the wheel, and I'm losing hours in the spirit realm and barely being able to walk when I come back. Something is going wrong, Cordelia, and it's to do with the ritual you let Lady Harper use on me."

Keir's mouth parted in surprise. "Lady Harper?"

Cordelia scowled. "Evelyn told you."

I glared at her. "You couldn't even be honest with me about my mentor—the woman who looked after me for six years of my life. I guess it irked you that she was closer to my family than you would ever be."

The forest began to fade, the hole in the cave wall closing up. "Is that what you believe, Jacinda?"

A road lay ahead of me. Edinburgh. *No. I was trying to get to the other side, to Lady Harper's house.* I swore under my breath, and then looked up at the sky.

Burning red streaks marred the clouds, and the deafening sound of thousands of screams ripped through my eardrums. I wasn't on the bridge, either, but on a cobbled street that was elsewhere in Edinburgh.

"Not this," hissed Evelyn, so close I jerked my head to the side. She floated next to me, her transparent form a jarring contrast to the blood-splattered brick wall behind her.

"Since when could you talk to me in visions?" I said.

"Get out of my memories," she growled through her teeth.

"Believe me, if I could, I would." My voice grew more distant, and I became aware that the person whose eyes I watched through had dropped to their knees, blood spilling onto the cobblestones. Purple light flared to life in my hands: a healing spell.

"No," Evelyn's voice said, through my mouth. "I will not die."

Then I was I was on my feet, looking back at the house behind me. Bodies filled the entryway beside the blood-splattered wall. The right-hand side of the house was a gutted ruin.

One of the bodies stirred. A young woman, whose bloody face bore the same features as Evelyn. With a soft gasp, Evelyn crouched at her side, and let out a low moan of pain. "Not you."

"You're dying, too," whispered the woman. "They killed us all."

"No…" I gripped the tarmac with my bloody hands. "I can't die. I can't."

I lurched upright, running through the street, shutting out the cries and moans of the nearly-dead. Ghosts hovered all around me, moaning and screaming. The sky cracked open, spitting winged monstrosities out of its depths, but through it all, I kept moving. Rippling currents of energy crisscrossed the street, and my stomach lurched as I realised they were spirit lines. Wrecked spirit lines, torn open like exposed veins.

I walked into the open maw of a hole in the universe and stumbled to my knees on the forest's path. In front of me, a figure appeared, leaning heavily on a wooden staff. Lady Harper's clothes were torn and bloodied, blood caked one side of her head, and her hands trembled on the staff, but even twenty-something years younger, I knew her face as well as I knew my own.

"Are you the only survivor?" Her voice was quiet, but the trees caught every word and echoed them back at us.

A croak tore from my throat. "I will not die. I will not. I won't..."

My vision faded at the edges, the world shrinking to this small corner of the forest. While the tangled tree roots and the undergrowth cushioning me looked real, the smell of magic surrounded everything, and beyond that, death. *My* death. A shadow fell over the forest path as someone else approached.

"It's time," Cordelia's voice whispered. "Forgive me."

I jerked my head upright and my mouth dropped open. Lady Harper held a baby in her arms—sleeping, quiet even as the world outside burned and died. The incongruity struck me like a whip, the sight of the old mage holding a child in her bloodied arm, her free hand resting on her staff.

"Save our coven," croaked Cordelia. "If she dies... that child is our last hope. If Evelyn perishes without an heir, we die out. And then..."

A shadow passed over Lady Harper's face. "I can't promise both of them will survive this."

"Do it."

Lady Harper put the baby down in a nest of branches. My body tensed, though the child didn't wake up. She slept on, oblivious.

No. Make it stop. I don't want to see this.

Evelyn's hand gripped mine, startlingly solid. Both of us were ghosts, trapped in a nightmare. I looked at her rather than at the scene, and her eyes shone with tears she'd never be able to shed. Through them, I glimpsed flickers of the people she'd lost—the bodies in the street. The young woman, a sibling maybe.

In that moment, I understood her more than I ever had before. I understood her desperate loneliness, and why she'd come to care about me enough that she'd even kept Keir alive for my sake. Her entire world had crumbled, and here I was, her only anchor to life, a cage and salvation all at once.

"Get out of my memories," snarled Evelyn. "You have no right to be here."

"It's my history, too." I wrenched my gaze from hers, to the sight of her body lying dead on the tree roots below, as the baby—*me*—lit up with the glow of Hemlock magic for the first time. "Cordelia—*stop.*"

Mercifully, the scene faded out. I came to, on my knees on the forest floor, my face wet with tears and my heart aching.

Keir's arms came around me. "Jas, it's okay—I'm here."

I shuddered, gasping for breath, unable to stop the tears from flowing.

He paused. "Please tell me you're not Evelyn, otherwise this would be really awkward."

"No, it's me," I mumbled. "Cordelia—who was the other person in the vision? The one who handed me over to Lady Harper?"

"She came from the Briar Coven," said Cordelia, her voice quieter than usual.

"I thought you didn't know where they lived. Do you have any memories of *them* to show me?"

The trees disappeared, leaving nothing but rolling hills, and silence.

15

"Well," I said to Keir, trekking up the hillside. "That would explain why the Briars didn't stick around for a chat. They condemned me to be bound to Evelyn, even when they saved my life."

"Yeah." His mouth pinched. "Are you okay?"

"I just witnessed my own death and rebirth—again—so I'm doing swimmingly. I think Evelyn's worse off than I am." I hadn't heard a word from her since the Hemlocks had unceremoniously dumped us on the hillside down from Lady Harper's old house. "I hope they let us back through because I'm not staying here for long."

I couldn't forget the raw memory of Lady Harper holding me in her arms. Not only had she lost almost her entire family that day, she'd also had to bind Evelyn and me at the risk of one or both of us dying in the process. No wonder she'd kept me at arm's length for all the time she'd known me.

Keir and I walked up to Lady Harper's house, and I undid the wards on the door so I could let us in. "I know it smells like a winery in here. There used to be several dozen bottles of old wine in the basement. Guess it's a good thing they didn't leave them behind, because I'd have probably drank them all out of boredom."

He gave a soft laugh, taking in the ghastly-coloured furniture of the living room. "Looks cosy."

"I've been living in front of the fireplace." I paced over to where I'd left Lady Harper's journal and slipped the map inside it before picking it up. "I'm not exaggerating when I say this has been the longest day of my life."

Keir stepped in behind me. "You sure you want to do this now?"

I shivered as his vampire's touch brushed against me. "If the mages steal the mirror before I can find the Briars, I'll be seriously pissed off."

"Hmm." He gave my shoulder a squeeze, and when I tilted my head, his mouth came down on mine. He kissed me long, deep, his fingertips caressing my chin. "I'm glad you're back."

"Me too." I raised my hand to his cheek, tracing the stubbled edge of his jaw. He needed a haircut again, and the soft strands brushed my fingertips. "I didn't have time to miss you, but I would have. That dragon wasn't the best company."

"Obviously." His vampire's touch ran down my spine, a wickedly fast stroke that brought a gasp to my lips. "I'm friendlier."

"You're insufferable." I gave him another swift kiss on the lips, getting a quick brush against him in the spirit realm in for good measure.

He exhaled in a curse. "Damn, Jas, you're not making it

easy for me not to lay you down in front of that fireplace and do everything I've been dreaming about for weeks."

I nipped his lower lip, enjoying teasing him. Anything to forget the forest, and the emptiness of that other realm. "We'll have plenty of time when we're back."

———

"Hey, you're the vampire, right?" Drake said, letting us into the hotel room. "I've always wanted to meet one of you."

"Enough, Drake," Vance said, with an appraising look at Keir. The two of them hadn't exactly got off on the right foot, since Wanda had gone missing at the same time as Vance had witnessed my secret being exposed. His tone was crisp and polite, though, when he extended a hand and said, "Mage Lord Colton. I don't believe we've been formally introduced."

I suppressed a snort at Keir's incredulous expression as he shook the Mage Lord's hand. "Keir Langford. Have you been through the mirror to make sure there's nothing waiting to ambush us on the other side?"

"Nah, we haven't been in town," said Drake. "Can I—"

"No," said Vance. "You're to guard the mirror from this side while I call Ivy."

"She's still in Faerie," Drake added to me in explanation. "If you end up in the dragon realm again, can you send me a postcard?"

"I'll think about it." I walked to the mirror, which carried a faint whitish glow. No reflection faced me, making me feel oddly like I was on another midnight tryst around the mages' headquarters—were it not for the vampire at my side.

I pressed my hand to the mirror. *Take us to the Briar Coven. Take us to the other mirror.*

The mirror turned transparent, and my hand passed right through. Then I walked into nothingness.

Fluorescent lights came on overhead, banishing the dark and revealing a small, empty room with tiled floors and plain grey wallpaper. A door lay half open ahead of us, revealing a corridor. The walls, floor and ceiling were the same shade of pale grey, giving our surroundings a lifeless quality. Like a more solid version of the spirit realm.

"I don't think this is Foxwood," I whispered. "Ilsa said it was a small village in the middle of nowhere, not... whatever this is."

"You think someone stole the mirror?" he whispered.

"Must have." I trod forwards, my boots clacking on the cool tiles. "I guess this must be the place the mages were connecting with when they had the other mirror at their headquarters. Not the dragons' realm." I'd had it wrong. But what in hell was this place? It put me in mind of the necromancer guild with its echoing corridors, but the lighting struck me as much more modern.

A ghost walked through the wall, male, with vaguely defined wispy hair.

"Ah," I said, taking a step backwards.

The ghost's eyes locked onto us, glowing silver-white. "You," he said. "You're not alive."

"Uh... yes, we are," I said. "Definitely alive and kicking here. Who are you?"

"I... can't remember." He turned on the spot, looking

through the wall as though staring at something invisible. *Oh, boy.*

I looked incredulously at Keir. "I travelled into another dimension and I'm still being haunted by annoying ghosts. How is this possible?"

"I'm not annoying," said the ghost. He turned back to face us, his transparent eyes crinkling at the corners.

"Do you remember anything about your life?" I asked.

"Cold," he said, with a faint shudder. "So cold. Bright. And cold. So long… so long… so many years…"

"Years?" Ghosts shouldn't be able to stick around that long. He must be totally addled. *We don't have time for this.*

Keir caught my arm. "Jas… check the spirit realm."

I turned on my spirit sight and jerked backwards in alarm.

The entire space around me was swarming with the dead. So many ghosts, overlapping, a mass of grey shapes that hardly resembled the living people they'd once been. Murmurs, moans and whispers echoed, like a distorted recorded tape played at a faint volume.

I'd been banishing spirits for a third of my life and I'd never seen a ghost who'd stuck around longer than a few weeks, but these spirits were so faded, they might have been here for months or more. Fear clawed at me from within. Whatever had killed all those people, instead of moving on, the ghosts had been trapped in an eternal hell.

"I think it's probably safe to say the mages don't have any necromancers working here." My voice was shaky. "They'd lose their minds."

"Can't disagree there," Keir said.

Even people who banished the dead on a daily basis could only tolerate so many spirits before they started to crack. But for all the ghosts, I hadn't sensed any *living* people during my brief scan of the spirit realm. Then again, Vance and the others had taken the mirror at least six weeks ago. Nobody had come here since.

"Do you remember seeing any mages?" I asked the ghostly man. "Or… any other humans? When was the last time you saw someone living?"

The ghost flickered and vanished. Creepy was par for the course when it came to the dead, but the stifling stillness of the narrow, clinical-smelling corridors made the small hairs on the back of my neck stand on end.

I released a slow, steady breath, and imagined Lloyd cracking up laughing at me for being afraid of a single ghost. "Want to look around?"

"Sure, but we should be careful," Keir said. "Someone really screwed up here."

"Coming from the guy who tried to take on five hellhounds single-handedly."

He gave me a smile, but his eyes were wary as he walked out of the room, past the spot where the ghost had vanished. Fighting the instinct to turn heel and get the hell out, I followed.

Outside the room, the corridor was lined with glass-windowed rooms filled with shattered glass and broken machinery. The smell of decay underlaid the clinical scent, suggesting some of the ghosts were recent after all. The spirit realm didn't tell me how big the facility was, but the lack of windows suggested it might be underground for all I knew.

"How far did we travel?" I whispered to Keir. "Ilsa said the mirror was with someone she knew, and she wouldn't have had any reason to lie. This sure as hell doesn't look like the Highlands."

He made a small noise of assent and carefully climbed through the glass frame of a shattered window into one of the labs. The movement stirred up a flurry of dust, making me cough as I climbed into the room behind him.

"Thirty years," Keir said, reading the topmost page of a stack of papers on the desk. "No, thirty… thirty-one years. That's when this place was set up."

Three decades, some of these ghosts had been trapped in here. The mages might not even know, if they could only see the bones, not the screaming dead.

At the back of the lab stood a row of three tall glass cases, each big enough to fit a person inside. A long-decomposed skeleton lay in one of them. I pressed a hand to my mouth, fighting nausea.

Pages rustled as Keir lifted the notebook from the desk. "This place was an old Orion League stronghold. They—captured humans."

"Supernaturals." Fear squeezed my chest, imagining what it would be like to slowly suffocate here in a tank inside this cold, window-less lab. "The mages were in on this."

"Not always," said Keir. "Lord Sutherland wasn't Mage Lord thirty-one years ago. I'd say it's more likely that he found this lab later on and decided to steal some of the equipment for himself."

"Out of academic interest, I suppose." I gave a brittle laugh, thinking of the book Asher had said Lord Sutherland had stolen from him. "The League captured witches and forced them to use dark magic on humans, and the mages decided they wanted in on it."

I climbed through the shattered window into the corridor, taking in a long breath. My lurching heartbeat kept me anchored to the present, if nothing else. Keir's hand slid into mine and squeezed. "You good?"

"If I was, I'd be worried." I let go of his hand. I'd nearly said *I'd be worried I was turning into Evelyn,* but that was a bit unfair. It wasn't that she didn't have feelings, but that she prioritised her own above all others.

I made for the next room. Old bloodstains the colour of rust marked the floor, along with heaps of disintegrated bones. "Ugh."

Bodies, some still rotting, were heaped carelessly into a corner. In the room's centre, chalk lines formed circles on the ground, hastily erased.

Keir swore. "Look at those marks."

I didn't want to, but I forced my gaze to the nearest corpse. His arm was covered in faded symbols. So was his neck. As a necromancer, it was my job to ease their suffering, and yet there was absolutely nothing I could do to help the lost spirits trapped in this place.

Shivering, I tentatively turned on my spirit sight. Evelyn appeared at my side, her hands pressed to her ears. "Get me out of here before I lose my mind."

"How am I supposed to do that?" I grimaced as the chorus of the dead rose in the background, eerie, insistent.

"Who are you talking to—right, Evelyn," said Keir. "I guess it can't be fun to be surrounded by ghosts even if you are one."

"You're telling me." My hands lit up with Hemlock magic, unexpectedly. "Whoa. My magic... it's reacting."

A tugging sensation, like the tracking spell, spun me on my heel like the point of a compass.

"Reacting to what?" Keir walked at my side as I backed out of the room, turning in the direction of the faint tugging sensation. Wards rippled against my skin like static, coming from a locked door at the corridor's end.

Instinct screamed at me to get out. Necromancer I might be, but I did have some sense of self-preservation left.

Curiosity won. I opened the door.

More glass tanks filled the space within the room. Inside each, a circle of candles lined the edges. And between each candle circle was a ghost.

Young, old, faded or clear... everyone in the lab was dead. A thousand transparent stares turned in our direction, pleading, desperate, trapped within their glass prisons.

"This shouldn't be possible." The words stuck in my throat. "How...?"

I knew how. For a ghost to be imprisoned in a cage, they must have been torn from their bodies while they were still alive. Even if their bodies rotted away, they'd endure. Forever.

Keir swore under his breath. "This is what the mages were doing."

Separating bodies and souls. The spirit inside the nearest tank looked at me with faded blue-white eyes. His hands brushed the glass and I jerked back. "Is he... is he a vampire?"

"They all are." Keir's hands curled into fists at his sides. "Every last one."

"Bastards." I scanned the tank in front of me in search

of a way to open it, but there didn't seem to be one, and the candles were on the inside of the glass.

I called on my Hemlock magic, my hands tingling with static as I touched the metallic edge of the tank.

"Watch it," Keir murmured. "There'll be defence mechanisms."

"I know that." My voice shook, and so did my hands. Magic sparked from my fingers, bouncing off the tank's glass front.

Then a live current slammed into me, sending me sprawling onto my back. Keir exclaimed, crouching at my side. "Jas. Speak to me, Jas."

"I'm fine." Shaking off the shock, I clambered to my feet and found myself face to face with the vampire inside the tank.

"Watch yourself," said the vampire, his voice quiet but echoing. "Unless you want to join us on the other side, that is."

"Who put you in here?" I asked. "The mages, right?"

"Does it matter?" The vampire shook his head. "Human, supernatural, dead, alive, you all look the same from here."

"I can set you free," I said. "I can help you to the afterlife. To move on. But first, can you tell me... why did they put you in the tank? What did they hope to learn?"

His mouth moved, but I didn't hear a word. He was fading. My magic reached out, pushing at the tank's edges. This time, I felt a spark, and stifled the current before it could shock me.

A splintering noise sent a jagged crack upwards through the glass exterior. Encouraged, I directed my magic into the tank, pushing the candles apart.

The ghost, however, didn't move. He remained floating on the spot, his eyes glassy, almost empty of life.

"Hey," I said to him. "You're free now."

The vampire floated out of the circle, through the place where the tank's front had been. Then his hands latched onto me, and he began to feed.

Coldness pierced me through to the very core, rendering me still. Icy hands gripped my already-depleted spirit, and while I tried to back away, my body wouldn't obey me.

Then Keir's hands locked around the vampire's ghostly arm, pulling him off me. I staggered, forcing my legs to keep moving away from the vampire's pale, empty stare. The lucidity in his expression from earlier had vanished, and his form grew more shadowy as my spirit gave him life.

An incoherent growl slipped through the vampire's teeth and he spun on Keir, hands reaching for his throat. Keir calmly sidestepped, wrenching the ghost's arm behind his back. While he couldn't feel pain in that state, neither could Keir.

"Don't make me drain everything you have left, vampire," he said.

"Shade," growled the vampire. "You're one of them, too."

"What're you talking about?" I rubbed my hands together to get some sensation back into them, both eyes on the restrained vampire. "You were talking to me just then—you haven't completely lost your mind."

"He might as well have," said Keir. "He's half-dead. There's no coming back from this state."

The vampire made a half-wild lunge, breaking out of

Keir's grip. Cursing, he snagged the vampire by the leg before his grasping hands found my throat. "I banish you beyond Death's gates, vampire."

The vampire vanished—then he reappeared again, directly behind me. His hands went through my chest, straight to my soul.

"I banish you beyond death, vampire." I choked out, fighting the chill.

"I am already beyond death," he snarled.

Keir crashed into him from the side, locking his arm around his neck. "Go peacefully or by force, it's all the same to me, vampire."

"You're dead," I said. "No matter how long you try to feed on me, you can't come back to life. It'll be better for everyone if you move on."

"No," screamed the vampire. "I won't!"

He broke free of Keir's grip and vanished once more. Tapping the spirit realm, I recoiled from the solid wall of ghosts. Hands grabbed at me—ghosts, not vampires—and I turned off my spirit sight. But the vampire had vanished among the other lost spirits, fleeing the room.

Keir swore under his breath. "The mirror."

Shit. The vampire might not even know the mirror was there, but if I were him, I'd head straight for the nearest way out. Right into Edinburgh.

Turning my back on the other tanks, I broke into a jog, retracing our steps. The vampires' moans and whispers pursued us, trailing like ice on the back of my neck, but I'd learned my lesson from freeing the first guy. As awful as their punishment was, if they got out into Edinburgh, just one vampire could kill multiple people in seconds.

I skidded into the room with the mirror to see the

vampire's ghostly form pass through the mirror's rippling surface.

"Fuck," said Keir, echoing my own thoughts. "If he possesses a vessel, we'll have a hell of a job finding him."

"I'm more worried for my friends on the other side." I ran to the mirror, and Keir caught up with me as we passed through the glass into the hotel room.

In front of the glass, Drake lay in a crumpled heap on the carpeted floor. I clapped my hands to my mouth. "No. Drake—"

"He's alive," Keir said.

Sure enough, I tapped the spirit realm and found a faint but strong glow above Drake's body. The expanse of grey seemed blank and quiet after the chaos of the trapped dead in the lab.

Keir shouted a warning, and the vampire slammed into me from behind, his ghostly hands locking around my throat. Once again, a chill permeated my blood, needles prickling at every inch of skin. "Get off me!"

"Let her go," Keir said, grabbing the ghost from behind. "I banish you, vampire, beyond Death's gates."

"Likewise." I twisted out of the vampire's grip, flying out of my body to face him directly in the spirit realm. Necromantic power suffused my hands and I pushed it all at him, willing him to calm and move on. "I banish you. Go to rest."

"I will *not* be beaten," roared the ghost, and necromantic power exploded from his hands, knocking me flying backwards into the air.

By the time I'd caught my balance, he was gone.

"Damn, he's a shade," said Keir.

"Come again?" I shook out my hands, wishing I had a warm fireplace to hold them near. "He's dead."

"I know," he said. "But he's been brought back from the edge at least once. He's not bound to a body, but he can't be that strong without being a shade. That banishing ought to have worked."

No kidding. The guy was so faded, he ought to have disappeared right away. "Was that what Lord Sutherland was doing in the lab? Bringing vampires back from the edge and then… turning them into shades?"

"There were at least a hundred in that lab," Keir said.

A hundred. Every one of them furious, ravenous, deadly.

"He wasn't just conducting experiments," I said. "He was building an army."

Had anyone ever destroyed a shade before? Even for the guild, it was unchartered territory. But if the vampire's ghost showed himself in front of the mages, Lord Sutherland would know where he came from right away. Then it was one step from there to tracking down the mirror… and he'd be able to set the entire army of vampire shades loose into Edinburgh.

Drake groaned, stirring at my feet. "It feels like I took an ice bath," he mumbled into the carpet.

"Not quite," I said, relieved he seemed okay. "An angry vampire's ghost escaped through the mirror. Sorry."

"I thought you were going to find your coven's friends, not the vampires." Drake pushed to his feet, looking around the hotel room in confusion.

"That mirror doesn't lead where we thought it did," I said. "Is Vance around? And Wanda?"

"Wanda's outside," he said. "I'll call her back in. What's on the other side of the mirror?"

"Lord Sutherland's army," I said. "Vampires. Starved, angry vampires, pushed into Death and brought back to life."

"Vampires have been disappearing off the streets for ages," Keir added. "Everyone assumed they didn't leave a trail deliberately, so nobody would be able to track or follow them. I didn't know..."

None of us had known. And if not for my allies taking the mirror back, those vampire ghosts would have been the next monsters to fill Edinburgh's streets.

"I'm sorry, did you say an *army?*" Drake said, his eyes wide.

"They're dead vampires," I explained. "Trapped in summoning circles inside warded tanks. The instant they get free, they'll attack. If we tried to banish them all at once—I'm not sure even the guild can handle it."

Keir sucked in a breath. "And we don't know if their bodies are still alive."

Oh. "Do you think he might be there?" I asked. "Aiden?"

"I don't know." He delicately averted his gaze from mine, pacing to the hotel room's door.

Given the state of the other ghosts, the chances of finding Aiden alive and sane were dwindling by the second, but I wouldn't take away the last of Keir's hope. I hadn't checked every single tank, and a lot of the spirits had been there a long time. The spirit devices, and the Soul Collector, proved that it was possible to separate body and soul without causing damage—hell, even my own blood magic mark proved it, too—but those vampires had been anything but whole.

"I'm going to free them," I said. "There'll be a way, we just have to be cautious about it. If I blow up every tank, living people will die unnecessarily. Those vampires haven't fed in months if not years. I don't know how they survived."

"They're shades," said Keir. "They survived death, and they came back stronger. And… perhaps their sanity can be revived, I don't know. But I doubt the two of us can free every single one without one of us suffering the backlash."

"Meaning me?" I tilted my head on one side. "Keir Langford, are you actually suggesting we hire the necromancer guild to help us?"

"Maybe I am." He turned to face me, and while his eyes retained the wary, haunted look he'd worn in the lab, a smile tugged at the edges of his mouth. "Are you ready to face your boss?"

16

"I can't believe you went to a creepy lab and didn't invite me," Lloyd said, sitting across from me on the sofa in Ilsa's living room.

"I'm rubbing off on you, aren't I?" I picked up my coffee mug to get some warmth back into my hands. "You're supposed to say, 'why did you go into the creepy lab, Jas? Don't you know that's the quickest way to die in a horror movie?'"

"Jas, you've died more times than anyone I know," he said. "I'm pretty sure you can waltz into the Devil's lair and walk out in one piece."

"Don't speak too soon." The combination of exhaustion and caffeine set my nerves jangling, and despite the long day I'd had, I was wired. "I'm sorry I ran off before coming to tell you I was alive. I was expecting a quick visit to family friends, not a dive into NightmaresVille."

"Have you met you?" Lloyd glanced sideways at Keir, who sat in the armchair on our right-hand side. "Setting a vampire shade loose in the city is a new one, though."

"I didn't realise he'd lose his shit the instant I freed him and would be immune to banishment."

"I bet he's not immune to my Gatekeeper powers," said Ilsa, who occupied the other armchair. She and Lloyd had received Isabel's messages about my unexpected return from the other realm, and Keir and I had spent the last half-hour bringing them up to speed on our latest adventure. "Are you absolutely certain you want to bring the boss into it? Because once you do, Lord Sutherland will have no reason to hold back any more."

"Lord Sutherland already had a fury drag me through the spirit lines in an attempt to get rid of me," I said. "He isn't holding back. And if he is, it's because we took the mirror. If we wait, he'll find it first. We have to take out his army before he can set them loose."

"You had trouble with one ghost and you think a small group of us can beat an army?" said Lloyd sceptically. "Your vampire friend might think he's invincible, but the rest of us aren't."

"None of us is suggesting taking them on all at once," Keir said. "That's why we need the guild."

"But that place is hellish for necromancers," I added. "The whole facility is swarming with ghosts. I think some massive tragedy happened there and everyone got stuck on the wrong side of the veil."

Ilsa grimaced. "It's not a liminal space, is it?"

"Not that I can tell," I said. "I didn't even see any windows or doors. It's a secret lab, so it might be underground. It also can't have been too far from wherever they stole the mirror from, right?"

"Near Foxwood." Ilsa's mouth pinched. "Yeah, the mages have gone nuts over the Ley Line, otherwise I'd run through and check on Agnes and Everett. They were the ones who had the mirror, so I assume the mages took it from them. But we have bigger problems."

The doorbell rang. Everyone looked at one another.

"If it was a bad guy, they wouldn't ring the doorbell." Ilsa got to her feet. "Back in a second."

I looked at Lloyd. "What're the odds the boss already knows I'm back?"

"She does," Ilsa said over her shoulder.

I walked out to join her. River Montgomery stood on the doorstep, his golden hair and pointed ears standing in contrast to his black necromancer coat. Ilsa's boyfriend… and the boss's son.

"So it's true." He looked me up and down, taking in my dishevelled appearance. "My mother told me she sensed you in the spirit realm. She wishes to speak with you."

That's promising. "Better hope I'm not getting arrested again. I think she's going to want to hear this."

———

My nerves spiked again as I walked to the guild's headquarters with Lloyd on one side and Keir on the other. Ilsa and River led the way. The boss's son had remained tight-lipped on Lady Montgomery's reaction to my sudden return, so I didn't know what sort of mood to expect her to be in. Either way, I doubted she'd shower me in praise for setting a vampire shade loose in the city.

"I'll get worse than a stint in the archives for this, won't I?" I said to Lloyd.

"You'll be cleaning the toilets for a month."

"Not helping."

"I'd say it's more likely that she sends you to banish that shade in person," said Keir. "Which I'll help you with, of course."

"I hope it hasn't attacked anyone." The shade could have killed me, and given recent events, I could no longer count on my own shade powers to save my neck.

Keir frowned up at the guild's warded exterior. A rush of nostalgia swept through me at the sight of the smooth brick façade laced with iron, and the glimmering wards enhanced with my own magic. I kept my head down as we entered the wide lobby, but felt the stares of curious novices scrutinising me.

River halted, checking his phone. "Change of plans. The boss wants to meet us in one of the summoning rooms."

Oh, boy. What was she planning to do, lock me in a room with a poltergeist, like they did in advanced exams for high-ranked necromancers?

"You don't have to come," I said to Lloyd, who looked mildly unsettled as we entered a corridor lined with locked metal doors. "You shouldn't take the heat for what I did."

"Look, I've worked for the necromancer guild for a third of my life. I'm not afraid of the—" He broke off as Ilsa opened the door on our right, staring at the summoning circle inside the room. "What the bloody hell is that?"

"I take it you're responsible for this, Jas?" Lady Montgomery said, indicating the circle.

Trapped between twelve candles, the vampire shade floated in the circle, considerably less transparent than he'd been before. He'd fed on someone. Several someones.

"He attacked the guild?" I guessed.

"He tried." Lady Montgomery eyed the others. "Jas, Lloyd, come in here with your friend and explain yourselves. Ilsa, River, find the psychics and tell them to stay away from here until I tell them it's safe."

"All right," said Ilsa. "Call me back if you need me to take care of that guy."

Ilsa and River left, and with their departure, the room seemed to grow several degrees colder. Or maybe it was the presence of the vampire's hungry stare. More worrying was the boss's silence. She looked the same as ever, none the worse the wear for her narrow escape from losing her soul at Lord Sutherland's hands. Her floor-length cloak was adorned with decorative medals and her greying hair swept back in a bun. Her stern, wrinkled face was as familiar as someone from my own family, and a fist clenched around my heart. *Please don't kick me out.*

"Sorry," I said when she didn't break the silence. "It's my fault he got loose in the city."

"I think that's the least of your recent transgressions, Jas," said Lady Montgomery. "You have multiple arrest warrants on your head."

"I know," I said. "I mean, I guess about half of them are for the spirit of my dead ancestor, but she doesn't exist on any records, it'd be hard to prove."

Her eyes narrowed. Ah. Maybe joking hadn't been a good move, but the silence was seriously getting to me. And did we have to do this in front of an insatiable ghost who wanted to eat my soul?

"I thought Jas was listed as dead or missing," Keir ventured. "I also thought a number of witnesses saw Lord Sutherland send a fury to drag her through the spirit line."

"That is not, unfortunately, what the witness accounts say happened," said Lady Montgomery, with a sideways glance at the vampire's ghost. "All accounts of the incident claim that Jas used her magic to open the spirit lines, at which point a number of monsters came through and carried her away with them."

A wave of indignation rose within me. "That is such bullshit—"

"I agree, Jas, but it's your word against someone who has the letter of the law on his side." She took in a deep breath. "That is the only reason I am willing to assist with this absurd plan of yours. Ilsa tells me you found a laboratory in use by the Mage Lord—and this man backs up your story."

I turned to the vampire's ghost with some surprise. While his eyes retained the ravenous stare of a half-starved vampire, he stilled under the boss's stare. "He trapped me. He tore out my soul and left me to die."

My stomach lurched. "None of them can remember how long they've been there. That lab's been in use since before the invasion. Would that count as proof?"

"Considering the mages have made no secret of the fact that the mirror is their possession and was at their headquarters until recently?" she said. "Yes, it would, but only if we can capture and gain testimony from some of the trapped vampires after the threat is eradicated."

"You mean... banish most of the ghosts and bring some of the others back to testify against the Mage Lord?" Would that work? It carried one hell of a risk, and yet—she'd managed to get the vampire into a summoning circle even with him being a shade.

"Yes," she said. "However, that would not rid us of the

price on your head, Jas. I take it you were aware of Jas's situation, Lloyd?"

He shifted from one foot to the other under the boss's attention. "I didn't think it mattered, since nobody knew Jas was alive."

"In case you're unaware," said Lady Montgomery, "Lord Sutherland is making a compelling case against the need for a necromancer guild at all. I'm weeks from losing my job, if he decides that disbanding is the best way to go. I have every intention of putting up a fight, but it's not one I expect to win."

"He stole those spirit devices from you," I said heatedly. "He turned your own people against you and—and ripped out their souls. And he gets away with it?"

"No perpetrator was found for any of those crimes," she said, her jaw clenched. "As there were no surviving witnesses."

I get it. If she openly accuses the Mage Lord without enough proof to back it up, she loses her job for sure. Then every single necromancer at the guild would be out on the streets and a potential target for the Mage Lord's twisted schemes.

"And he blamed me for the furies and hellhounds running amok around the city?" I guessed. "If I'm supposed to be dead, he'll run out of people to blame."

"The spirit devices were destroyed," said Lady Montgomery. "Which I can thank you for, at least, Jas... however, I don't doubt he plans to make others. They were the hallmark of the Ley Hunters, after all."

"The Ley Hunters?" Lloyd frowned. "I thought the Ley Hunters was like... a cover. For those vampires who worked for the Soul Collector."

"That wasn't the first time," said Lady Montgomery, with a glance at Keir. "The Ley Hunters was also used as a cover in pre-invasion days by a group of humans who possessed the spirit sight but had no prior connections to the supernatural world. Eventually, those so-called Ley Hunters sold their secrets to the Orion League, who took their resources and used them to fight against supernaturals. Most significantly was their decision to take the Ley Hunters' practise of inking runes onto themselves to link their spirits to the realm of Death and combining that with an art stolen from the witches…"

"To turn them into zombies, raised by witchcraft," I concluded. "The Ley Hunters were the first people to create those spirit devices?"

"Yes, but they got the idea from an old practise," she said. "Every couple of decades seems to bring a new attempt to break open the spirit lines in an attempt to gain knowledge or enlightenment, which usually ends in disaster. I need to know, Jas… *was* it you who opened the spirit lines?"

I started to shake my head, then faltered. "My magic… it links to the spirit lines. I can open and close them at will. But when the spirit devices blew up, they hit the lines of their own accord. I tried to *close* the lines, not open them."

Lady Montgomery's expression shuttered, but somewhere in the depths of her eyes, I saw a flicker of fear. *It's not me you should be afraid of.* I was kind of surprised Evelyn hadn't stepped in to say her piece, but she'd been all but silent since my return from the lab.

I licked my lips. "Has anyone ever travelled to the realm on the other side of the line before? Do you know?"

Lady Montgomery shook her head. "Travelling to other realms… that has never been an area of expertise of the guild. We deal with Death, nothing more."

"And the mirrors?"

"An Ancient creation, I would guess," she said. "The League stole many artefacts from the Ancients. It's not hard to find them if you know where to look—or it wasn't, before Lord Sutherland started hoarding the information for himself. I suppose now I understand why, if he was conducting similar experiments."

"Question." I darted a quick look at the vampire, who was intently listening in. "Do you know how to banish a shade? A regular banishment didn't work."

Lady Montgomery strode up to the circle of candles. The vampire, while retaining his ravenous expression, moved imperceptibly backwards. "Yes, I can. Watch very carefully, Jas, and remember that vampires have access to the same tools that we do."

She reached through the circle's boundary, her hands touching the vampire's shadowy outline. A glowing blue light travelled from the vampire to her hands as she removed them from the circle. Like when a necromancer reanimated a corpse, except the thread of light travelled towards her, not the other way around. The light around her hands brightened, and the vampire dimmed.

I watched, my eyes widening. Lloyd stood frozen at my side, and even Keir's attention was entirely fixed on the vampire.

"No," he whispered. "I will not… die."

He was already fading, becoming more transparent until the blue light died out. The last shadow dissipated, and every last trace of the vampire was gone. She hadn't even used the banishing words.

Note to self: don't get on her bad side. My former boss had reached out and drained his life force like... well, a vampire. "How in the world did you do that?"

Lady Montgomery lowered her hands. "Energy transfer. *Not* a skill we teach on our curriculum—it requires opening a direct connection between yourself and the vampire, and it's generally only necessary to use it on shades. The transfer removes the energy tethering them to life."

"You took his spirit essence out," Keir said. "Didn't you?"

"Yes," she said, looking from me to Keir. "I suppose another vampire would be able to do the same, since the transfer of energy is your area of expertise. That's likely why you were chosen as subjects of the experiment."

"Maybe." Keir caught my eye for a brief second, enough for me to be certain we'd both had the same thought at the word *energy transfer.* Lady Montgomery had managed to turn the spirit from a shade back into an ordinary ghost again. What if the same magic could be used to separate Keir's spirit from mine—and mine from Evelyn's?

———

Keir didn't speak a word as we re-entered the lobby, leaving the cold room behind. His brow was furrowed as though lost in thought.

"What now?" Lloyd asked me. "Are you and Keir gonna—"

"Not now." The words came out sharper than I intended. "Sorry. I have to think about this."

"Me too." Keir turned to me. "I need to check on my brother. I'd invite you back with me, but you want to catch up with your friends, right?"

My objection died on my lips. If we were to do the energy transfer, it would take away Keir's resilience and might make him more vulnerable than before. The decision should be mutual—which meant giving him the chance to make up his mind first.

"I should stay at the guild tonight," I said. "It's safer, and I have everything I need with me."

Except you.

He tilted his head as though he'd heard the unspoken words, and lowered his head to press his lips against mine.

He didn't drain me, and I didn't, despite our direct connection, try the energy transfer. The last thing I wanted was to weaken him right before our mission. But if there was a way to ensure that our link never hurt him again…

He broke the kiss, wrapping both arms around my back. "I'll see you tomorrow, Jas. I'll call… no, I'll contact you through the spirit realm. Okay?"

"Better than okay." I dug my hands into the fabric of his thick, spell-strengthened coat, then released him. "I'll see you tomorrow."

He gave me a faint smile before leaving the guild.

Lloyd cleared his throat. "You're seriously not going to remove the link? You like him that much?"

"I haven't even tried the energy transfer yet," I said. "I

need to practise, and I definitely don't need to take any more risks when we have an army to banish tomorrow."

"Uh, about that," said Lloyd. "Lady Montgomery didn't say who would be going through the mirror with you, did she?"

"Keir and I are going to have to take the lead. And Ilsa, I bet the energy transfer is no problem for her. Maybe Morgan, too, but the number of ghosts in there is probably too overwhelming for anyone with psychic tendencies."

"And not me?" He raised an eyebrow.

"I don't want you to get hurt on my account," I said. "Those shades are powerful—even Keir and I couldn't stop that vampire getting through the mirror."

"You do realise that if it all goes tits-up, we'll be fighting those vamps out in the open rather than a safe enclosed tank, don't you? I'm going with you." He wrapped me in a bear hug, muffling my protests, then released me.

"We'll see what the boss says." I headed for the stairs. "Where's Ilsa, do you know?"

"Either the training room or the archives, I'd guess."

I headed upstairs with Lloyd. "I'll tell her how to do that energy transfer thing, if she doesn't already know."

Considering she'd learned of the existence of vampires around the same time as I had and had only read about shades in the textbooks before she'd met me, I had my doubts she did. We were going in with so little knowledge compared to the enemy, but what choice did we have? If we didn't handle the lab as fast as possible, the entire city would be overrun with vampire shades.

We found Ilsa in the archives with Morgan and Mackie.

"About bloody time." Mackie bounced to her feet. "I knew you were alive as soon as you came back, Jas."

"That's because you took the iron off." Morgan put down the textbook he was reading.

Mackie shrugged one shoulder. "So did you."

"Ilsa asked me to." He jerked his head over his shoulder at his sister, who stood on a footstool to reach the highest bookshelf. "She insisted that I'd be able to sense if Jas came back from the other side."

"Lloyd's idea," she said, without looking up.

I raised an eyebrow at him. "You all took the risk for my sake?"

"Hardly a risk," said Mackie, rocking back on her heels. "It's not like there are any evil vampires around to mess with my thoughts."

"Uh… about that." *Crap. I can't tell her the Soul Collector might be back.* Not without concrete evidence. If he'd been there in the lab, he'd have found Keir and me. I doubted a tank could hold *him.*

"Aside from the vampire shade army?" said Morgan. "We're on the first patrol, obviously."

"You aren't." Ilsa lifted a hefty textbook down from the topmost shelf. "Nor's Mackie. We're not prepared to deal with them."

"Did Lady Montgomery tell you how to banish a shade?" I asked.

"River did," she said. "He's giving instructions to the others, too. In case any of them escape through the mirror into the city."

Worry squirmed through me. "It's a high-level skill, isn't it?"

"Not when they're stuck in tanks," said Morgan. "A kid could do it."

"I'm not a kid, I'm eighteen," Mackie said. "And yes, I can do it, thanks. I'm top of my novice class now, Jas, did you know?"

"That's awesome," I said, with a rush of genuine pride at her enthusiasm.

"At this rate she'll catch you up, Morgan," Ilsa said. "And you, Lloyd. If you keep getting suspended from missions, anyway."

I frowned at Lloyd. "Why'd you get suspended? Did you store zombie body parts in your room?"

"Nah, we tried some questionable tricks to get you back from the hole in the sky," Lloyd said.

I chanced a look at Morgan, wondering if the two had finally voiced their feelings aloud yet. Judging by the distance between them, I'd guess not.

"Questionable meaning illegal?" I queried. To get Lloyd back, I'd have done the same, no question.

"Maybe." Morgan shrugged. "He said you might be stuck in limbo."

"Not anymore." I looked around the room at my friends. "Tomorrow will be risky. I'm not talking any of you out of coming with me, but it's bad over there. Really bad."

"I've probably seen worse." Morgan removed his feet from the desk. "Look, you need me there. None of you is psychic."

"That's why I think it'll be too overwhelming," said

Ilsa, with a glance at Mackie. "Those ghosts… how many were there, Jas?"

"Hundreds. Maybe thousands." I lived in a city of the dead and yet I'd never seen so many trapped souls. It was like the gates of Death didn't even exist over there.

"But they weren't all vampires, right?" Mackie's brash confidence faded a little.

"Most of them weren't," I admitted. "But the ones trapped inside tanks were vampires *and* shades. That's why we have to banish them one at a time. They were pushed to the brink of death, but the spirit circles are keeping them alive. They're stuck in limbo, reduced to nothing but hunger, and can drain you dry in a blink."

Mackie made a small noise, her head withdrawing into the shadows.

Morgan glanced her way. "What, have you seen them before? The guy who took you wasn't a shade, right?"

"Mackie?" I said gently. "Do you know something?"

She squeezed her eyes shut, her mouth pinched. "He… the vampires who captured me said they escaped from a lab somewhere. That's why they wanted to attack the guild. They… they blamed the necromancers."

A lab? The mirror was miles away, but… maybe they'd escaped from there a long time ago. Mackie had been a prisoner for years, and the lab had been around at least as long.

"Whatever the case, there's a lot of people who've been suffering for a long time trapped in there, and I owe it to them to at least try to set them free."

If we can, then maybe Keir and I can undo the bond making him dependent on me.

The memory of him nearly drifting beyond Death's

gate was still raw. I'd come so close to losing him, and I would never put him at risk on my account again.

"What about Lord Sutherland?" said Lloyd. "Don't get me wrong, I'm on board with the plan, but what if he attacks the guild while you're gone?"

"He didn't attack after he pushed me through the gap in the spirit line, did he?" I said. "I'm not even on his radar as a threat. It's insulting, to be honest."

He didn't even seem to care about the Hemlocks. At least, I didn't think he did. After all the Hemlocks' insistence—especially Cordelia—that there was an inevitable war, they seemed to be mistaken on who was actually going to participate. The battle was supposed to involve the Ancients and the Hemlocks. Not the mages and the rest of the supernatural community.

"He's a sick bastard," said Mackie. "We'll wipe out his army."

Ilsa put down the heavy textbook on the desk. "Shades and vampires hardly appear in the same sentence in any book in here, though. Did the mages confiscate every book on the subject? That's what River implied."

"I think they did," I said. "They also confiscated a book from Asher—Isabel's friend—which contained instructions on how to do ritual magic. Pretty sure the mages are using it as a guidebook."

But I hadn't found any signs of the book at their headquarters.

"Asher had a book on rituals?" asked Lloyd.

"He used to, years ago," I said. "It wouldn't surprise me if Lord Sutherland left it over there in the lab. It'll be what he was using to bind those vampires, I'll bet. And it wouldn't surprise me if that's another reason their plans are on hold until they find the mirror. They left the book behind, and without it, they can't summon the Ancients."

And if I found it, I'd be able to reverse the ritual binding my soul with Evelyn's and bind her to a new body—assuming I found one.

"We'll take everything they have," said Morgan.

"I'm not letting you lot have all the fun," Mackie added.

"I still think you're batshit, but I'm with you," said Lloyd. "Okay, if this is our last night alive, I think we should order takeout and watch Zombie Platypus Army Part Two."

"That sounds bloody terrible," said Morgan. "I'm in."

Ilsa snorted. "I'm going out with River, but have fun."

"Just like old times?" My throat tightened. I might be back home at the guild, but it wasn't really my home. Not as long as the price on my head existed.

But my friends would stick by my side. And tomorrow, we'd take down the mages' army before they could unleash it on the city.

17

To no surprise, I couldn't sleep. After staying up late converting all the ingredients I'd left behind in my old room into usable spells, I left my body in rest mode and floated through the roof of the guild. There, I found Evelyn hovering in silence, eyes trained on the shape of the castle towering over the city. A rush of emotion pierced me at the sight of the peaked roofs, the ribbon of rippling coastline in the distance.

"There you are," I said. "I wondered if you'd gone walkabout again."

"That place nearly wiped me out," Evelyn replied. "You have no idea what it was like in there as a ghost. They swarmed me."

"Oh, shit." That explained why she'd gone silent during the chase through the lab and hadn't helped me recapture the vampire. As a ghost, she'd have been swamped by the crowd of tortured spirits. Not a pleasant experience. "Sorry."

"I'm used to it," she said. "I'd rather not have their army overrun the city, so I'll help you be rid of them."

"Can you do the energy transfer thing? Even as a ghost?"

"Yes," she said tersely. Her eyes traced the flow of energy beneath us, the spirit line crossing to the abandoned train station and beyond. The memory of her death and rebirth crawled to the forefront of my mind. We hadn't had a real conversation since I'd been forced to relive her death in the forest, and if I were her, I'd be feeling pretty fragile, too.

"Just checking," I said. "You know, since those vampires survived so long in the lab, it's probably possible to bind them to new bodies. If they aren't out of their minds, that is."

"If there was already a soul present in the body, then they would likely perish like that unfortunate necromancer," Evelyn said. "Even another shade might fade away. Two souls would not make one another stronger. There's nobody quite like you and I out there in the world."

Says who? Did she not *want* to be separated? She'd done nothing but bitch at me for my entire exile, when I hadn't been wandering around in the spirit realm, anyway. Admittedly, we hadn't found her a substitute body yet— without a soul already attached. The body would either have to be recently dead or preserved by blood magic, which made it trickier. But then, look at Aiden.

Unless… unless she thought being removed from my body would cost her some of her magic? If it was true, then the same would happen to me. Together we were stronger. Both of us. Strength meant more to her than it did to me, but she'd made no secret of her desire to leave me behind and fulfil the Hemlocks' mission without me holding her back. Right?

"What is it you want, Jas?" Her eyes were sharp, cutting. "Do you think this is an easy way out for you? A chance to evade your responsibilities?"

"Excuse me? I'm about to take on an army of vampire shades with a bunch of people who only found out they existed just yesterday." What was her problem this time? Her comment about us being unique was a reminder that we were both outcasts, but that didn't mean it had to define us. I hadn't fit in at the witch orphanage, or with the mages, or even really at the guild, either. After all, I'd lived a lie most of the time I'd been here. Yet I'd made friends. I'd built a life for myself here.

Evelyn had never had that chance. Never had the choice. Was she *jealous* of me?

"If we separate," I said carefully, "you'll be able to start over. Become whoever you want to be."

She made a soft, incredulous noise. "I am a Hemlock witch, Jacinda. It's my life's purpose to destroy the Ancients and claim the power that is rightfully mine."

"All right, then." I gave up on trying to argue with her. "Feel free to do whatever you like. Just try to remember you're not the only person who's affected by your decisions, okay?"

Her head snapped up. "We're not alone in here."

A distant voice said, "Honestly, Arden, that doesn't help."

"Ilsa," I said, turning on the spot. "That sounded like Ilsa. No idea who Arden is, though."

I moved through the grey haze in the direction of the

noise. Further down the path, Ilsa floated, a leather-bound book open in her hands. Her talisman.

"Hey," I said to Ilsa. "What're you doing?"

"Oh, hi, Jas," she said, looking up. "I'm trying to wrangle answers from this book. It's supposed to contain the secrets of the Ancients, but it seems pretty damned reluctant to tell me how to stop those vampire shades."

"I didn't know you could actually read the book." I glanced at the page over her shoulder, but the glowing writing was too small to read.

My magic hummed to life, drawn towards the pages. I willed it to quieten down. *Stop reacting to Ilsa. She's my friend.*

She closed the book and opened it again. "The book's text changes depending on what I need to know."

I put my hands behind my back. "The text in the book changes by itself?"

"It has part of a living god in it," said Ilsa. "But it depends if he feels like sharing with me or not. Usually, he doesn't."

"Huh." The book itself looked unremarkable, aside from the faintly glowing cover, but Ilsa must be able to see something in its pages that I couldn't. "What exactly is it, a guide to being Gatekeeper?"

"Kind of," she said. "It contains basic info on most parts of necromancy, including vampires, but shades are different. Shades can be created. Vampires are born that way, from what I can figure out. That means the ones in the labs were captured from somewhere. Also, it would really have helped if Arden had told me beforehand that the only way to kill a vampire shade is to remove their spirit essence, turning them mortal again."

"You and this god were… friends?" I asked.

"More like master and apprentice, and I wasn't the master." She closed the book, shaking her head at the cover. A shimmering image of a raven was etched into it, its eyes oddly mesmerising. "Arden is still alive, in this book. Like all Ancients, he's hard to destroy."

"Was he involved in the war?" The question escaped before I could stop it. "I mean, the war between the Ancients and the Hemlocks?"

"Not that I know of." She frowned. "I don't think he was ever really involved with the other gods."

"My magic keeps reacting to your talisman," I admitted. "Like it did to the Moonbeam stones."

Her eyes widened. "What, in a hostile way? Why?"

"I don't know." I stuck my hands out, showing the sparking magic across my palms. "It just turned on by itself. My coven's being as unhelpful as ever. They didn't even tell me *they* created those rituals to contact the gods themselves. Not to fight them. Asher said… he said all magic had the same source. Ancients, witch magic, necromancy, whatever."

Her mouth opened slightly. "Maybe it does. It's a theory I've come across a few times in my readings… not that there's much on the Ancients. Just speculation. But they've been involved in this realm for years. I think they've always been able to cross over."

"Before they were shut out of this realm." *By my coven, apparently. No wonder they feel betrayed.*

But who was in the wrong? The Hemlocks had never been the most forthcoming of individuals, but every Ancient I'd met had tried to kill me and my friends. Not much of a contest there. And despite it all, Evelyn believed it was her duty to fight against the Ancients. Even if she gained a new body, a new life. Did she really not want anything for herself?

Even if I was unable to convince her of that, tomorrow, I might learn how to set both of us free.

———

The next morning, I woke early and took my time getting ready and setting up my spells ready to storm the castle. Or rather, the top-secret lab.

Lloyd knocked on my door to bring me a stack of toast from the cafeteria. "The mirror's here."

"The mages brought it?" I took the plate from him and munched toast on the way downstairs, feeling slightly odd dressed in my necromancer coat. Like I was just running a regular patrol, not a potential suicide mission that had never been attempted in guild history before.

In the lobby, I found Vance speaking with Lady Montgomery. *So that's how they smuggled in the mirror—using his teleporting power.*

"Oh, Jas." Vance turned to me, and I awkwardly swallowed my mouthful of toast. "The mirror is in a secure room. If the hotel we stored it in is discovered, Lord Sutherland's people won't find anything there."

"Good," I said. "Are you coming with us?"

"The situation seems better suited to necromancers, given the nature of the army." He nodded to Lady Montgomery. "We will be staying here to protect the guild in case Lord Sutherland gets wind of your plan."

"I hope not." The vampire shades were enough to deal

with. But I wouldn't put it past Lord Sutherland to mount a sneak attack on the guild while we were gone.

"I'll stay." Evelyn's voice startled me. "I can guard the guild from this side while you're in the lab."

"Are you sure?" At Vance's quizzical look, I added, "Evelyn, you can make yourself visible."

She appeared, flickering around the edges. "Ta da," she said, in sarcastic tones.

Lloyd stifled a snort, while Lady Montgomery and Vance both stared at her, probably bewildered by the resemblance between her and me.

"Meet Evelyn Hemlock," I said to Lady Montgomery. "She's... we're distantly related."

"And you're both shades," she said.

"Technically," I said. "I know my coven broke the law, but it's hard to arrest people when they're dead. And I was a year old at the time. So..."

"Nobody is getting arrested," said Lady Montgomery. "Except, that is, for Lord Sutherland and his contingent of mages. I've been compiling a list of disloyal mages and their potential replacements, and I've invited those replacements to meet for a summit in the next two weeks. I wish it could have been sooner, but given the circumstances, it's best not to make him suspicious until we have the evidence."

Oh, we'll bring the evidence, all right. "We'll have enough for a trial from the lab alone. Who in their right mind wouldn't arrest him after seeing what he did to those vampires?"

"He played his part well," said Lady Montgomery. "Not well enough, however. I have recorded evidence that he paid a visit to our guild some years ago and requested that we raise his wife from death. She died from a fatal illness, as far as I know. That's enough to prove the origin of his fixation on necromancy."

"I hope you're right." That explained his obsession with preserving his own life, even to the extent that he'd make deals with the gods to avoid death.

Banish the vampires. Gather the evidence. Bring down Lord Sutherland. When I saw my own determination reflected back at me in Evelyn's eyes, my resolve strengthened.

Let's do this.

———

Within an hour, our small group gathered in the spare room where the necromancers had stashed the mirror. Whatever argument Ilsa had used on Lady Montgomery had worked, because she let me choose the team myself. Ilsa, Morgan, Mackie and Lloyd joined me, while Isabel and Vance organised a defensive patrol around the guild in anticipation of trouble from Lord Sutherland. River and some of the other senior mages, meanwhile, worked on the guild's defences in case any of the vampires got loose.

My arms were lined with spells, and Isabel had also given me one of Asher's pens in case I needed to use blood magic in a pinch. Not that I'd let that one slip to the boss. If she realised I'd chosen to use forbidden magic, I'd rather handle the fallout after the battle, not before.

When Keir entered the room, Lady Montgomery's mouth tightened. "Are you sure taking another vampire with you is wise, Jas?"

"Absolutely," I said. "He'll know if the vampires can be saved or not." It wasn't a job I'd wish on anyone, but Keir merely nodded.

"I don't think she likes me much," Keir remarked. His jaw was set, and while I'd let him feed on me before we left, we were still bonded. If either of us disappeared during the fight… *don't think about that.*

Drawing in a deep breath, I walked through the mirror, with Keir at my side. We emerged into the same room as before. An eerie silence filled the air, all the stronger with Evelyn's absence. It was far from the first time we'd been apart, but she'd saved my neck when we'd gone up against the Whisper and almost lost her life for it. Facing the enemy without her made me feel vulnerable in a way I didn't care for at all.

Mackie stepped out of the mirror and immediately recoiled. "Can't you hear it?" she gasped. "They're screaming. They're all screaming."

"You're still wearing the iron, right?" said Morgan.

"Of course I'm wearing the bloody iron," she snapped. "Can't you hear them?"

"Yeah." He stepped backwards. "I hear them."

"Mackie, I think you should head back," said Lloyd.

"Says who?"

"Says me," said Morgan. "Lloyd, take her back home."

"I'm not your little sister," Mackie informed him.

"Thank god. I have too many of those already," said Morgan. "Ilsa, back me up."

"Guys," Ilsa said. "If you want to bicker, do it somewhere that isn't swarming with ghosts."

"There's nowhere on this side of the veil that isn't

swarming with ghosts," Mackie said, her eyes wide. "They're so miserable… you have to let them out."

Keir, who'd peered out of the room, withdrew his head from the corridor. "Show yourself, vampire," he warned.

A shadowy form appeared, hovering in front of us. He was male, maybe Keir's age, and faded around the edges. *Huh? He's not the one I set free.* Had another vampire got out of his tank, too?

My shoulders tensed as the ghost approached, hands outstretched. Keir caught his arm, and I lunged, my hand passing right through his chest. *Okay. Spirit drain… now.*

My Hemlock magic tried to react instead, but I pushed it down, reaching for the energy humming through the ghost's body, keeping him alive by a thread. Catching the thread, I pulled it loose. The ghost made a faint gasping noise and my stomach turned over.

"It's okay." I drew in a breath, pulling the current of energy into my hand. "I'm saving you. I banish you beyond the gates of Death."

Please let this work. I'd had no chance to practise the spirit-drain technique, and I'd thought we'd be banishing the vampires inside the tanks, not loose in the lab. How had he got free? Whatever the reason, the energy flowing into my hand reacted like a live wire. I startled as the current zipped up my arms, flooding my veins like icy liquid. *Is this supposed to happen?*

Keir tightened his grip, his own hands glowing the same as mine. The ghost struggled, arms flailing, but growing weaker.

"I banish you," I said.

The vampire remained there, so transparent he was barely visible.

"That should have worked," said Ilsa, frowning. "Are you sure we aren't in a liminal space?"

I shook my head. "Keir and I only explored two corridors before the ghost got out and we had to run back. We don't have a map of the place. But both corridors from here end up in the same place. The only way through went past the lab where we found the—"

"Vampires," Keir said, staring ahead into the corridor. "I think we may have a problem."

I let go of the energy, following him to the door.

The entire corridor outside was filled with ghosts. Not the trapped, tormented spirits, but an endless flood of ravenous vampires.

18

Had one vampire somehow managed to set the others free? Or had my freeing the first vampire had a knock-on effect and somehow broken the defences on the other tanks? Either way, we had to stop them from getting through the mirror. The vampires formed a faded shadowy mass, a hundred or more of them crammed into the narrow corridor. If they all entered the guild at once, there'd be a massacre.

Ilsa pulled out the Gatekeeper's book. At once, the ghosts recoiled from her, floating into the destroyed labs.

"They're afraid of the book," she said. "Morgan, take Mackie back through the mirror."

"I vote we all get out," said Lloyd.

"Bit late," I said. "If we do, they'll follow us. For some reason, we can't banish them here. Either it's a liminal space, or—"

"A spirit barrier," Ilsa said. "Around the whole lab. Knowing our luck, it'll be on the outside."

Bugger. I bet she's right.

"We can handle this," Keir said. "Ilsa, if they're afraid of the book, you'll have to lead the way. You guys, stay back here and guard the mirror."

"Shouldn't Ilsa be the one who stays behind?" asked Mackie.

"No, because then we'd get mobbed by vampires," said Lloyd. "We should set up candles. Right, Morgan?"

He nodded, not arguing for once. "Sure, I brought candles. Put them by the mirror. Might not be strong enough to keep out a whole army, but it can buy us time. Mackie, go and warn the others. That's an order, okay?"

Mackie opened her mouth to argue, then took another look at the ghost-filled corridor. "All right, whatever. Don't get killed."

"We'll try not to." Lloyd stepped beside Morgan, who looked a little surprised. "We'll set up a salt barrier, too, in case that discourages them. Jas, you've got this, right?"

"I sure hope so. Ilsa, lead the way."

"Be careful, you two." Ilsa took the lead, and the ghosts recoiled again, floating backwards out of her path. They were scared of the book—or more accurately, scared of the Ancient's power contained inside it.

Ghosts fled as Ilsa walked, following my directions to the lab.

When we reached it, I halted, staring into the gutted interior. Every single tank inside the lab had shattered, and their inhabitants were drifting around like balloons released into the sky. Surely I'd have noticed if my magic had shattered every tank when I'd set the first vampire free, but nobody else had been here since Keir and I had chased the vampire shade through the mirror. Right?

"It'll be quicker to find the edges of the spirit barrier if one of us leaves our body," I said to Keir. His eyes had glazed over, suggesting he'd got the same idea.

Ilsa tightened her grip on the book. "All right, but be quick."

I joined Keir in the spirit realm. At once, a mass of ghosts surrounded me, like a crowd jostling me from all angles. I gritted my teeth, pushing them aside with a gentle use of kinetic power. The lab didn't go on forever, so it must come to an end somewhere.

Sure enough, when I reached out my awareness, a solid barrier blocked my path, confirming Ilsa's suspicion that the mages had put a spirit barrier around the outside of the lab. No candles shone inside the walls, so I'd have to break the outside walls to move them. Someone really didn't want trespassers wandering in, living or otherwise.

A pair of hands grabbed me, yanking me around. I pulled myself out of the grip of a vampire shade, his fevered eyes glowing with blue-white light, and a burning sensation in my wrist jolted me back into my body. My blood magic mark must have kicked in.

"Jas." Keir caught my shoulders. "Did you find the edge? I couldn't see any candles."

"Nor me," I said. "It's a spirit barrier, all right, but we'll have to blast the walls down first. If anything, the mirror's a safer bet. We don't know what else is out there."

Ilsa swore. "Never mind what's out there—we have bigger problems in here."

A human-shaped figure stood in the doorway, eyes glowing with the bright awareness of a vampire. Not an undead at first glance—until I saw the mark on his collarbone.

Oh, crap. The vampires might be dead, but they retained enough awareness to inhabit a vessel. Specifically, a vessel preserved using blood magic.

The vessel moved, arms swinging, but Keir got there first. He blocked the vampire's strike with his forearm and casually tossed him sideways. His skull hit the wall, but he was on his feet a second later, aiming a punch at me. I dodged and hit back, sending him flying backwards into a second undead.

I called my Hemlock power to my hands, forming a shield between us and them. Their eyes glowed with blue-white light, their hands grasping, begging to feed.

"Hold on." Keir kicked the first undead to the ground, then grabbed him through the spirit realm. There was a bright flash, and the undead's body fell back, limp, the insubstantial vampire rising as a ghost. "I banish you beyond the gates of Death." Nothing happened. "Guess it was worth a shot."

I dropped to my knees beside the body, Hemlock magic searing my hands. I pressed my palm to the mark on his collarbone, pushing my magic directly into the symbol. The dead man crumbled, rotting away, and I did the same to the two undead grasping at the shield. When they collapsed, Ilsa ran forwards, holding her talisman in outstretched hands. The vampires' ghosts cringed away from the book, but behind them, more waited, eyes aglow, hands reaching out, begging for our souls.

Ilsa tensed, gripping the book like a shield, but the undead swarmed her, faster than any dead had the right to move.

"Ilsa!" I shouted.

Dead, clammy hands grabbed at us. I kicked out, and a

heavy blow collided with my skull. Keir caught my hand, pulling me after him and dragging me down a side corridor.

"We can't leave her!" I said.

"Jas—it's a dead end. We're stuck."

I turned on the spot. The corridor ended abruptly where the floor had collapsed into a giant hole which covered a huge section of the building, the splintered remains of machinery dangling into its depths.

"Shit. Do you know how to fly?" I called my Hemlock magic, conjuring a shield between us and the relentless dead.

Keir approached the pit behind us, his face pale. "I can't see the bottom, but we might be able to climb down."

As he turned his back on the pit, a dark mass rose behind him. "Keir!"

The dark mass resolved into a clawed hand, grasping Keir and yanking him out of sight. The hand belonged to something with long talons and jagged wings, an over-sized version of one of those shadowy furies. Malevolence simmered in its eyes, and my body locked to the spot, raw terror permeating every nerve. *Keir... no.*

Twisting, Keir slammed a knife into the claw holding him captive. The beast turned to shadow, dropping him. Keir landed on his feet, inches from the pit, his face ashen. "What the hell?"

The beast opened its mouth, and growled, "I will devour you."

Crap. It could talk as well?

"Sorry to burst your bubble, but no thanks." I conjured my Hemlock magic, pushing a second shield towards the pit in an attempt to get Keir out of harm's way.

The beast's claw reached out, through the shield—through *me*. I stared at the claw sticking out of my chest with a feeling of detached disbelief. There was no blood, and the claw didn't look solid at all—yet that same claw had grabbed Keir. *What the hell* is *this beast?*

The fury yanked its claw out of my chest, and my spirit came away with it. My body remained where it was, but the beast's claw had hooked my soul like a fish on a line. The monster pulled me towards its huge mouth, my transparent limbs flailing.

"Put me down." I squirmed, wincing as its claws dug into my non-existent skin. "You can't eat my soul. It'll give you indigestion."

Keir wasn't looking at me, but at my inert body. He gave me a firm shake, and a burning sensation shot up my arm. I vanished from the fury's grip, blinking back into my body. The blood magic rune had saved my skin, but Ilsa was gone, and the only way out of the corridor was past the shield I'd conjured to keep the zombies back. The instant we ran, they'd swarm.

Rather them than that fury beast.

I turned on my amplifying rune. "I'm gonna blow them up. Ready to run?"

Keir gave a short nod. I raised my other palm and blasted Hemlock magic at the zombies, knocking them into one another like skittles. Taking Keir's arm, I ran at the wall of undead. Between reanimated bodies and that shadowy monster, I'd take the zombies any day of the week.

My shield collapsed, and a wave of zombies descended on us, pushing me back towards the hole in the floor. Keir's arm was wrenched from my grip, and he disappeared beneath the flailing wall of zombies. I gave one last desperate lunge and the floor ran out, casting me into darkness.

———

Everything hurt. My body throbbed all over, and so did my spirit. On the plus side, my soul was still attached to my body. I hadn't gone floating off... or been devoured.

Keir. Please tell me he made it out. I raised my head, but all I could see were the wrecked remains of the machines and tanks which filled the room that must have stood beneath the corridor whose floor I'd fallen through. Judging by the size of some of them, they'd been holding that monstrous shadowy fury captive. The spirit barrier around the lab was probably the only thing keeping the beast from roaming throughout the Highlands, devouring everyone it ran into.

I groaned and rolled onto my back. My head pounded, and something sharp dug into my spine. Something book-shaped. Lady Harper's journal. I'd forgotten I even had it. What would she say if she found out I'd met my end in the ruins of an old lab, without ever fulfilling my duty as a Hemlock witch?

No. I wouldn't give in that easily. I had too much to lose. Evelyn was fighting for both of us back in Edinburgh, and so were my friends.

Climbing to my feet, I squinted into the gloom. There was no sign of the shadow-fury, which I hoped meant it had assumed I'd fallen to my death. *Another life gone, Jas.* Aside from the pain, I didn't feel quite as out of it as last time I'd died. I conjured a spark of magic to my hands to light the way, revealing marks on the glass-strewn floor.

Witch runes. Wards. Powerful ones, none of them active.

"Oh, no," I whispered.

Somehow, when I'd broken that tank with my Hemlock magic, the aftereffects had undone the wards around everything else in the lab as well. Including the spell imprisoning that monster.

My foot crunched in something hard. Bone, brittle enough to snap. Broken glass. Machinery. I walked through the ruined lab, wincing at every sound, but the giant fury didn't reappear. I found a book lying half-open at the edge of one of the faded chalk circles. I picked it up, staring at the numbering system on the spine. I'd volunteered in the archives enough times to recognise it as the guild's property. And the title—*Ritual Magic*.

Asher didn't mention he stole it from the guild. But this must be it. A ritual book, which *someone* must have used to summon a giant shadow-fury and imprisoned it here in the lab. If it escaped into Edinburgh, we were all screwed. The monster looked too big to physically fit through the mirror, but who knew, when it came to the Ancients? The Whisper had managed to exist in a single symbol, while the Soul Collector had existed without a body for years. I wouldn't put anything past them.

Looked like my assumption that the mages would never have been able to keep an Ancient caged in the same way as they had the vampire shades was dead wrong. And now it was roaming free somewhere in here, hungry for my soul.

I spotted a pile of machinery which looked stable

enough for me to climb to the upper corridor. Finding hand-holds, I gingerly pulled myself up, holding my breath whenever my feet slipped. For once in my life, I was glad of being short, lightweight and agile enough to balance on flimsy machine parts until my feet hit solid ground. *If the guild doesn't take me back, maybe I have a second career option as a stunt double.*

I walked tentatively through yet another lab filled with broken equipment, only to find myself at yet another dead end. "Seriously?"

"Seriously," a voice replied from the gloom.

Great. Another vampire. At least this one had the courtesy of announcing his presence.

"There's a monster blocking the other corridor," I told the disembodied voice. "Can you tell me how to get out without being maimed or killed."

"No."

"Really helpful."

"Look, that thing is an Ancient, and if you had the slightest idea what it's capable of—"

"I reckon I do." Unfortunately.

"Well, that makes things easier," he said. "It can't break the iron walls of this place, which is good news for the people outside. Just bad news for us."

"Fuck me," I muttered.

"I'm a ghost, but hey, I won't back down from a challenge."

"Oh, lord." Just what I needed. A ghost with a dirty sense of humour. I supposed he *was* a vampire. I heard him chuckling as I picked my way through the lab in search of a door.

That giant monster was immortal. Just like the other

gods. No wonder my fellow Hemlocks had kicked out the Ancients into other realms. They'd never been dead. Only imprisoned. "Please tell me there aren't any more of them in here."

"Isn't one enough?" he said.

"Is there a way to reactivate the binding spells, then?" I'd rather that Ancient be trapped in a spell than roaming around snacking on my friends' souls.

"I don't know, you tell me," said the ghost. "You're clearly a necromancer, not a vampire or... oh. *Oh.*" He appeared next to me, a transparent outline barely visible in the gloom. "You're a shade, too? How did you get out?"

"I wasn't captured," I said. "I'm the one who accidentally set you all free, I think. I was trying to put you out of your misery, but it backfired."

"I'm not miserable," said the vampire. "I'd like to find my body, though..."

"Sorry, but I don't think that's likely." *It was probably among those zombies who attacked me.*

And Keir. If he hadn't made it out... dammit. I never should have brought him here.

My fists clenched at my sides, and I kicked at the nearest piece of equipment. I was going to die here, too soon to win the Hemlocks' war, because some dickhead had decided capturing a giant god was a great idea. *Why did I leave Evelyn behind?*

"What is it this time?" the vampire asked. "You look like you're about to cry."

"My friends might have died for all I know, and I can't reach them," I said. "Instead, I'm stuck here with a monster and a bunch of ghosts. No offence."

"To me or the monster?" he said. "I'm not exactly in

heaven either. Most of *my* friends were suspended in those tanks and lost their minds years ago."

"I'm sorry."

"Don't be. I've had years to accept my fate." He hovered in mid-air. "I stopped counting the days after they removed me from my body. You will, too, if you're lucky to last long enough for that beast to forget about hunting you. Kinda hard to keep track without a clock."

Apparently, he was a talker. Not that I minded having someone to speak to. There was no danger of him disturbing the fury, because they couldn't sense or hear ghosts, as far as I knew.

"Why does that fury eat souls?" I asked.

"Because it does," he said. "I don't know. I've been researching the Ancients my whole life and I haven't come close to understanding them."

"Research?" I asked. "Is that why the mages took you?"

"Pretty much," he said. "The other vampires didn't care, when I told them, but you strike me as a good listener."

"Not like I have any other options at the moment." There was no way out except back the way I'd come. I'd have to climb back over the pit to reach the other corridor, which had been overrun by zombies the last time I'd seen it. And the fury was still roaming around somewhere.

"Vampires are all descendants of an Ancient-human hybrid," said the ghost. "Not sure which Ancient. I've never met them. Probably for the best."

"Given my experience, I'd have to say I agree." I scanned the lab again. "Is this room warded?"

"Why?"

Hemlock magic sparked to life in my hands. "I'm going to blast the wall down. Can you warn me if the Ancient is on the other side?"

"It isn't," he said. "But I don't see any explosives."

I pushed up my sleeve, revealing my witch spells.

He whistled. "I stand corrected."

I was about to tell him to stand back, then I remembered he was a ghost. "Get ready to run."

I reached out my hands, searching for the wards humming inside the building's foundations. Resistance pushed back, but I gritted my teeth, finding the pattern of magic forming the wards. My hands moved over the wards, unravelling them one at a time. Just enough to leave a gap ahead of me.

Then I threw an explosive spell and blasted a hole through the wall.

The vampire whooped and cheered, doing a back-flip in mid-air. "Nice one."

"Let's see what we have here." I walked towards the newly created window and climbed through. "Do you know the way back to the room with the mirror inside it?"

"The lab runs in a circle," he said, pointing. "Keep going that way and you should get back to where you started."

"If you don't want to be eaten, you should probably come with me."

The vampire kept up a stream of directions as I moved through the labs, dodging zombies and the occasional vampire-shade. When we ducked into a room lit with fluorescent lights, he grimaced and tried to hide in the shadows. "Ah. That's too bright. I really need to feed, by the way. Just so you know."

"It won't be long now," I said, squinting in the brightness. He appeared clearer than he'd been in the dark. And his features were startlingly familiar.

"Holy shit," I said. "Aiden Langford? Is that your name?"

19

Keir's brother blinked at me. "You know me?"

"I know your brother."

He shrank back. "You're lying."

"Keir," I said. "That's his name. You remember him, right? He's here—or he was, anyway."

His eyes widened. "I have to see him before it's too late. I can already feel myself fading."

"Hang on." Was there a way to temporarily strengthen him long enough to get him to his body? "Can you grab a vessel?"

"Not without letting myself get caught in that swarm of zombies."

And more vampires might be on the other side of the mirror. "Is there a way to stop that from happening?"

"You can bind me to yourself," he said. "Temporarily. Just to stop me from drifting off. But I don't know if that's magic you can do."

"Would it be in here?" I pulled out the ritual book I'd

found in the pit. Its leather-bound cover was marked with symbols, too. Witch runes.

"Where'd you get that?" Aiden peered over my shoulder as I skimmed through the book. It wasn't hard to find which rituals had been used recently, because those pages were stained in dried blood.

"That one." Aiden pointed at a faded heading inked in black, and I stopped flipping pages. "A temporary binding. It won't endanger either of us. It'll keep me alive, relatively speaking, until you find my body."

After reading the printed text, I didn't see any harm that might result from trying the binding. No blood sacrifice requirements, and nothing that might screw up my bond with Evelyn and Keir. I dug in my pocket for the blood magic pen, then I copied the design onto my arm.

Energy rushed to the surface of my skin, and the rune glowed around the edges. "Oh," said Aiden. "That feels... strange."

"Did it work?"

"Ah." He moved, and when he did, so did I.

"Well, this is awkward," I said. The spirit was kind of... stuck to me. At least he wasn't trying to eat my soul, but the last thing I needed was another permanent hitchhiker sharing my body.

"Fair warning, I'm not alone," I told him. "Don't be alarmed if another spirit shows up. I'm a shade with a split soul."

"You're telling me this now?" said Aiden. "Are you absolutely sure you're not one of the mages' lab experiments?"

"No, just a freak of nature." To say the least. "Can you sense Keir in here?"

"No, but your mirror room is that way." He pointed. "Better hurry."

When we came to an area I recognised, I took the lead until we reached the room with the mirror. Then I checked the spirit realm. No sign of the others—Keir included.

"I can't sense my brother," Aiden said. "Can that mirror really get us out of here?"

"Yep. Welcome to Edinburgh's necromancer guild."

I leapt through the mirror, finding myself suspended in mid-air, legs flailing. The door lay open ahead of me, and the mirror had fallen onto its back. My feet snagged on the edge and I caught myself before I tumbled back through the mirror again. Bits of dismembered zombie and discarded candles littered the floor, while shouts echoed from the lobby. I ran into the corridor and turned right, my shoes crunching in salt. Kicking a rotting zombie arm aside, I led the way into the wide space of the lobby.

Cloaked figures ran in all directions, and Lady Montgomery stood in the centre of the chaos, her hair streaming loose from its bun. Groups of necromancers hurried up and downstairs, carrying armfuls of candles, including—

"Hey, Lloyd." I waved at him as he reached the foot of the left-hand staircase.

Lloyd dropped the candles. "Jas!"

I ran to him and he hugged me tightly. "I'm glad you got out."

"Did you die *again?*" interrupted Morgan, also laden with candles.

"You're cold as the grave, Jas," Lloyd said. "What in the

world happened back there? Keir said he saw you fall into a pit—"

"Keir's alive." I let him go, overcome with relief. "Did the others get out, too?"

"You bet," said Mackie, running past with an armful of candles. "I already screamed at two of those bastards and scared them into letting go of their vessels."

"She did." Lloyd grabbed some of the candles he'd dropped. "Problem is, a bunch of them still got out into the city. It's a mess out there. Ilsa went to round them up."

"I'd better go and help. Is Keir out there, too?"

"Last I saw. Be careful."

I ran towards the guild's doors and pushed them open. A row of cloaked figures guarded the entrance, and on the other side, a number of winged shapes circled the guild. Furies. No, shadow-furies. What did they want? Did they know a giant version of one of them was on the other side of the mirror?

"This is beyond creepy," Aiden whispered in my ear, making me jump. "Uh, Jas, is my brother somewhere behind those monsters?"

"Quite possibly." I tensed, readying my Hemlock magic.

"They aren't trying to get in," Lloyd said from behind me. "They're just... hanging around there. They attack if you get too close. Isabel took out three of them and used up half her spells in the process. What're they playing at, do you know?"

"They're waiting," I said. "Let's just say zombies and vampire ghosts weren't all I found on the other side of that mirror."

And I think they want to meet their big brother in person.

A blast of fire hit one of the furies, knocking it out of the air. Drake appeared a second later, his hands blazing.

"Hey there, Jas," he said. "Heard the guild had a bit of trouble with unwanted guests."

Two more furies descended, and Vance appeared beneath, a blade in each hand. At his side, Ivy Lane readied her weapon, blue light igniting as she leapt into the air. My jaw dropped as she cleared ten feet, swinging the sword into a fury's neck. Lloyd jumped behind the guild's doors as its head went flying, bouncing off the wards.

Ivy landed on her feet. "Hey, Jas. Sorry I took so long. I had a situation in Faerie to sort out."

I stepped back to avoid the spray of blood as the fury's headless body hit the earth. "And now you have a situation here to sort out."

"Keeps life interesting." She jumped, using the fury's body to propel herself upwards and knock another low-circling monster out of the air. I ran to help, conjuring a whip of Hemlock magic.

"I think I know why these bastards are at the guild." I circled the beast's leg and gave the whip a tug, pulling it to the ground. "There's a giant shadowy fury on the other side of the mirror. Not sure if it was Lord Sutherland who imprisoned it or the Orion League, but I think those furies must be able to sense it."

Ivy jumped at the falling fury, sinking her blade into its spine. "Not an Ancient?"

"You've got it."

Ivy climbed onto the fury's back to ride its descent back to earth. "Should have figured something spawned those monstrosities. I'll introduce it to Helena."

"Who's Helena?"

"Her sword," Vance said, displacing his own sword so it sank into another fury's neck from behind. As it fell, the sword vanished and then reappeared in his hand.

I swung my whip at another fury, catching it before it disappeared into the shadows. "You mean the same sword which contains an Ancient's magic? What does the god think of you giving it a nickname?"

"He never asked." Ivy sank her blade into the fury's side as I tugged it out of the sky. Freeing my whip, I gave it another swipe, slicing the fury's head off.

"Nice one," said Aiden's voice from thin air.

"Who said that?" asked Ivy. "Not Evelyn? That sounded like a guy."

"It was." Apparently, Aiden had figured out how to make himself heard by non-necromancers. "He's a vampire ghost I saved from the lab. Have you seen her, by the way? Evelyn?"

"Isn't she tied to you?" Ivy shook droplets of blood off her sword, which glowed bright blue.

"I left her back here while I went through the mirror," I explained. "She was pretty badly affected by the flood of ghosts in the lab the last time, so she wanted to stay here and defend the guild."

"Haven't seen her," said Ivy. "I did see that vampire, Keir, running across the bridge, but he didn't stop to chat."

"He must have gone to Clancy's." I fed more power into the whip in my hands, which glimmered, slicing through the furies' skin like paper. The remaining furies shrank back, and Vance appeared behind them, his blades flashing.

"Oh, Clancy," said Aiden. "He's still around?"

"Clancy's supposed to be keeping an eye on Aiden's body in case anyone steals it," I said to Ivy. "Aiden is Keir's brother, and he's bound to me until I get his body back."

"And I thought I'd had a bad week." Ivy dodged as a pair of claws appeared from the shadows behind her.

I snagged the beast's clawed hand with my whip. "How do you kill a god? You saw one die, didn't you?"

"A super-powered Sidhe killed him." Ivy leapt forwards, sinking her sword into the trapped fury's neck. "Same for the god whose magic is in Ilsa's talisman."

"I'm guessing no human has ever killed one?" I ducked to avoid the spray of blood. "No wonder the Hemlocks cursed themselves into a forest to opt out of the war."

They cut us off to save their own skins, the Soul Collector had said. Not surprising, given that the Hemlocks weren't immortal in the same way the gods were.

"Incoming," Ivy warned, as the guild's doors flew open and three zombies ran out behind me, driven by vampire shades.

"Oh, hell." I disentangled my magical whip from the dead fury. "They're still getting out of the mirror."

"Damn, they're fast." Ivy swung her blade into a zombie's chest, blood spraying out.

"They're using blood magic. You can still use salt to destroy them, though."

"And fire." Drake threw a fireball at the nearest zombie, and he burst into flames.

"Now the vampire's gonna run for another vessel," I warned, tapping into the spirit realm.

Sure enough, the vampire reached out for me, hands grasping. I snagged him in my whip, holding him still.

"Stay there." I reached out with my free hand, calling his spirit essence into me. When the spirit essence touched my Hemlock magic, it shimmered, growing more substantial even as the ghost stopped struggling. A current of energy ran through my veins, sharper this time. *Can I draw on spirit energy? Like a vampire?*

"I banish you," I said to the vampire.

Death's gates appeared looming overhead. *I never thought I'd be so glad to see you.* I gave the vampire a cheeky wave as the gates swallowed him up. One down, a hundred more to go.

A crack in the grey fog of Death caught my eye, and I tilted my head. *That's not supposed to be there.* The spirit realm had split, just a little, creating a slim tear in the emptiness on a level with my head.

I halted, realising I'd drifted away from my body and into the grey. More cracks lay in all directions like tears in the fabric of the spirit realm itself. What the hell were they?

"Hey! You can't die now," Aiden said from behind me. "Otherwise I'll be bound to your dead body, and let me tell you, that is *not* how I wanted to spend the rest of my existence."

"See that?" I indicated the nearest crack in the spirit realm. "What is it?"

"Uh." He floated beside me and stuck his hand through the gap. "Damn. That's... I don't know *what* that is."

I floated up to join him, reaching out a hand. Like him, my hand passed through the air, feeling... nothing.

"Those shadowy furies," Aiden said. "I think they might be eating holes in the spirit realm. It isn't the shades, that's for damn sure."

I turned on the spot, towards the spot where the guild lay, and gasped. Around the guild, the tears in the spirit realm were even worse, overlapping where the furies circled overhead. Wherever they were appearing from, the effect was damaging the spirit lines.

I blinked back into my body.

"There you are," Ivy said, shaking blood from her sword. "Where'd you go, Jas?"

"Had to banish one of those vampires. Where the bloody hell are Edinburgh's Mage Lords? Aren't they going to take control of their own vampire shade army?"

"Of course not," said Ivy. "Last I heard, they barricaded themselves in their own headquarters."

"Behind a spirit barrier, I'll bet." I'd missed one crucial part of my prediction of the enemy's plan. Lord Sutherland didn't want to participate directly in the war. Terrorising the public from behind a barrier was more his style.

"Does *he* have my body?" Aiden asked. "Because the spell binding us has a limit."

"I hope he doesn't," I said. "Right—I'm off to Clancy's. Vance, can you teleport me over the bridge?"

Ivy waved him over, and Vance walked to my side, his suit barely rumpled from the fight with the furies.

"Where should I drop you off?" he asked.

I gave the spirit realm a brief scan. "Princes Street will do."

Vance gave a nod. An instant later, we appeared in front of the abandoned train station.

On the other side of the road, humans cowered inside shops and cafes as a line of zombies ambled down the middle of the road in a steady line, not breaking formation even to attack.

I wouldn't call them a swarm, more a procession. They were too well organised to be moving at random, all of them shuffling in the same direction. A breeze from behind told me Vance had gone to re-join Ivy, leaving me alone with the zombies. *They can't be moving of their own accord.*

"My body isn't there," said Aiden.

"Don't complain. It might mean you've been spared." I dragged my gaze away from the undead and found a zombie-free spot to cross the road near the Scott Monument. Then I took off for Clancy's shop at a run, skidding to a halt in front.

A dismembered zombie lay in the entryway, and Clancy gave a threatening growl as I approached, his hands sheathed in claws.

"Oh, it's you, Jas." He lowered his hands. Claws aside, he was a big man who put me in mind of a bear—both cuddly and deadly depending on whether or not he liked you.

"Keir's not here?" I peered into the shop. "I found Aiden, and I know how to get him back to his body."

"Ah, shit," said Clancy. "Aiden's body—it got up by itself and walked outside. Knocked me out cold. Next thing I know there are zombies beating down the doors. Keir... soon as he found out, he went to follow. I told him not to."

"Shit." Might some of those zombies still be alive? If they were missing their original souls, it was impossible to tell. Either way, they were all controlled by hungry, murderous vampires... which made their precise formation even creepier. They could only be going to one location: the mages' headquarters.

"I guess I'll have to haunt you for a bit," Aiden said from beside my ear.

"I'll take you with me. Stay safe, Clancy." I headed down the road, eyes following the long line of zombies. They must have swarmed out of the lab the instant they'd realised they had a way out, and surged straight through the mirror. I'd bet there'd been a backup army of undead waiting on this side. Apparently, Vance and his council weren't the only ones with secret bolt holes.

Evelyn. Where are you?

A sudden tug gripped my spirit, pulling me out of my body.

"What the—?"

A loud, clear voice echoed through the spirit realm. "I summon you, Jacinda Hemlock."

Lord Sutherland.

Aiden shouted in alarm, but the tug grew in intensity, yanking me through the grey fog, past screaming spirits and tortured souls—then down, into a circle of spinning lights.

I halted, suspended between twelve candles in a darkened room. A spirit circle held me captive in mid-air.

"There you are," Lord Sutherland said. "I confess, I rather hoped you'd died. It shouldn't take this much effort to get rid of a single junior necromancer."

A cloaked feminine figure at his side nodded in agreement.

"Now I have you," said Lord Sutherland. "It's time for you to die, Jas."

20

"No, thanks," I said. "I think I'll pass."

"Do you find this situation amusing, Jas Lyons?" he enquired. "Or is it Jacinda Hemlock? When I probed into the lists of those who died in the invasion, imagine my surprise when I found the name Jacinda Hemlock was listed among the dead. Yet records show that Jas Lyons moved to this city and joined the guild seven years ago."

"I'm well-travelled." I peered at the woman at his side, trying to make out the face underneath the hood. Not a witch this time. From the glow around her eyes under the hooded cloak, I'd guess a vampire. "And I have this annoying habit of coming back from the dead."

"A vampire would fix that problem," he said. "As for your other soul… where exactly is Evelyn Hemlock? I should summon her to join you, but it seems a waste of effort since she'll perish when you do."

Evelyn. She must still be out there somewhere. So was my body, and the rune on my arm, but it hadn't reacted yet. *Shit on a stick.* Was there a limit on the number of times I could use its magic to return to my body? Or might the summoning circle have cut me off entirely?

Until I knew for sure, stalling was my only option. "You can't hide anymore, Lord Sutherland. The entire necromancer guild knows that you were ripping vampires' souls out of their bodies in the Orion League's old lab, and so does the Council of Twelve. You're going on a one-way trip to jail whether I live to see it or not."

"Oh, am I?" He gave an unconvincing smile. Only then did I notice that he seemed to have deactivated his anti-ageing spells, and wrinkles marked his once flawless skin. Despite his position of superiority, he made no move to get any closer to the circle.

He's scared. From the lack of decor around me, I'd guess I was in a chamber somewhere in the dungeons. This must be where the mages had holed up while their army ran amok around the city. He was too frightened even to watch his own victory.

"I'm told the spirit realm is falling to pieces, Jas," he said. "Reports tell me a group of monstrosities is circling the guild, almost as though they sense something inside, calling out to them."

A chill raced down my back. "Who imprisoned that monster in the lab? You, or the Orion League? You're both as bad as each other—and by the sound of things, equally foolish."

He shrugged off my insult. "Is the necromancer guild equipped to go up against forces that existed before humans ever learned to channel the forces of nature? Perhaps you should have left it alone, Jas."

"You're talking like you're not screwing with those

same forces of nature yourself," I said. "Don't kid yourself into thinking you have the slightest idea what you unleashed. The League sure as hell didn't know, and they paid for it with their lives."

"The League died out because they were never supernaturals," said Lord Sutherland. "They were never like us, and they feared us for good reason. We control the world now. That includes those who were once regarded as gods."

"Nobody is controlling that thing," I said. "And you can't claim the moral high ground when you imprisoned vampires in cages and ripped the souls out of their bodies."

"You truly believe those vampires are people?" He shook his head. "I suppose, being a hybrid abomination that you are, the definition is somewhat murky."

I gave a humourless laugh. "*I'm* an abomination?"

"You're certainly not human." He walked closer to the circle, scrutinising me. "You don't think I'm going to kill you without finding out what you are, do you? I want to know how you survived falling into the rift between realms. Are *you* an Ancient? You're more than a shade."

If I'd been in my body, my heart would have begun to beat faster at his words. "I'm a Hemlock witch. You're just pissed because I have a type of magic you don't. Same reason you want to shut the guild down and use vampires as guinea pigs. You can't stand not being in control, and you don't want to face up to the fact that you're no more special than anyone else is. You're nothing, Lord Sutherland, and you're going to be forgotten when you die."

"All of us start off as nothing," he said dismissively.

"What matters is what we become, and those of us who are more willing to adapt are the ones who survive."

"You're deluded if you think we all start out on the same level," I said. "You've probably never had to struggle for anything in your life."

"You know nothing about me," he said. "If you blame me for your woes, then you're setting yourself up for disappointment. The mages are the reason those Ancient abominations haven't driven humanity to extinction."

"I know enough," I said. "I don't hate you because you're a mage. Half my adopted family are mages. I hate you because you're a raging dickhead."

His jaw tightened. "You know, I did wonder if the guild and I might be able to work alongside one another, for a time. I even went to the trouble of funding their research, particularly on the nature of shades and such-like. Humans who can survive death. With the right application, every human might become the same. Yet they refused to take me up on my offer. Imagine that: an end to death. Why would Lady Montgomery deny that?"

"Because everything has a catch," I said. "Shades are the result of death going wrong. They aren't meant to exist."

"I might say the same of vampires, Jas," he said. "Do you know where they originally came from? Breeding humans with the decaying remnant of an ancient spirit. The taint spread like a virus among them, eating away at their souls until the only way they could survive was to feed on others. Tragic, really."

Nausea swept over me. *Aiden was right.* "Who did that —the League?"

"Oh, this was long before the League," he said. "The

League just revived the practice. But they were looking in the wrong place."

"Let me guess, that's why you took Aiden," I said. "Because he figured it out. He was researching the Ancients, and you didn't want word to get out. So you stole his body and left it on the other side of the mirror so he'd be doomed to die in that lab. Where is it now?"

"The vampire survived?" His mouth twisted. "His body will be with the others, at least until I no longer have a use for them."

Raw hate pulsed through me. "You're planning to betray them?"

"I owe them nothing," he said coldly. "It reflects badly on our society if we let such creatures roam around the city. Until now we've had trouble rooting them out, but with a reset of the spirit world, I'll be rid of all of them at once, and the shades along with them."

"You're the one who held them hostage!" Indignation burned within me. He'd captured and tortured them, ripped them out of their bodies and turned them into shades. And now he was waiving all responsibility by casting them into the afterlife. "Besides, you can't reset the spirit world. It's not possible."

"They were never supposed to escape," he said. "They weren't the end goal, but their inability to perish proved… taxing. No matter. It's certainly possible to cleanse the spirit realm, however. All I require is a sacrifice."

The cloaked woman stepped into the summoning circle alongside me, and I gasped as her hood slipped. "Lady Anders?"

"She served her purpose," Lord Sutherland said. "All of us must make sacrifices, Jas. I made plenty of my own."

The candle lights brightened, revealing bloody marks on the ground around the edges. Runes… for a blood summoning.

"Sacrifices?" I raised my head. "What the hell have you ever sacrificed?"

Lord Sutherland stepped forwards. Another spasm of nausea shook me as he raised his hands, exposing his wrists. Instead of witch spells, he wore blood magic symbols etched into his skin. Bindings… and one symbol that blurred when I looked at it as though I viewed it through tinted glass.

An Invocation.

He'd bound a god directly to himself. "You became a vessel yourself? What was worth that price?"

"A single life is little to give, in exchange for a simple name," he said. "That god you found in the lab has the unique ability to feed on souls, and when he's done, this city will be free of the likes of you, forever."

"You want to summon that Ancient back here?" My voice rose, echoing off the dungeon walls. "He already destroyed the labs. It'll be a massacre."

"He doesn't eat living souls," said Lord Sutherland. "Only the dead. Banishing him will be as simple as summoning him."

"Look, getting rid of a bunch of monsters by summoning an even bigger monster is not going to work out the way you think it is," I said. "People will die."

"People die at the hands of these monsters every day," he said. "I'll just make sure their deaths mean something."

The vampire piloting Lady Anders's body raised a bloody knife, pointed directly at me. Lights flared at my feet, igniting the blood magic symbols. A chill wind swept up, and the candle flames blew to the side.

No. I can't die here.

"Evelyn," I whispered. "Help." *Get here and stop him, otherwise that monster might eat us alive.*

My Hemlock magic snapped on, but the circle caught my power and pushed it back at me. The candles' glow was too bright to be anything other than the product of another blood sacrifice.

"Banish her, you fool!" Lord Sutherland yelled.

"Jas?" The voice was faint. Then a tug gripped me, pulling me into Death's embrace.

————

Lord Sutherland's furious shout pursued me as I drifted through the fractured greyness. Then a familiar, blessed pain shot up my arm from the witch mark. I landed on the pavement, back in my body.

"Nice of you to join us again," said Evelyn.

"You too," I said shakily. "Believe it or not."

I'd stopped Lord Sutherland's ritual, but he still had the god's name, which meant he was likely to try the summoning again with another innocent life.

"Don't thank her," Aiden's voice said. "She took control, and well…"

I straightened upright, eyeing the mess Evelyn had left behind. Bits of dead fury littered the pavement, surrounded by bloody puddles. She must have run all the way back to the necromancer guild and taken out her anger on the remaining beasts. Lloyd watched wide-eyed from in front of the guild's entrance along with several other necromancers. Relief crossed his face when he spotted me, realising Jas was in control, not Evelyn.

"I couldn't reach you," Evelyn said. "I found your body standing in the middle of the street, totally spaced out. I figured you'd gone to fight the vampires."

"Not quite. The Mage Lord summoned me as a sacrifice," I said. "Did you see where his army was going?"

Aiden's body is with them. I'd been so close, but the Mage Lord had been one step ahead. I hardly believed he'd gone to the trouble of creating an army only to kill them off. And if the smaller furies had left holes all over the spirit realm, I shuddered to imagine what the super-sized version would be capable of.

"The army of furies?" Drake walked towards me, kicking a piece of fury out of the way. "Your weird cousin took care of them."

"Not that army," I said. "Lord Sutherland is about to summon an oversized version of one of those furies which can eat souls, because he thinks it'll get rid of all the vampires in the city. He's lost his wits."

"He's *what?*" Wanda picked her way through the maze of fury guts, grimacing. "Where *is* Lord Sutherland?"

"Hiding in the mages' dungeon," Aiden said.

"Uh… Jas?" said Drake. "Who's that guy?"

"Hi," said Aiden. "You haven't seen my brother anywhere, have you?"

"You have two spirits hitching a ride in your body now?" said Wanda.

"Until we find his body," I said. "I don't suppose either of you saw where all those zombies wandered off to?"

"Watch out!" shouted a voice from behind me. I spun around, narrowly avoiding a shadow fury's claws.

A knife flew over my head, and Lloyd followed. "You okay, Jas? Found your vampire?"

"Nope." I called on my Hemlock magic, hooking the whip around the fury's neck. "Did this thing get *into* the headquarters?"

"Not for long," said Morgan, throwing a knife wildly and missing. "Try to kill Mackie, will you?"

The shadow fury vanished, slipping free of my whip. It reappeared behind Lloyd, and Morgan threw another knife, this time sinking it into the monster's leg. I snagged it around the neck, pulling it away before it landed on top of Lloyd. Morgan nodded thanks to me, and the fury strained against the magic holding it still.

And then another rush of magic joined mine. Evelyn. Two lots of Hemlock magic were better than one. Together, Evelyn and I pulled it down, our magic slicing through the beast's shadowy form.

"Nice one," said Aiden.

"Who's talking to you this time?" said Lloyd, picking up Morgan's knife and handing it back to him.

"Keir's brother," I said. "He had a slight mishap and ended up separated from his body, which is currently being piloted by another dead vampire somewhere."

"Jesus," Lloyd said. "A zombie disintegrated all over my shoes and everyone here is still having a worse day than I am."

"I'd take the zombies if only I had shoes for them to disintegrate on," Aiden added.

"Wasn't one ghost enough?" Morgan asked.

"I'm not a ghost," said Evelyn.

"Is this really the time to be pedantic?" Lloyd stepped

back from the dead fury. "Where is Keir's brother's body, then?"

"It wandered off to join Lord Sutherland's army. Keir followed, but Lord Sutherland summoned me before I could track him."

"He did what?"

"Summoned her," Aiden said. "Just like that. Man, if her other spirit hadn't stepped in—"

I switched on my spirit sight and tuned out his chattering, scanning the spirit realm for any trace of Keir's presence. The thin tears in the fog appeared even bigger now. Lord Sutherland was deluded if he thought inviting the giant shadow fury over here would help the situation at all rather than making it worse.

I directed my consciousness outwards. An army of vampires would be hard to hide, so I zeroed in on the flickering trace in the distance, coming from the spirit line running through the centre of town. *Gotcha.* Hiding his army on the spirit line was a smart idea, but not smart enough. Lord Sutherland must have rounded his vampires up like cattle ready to feed their souls to the shadow-fury. So much for commanding loyalty.

Aiden's body would be among their group somewhere, which meant Keir wouldn't be far behind. Question: how to get them out without alerting the rest of the army? Keir's trace was barely distinguishable from the hundred or more vampires the mages had drawn over to their domain.

Too close.

They caught him.

21

Sensation returned to my body, my chest rising and falling with quick breaths. *No. Keir.*

"What is it?" asked Aiden. "By the way, your spirit isn't in the best shape at the moment. Did a vampire feed on you recently?"

"Yes, and Keir—he's with the other vampire shades. I can't tell if they caught him or not."

Either way, how could I sneak up on the army without provoking an attack?

"And my body?" Aiden asked. "Don't tell me—he marched into the middle of the army to find it and got caught, didn't he?"

"You're not going after him?" Lloyd's brow wrinkled, anxious. "Damn, Jas. Be careful, okay?"

"I'll try to." I accepted his hug, my hands shaking. *Dammit, Keir.* If Death's gates took me again, he'd be dragged there with me—and so would Aiden.

Keir's trace guided my steps through the eerily empty streets of Edinburgh's Old Town. The stench of dismembered fury clung to me like an old coat, and Aiden's constant stream of chatter was a welcome change from the muted sounds of terrified humans fleeing the chaos.

Every time I checked the spirit realm, the tears seemed worse, merging to form man-sized rips in reality. The veil was the only barrier between this realm and the ones beyond. Never mind the furies—we'd have a full-blown Faerie War Part 2 on our doorsteps if someone didn't fix the damage. Hell if I knew *how.* Using my magic would paint a flashing target on my head and on Aiden by extension.

My steps halted beside a flickering street lamp. "I know this street."

"You do?" said Aiden. "Ah—a spirit line."

"Best hiding place for an army of vampire shades." The rippling current of energy smothered the row of terraced houses. The vampires must be in the tunnels because no sign of them showed aboveground. *Sneaky bastards.*

A single spark appeared on the line, moving towards me with the quietness of a vampire shade. I readied myself to attack—and looked into Keir's eyes.

His clothes were torn, a familiar mark glowing on his collarbone. Blue-grey light shone from his eyes, but the shadow who piloted his body wasn't Keir.

The vampires ripped him out of his body.

"Let him go," I snarled at the vampire shade. "This is your last warning."

"Get out of my brother's body." Aiden flew at Keir but passed right through him without touching the shade.

Keir lunged, aiming a punch at me. I blocked his strike, pain sparking from my forearm to my fingertips. From the angle, the vampire piloting him didn't have Keir's combat skills, but he was still stronger and faster than I was, while my stamina was depleted and my spirit felt pretty fragile, too.

Evelyn appeared, blasting Hemlock magic into the mark on his collarbone. I added my own magic, and the mark distorted into an inky smudge.

The vampire, however, stayed put. Using Keir's body, he lunged at me. I let him, catching his hand in mine as I slammed down onto my back. Unable to resist the opportunity to feed on a fresh shade, he didn't pull away. A mistake.

Blue light sprang to my palm, and I yanked the threads as hard as I could muster. Energy flowed from him to me, and he began to fade.

Panic suffused his expression. He tried to pull away, but the link didn't break. His mouth opened and closed, but my hand remained locked to his, through the spirit realm. I wasn't sure I *could* let go. His spirit essence flooded me, and I whispered, "I banish you. Go in peace."

The vampire shade vanished from sight. Hard pavement dug into my spine. I sat up, the back of my head giving a painful throb. Keir's body half-lay across mine, and when I gently pushed him onto his back, his eyes didn't open.

"They have his spirit somewhere in there," Aiden said, anxiously hovering on the spot. "How are we supposed to get him out?"

"I can summon him." I dug a hand in my pocket, not finding any candles. Just the blood magic pen. *I wonder...*

"What're you doing?" Evelyn demanded. "You can't perform a summoning with that."

"I know." I pushed up Keir's sleeve and drew a mirror

of the symbol I wore on my own wrist, courtesy of Isabel and Asher. *Please let this work.*

Keir might not be a witch, but I was, and my magic fuelled the spell. When the symbol was complete, I gave him a firm shake, jolting him with Hemlock magic. A spasm vibrated up his arm as the mark flared to life.

Keir's eyes flew open, and he drew in a gasping breath. "What the—?"

I threw my arms around him, and after a moment, he hugged me back. "What the hell were you thinking, going up against an army?"

Keir released me. "I wasn't. Thinking, I mean. How…?" He lifted his wrist, eyeing the glowing mark. "Is this a mage mark?"

"I had to use blood magic to shock you back into your body," I said. "It was that or summon you, and I'm all out of candles."

Keir started to speak, then he set eyes on Aiden. The remaining colour drained from his face. "This is a dream, isn't it? Or I'm dead."

"Nope," said Aiden. "Neither am I, come to that."

"Who the hell are you?" Keir said. "Why do you look like my brother?"

"It's not my best day," Aiden said. "I assume my body is somewhere under that spirit line? Please tell me nobody destroyed it. I'm kind of having an existential crisis here."

"It's him," I told Keir. "He was in the lab, and—it's complicated. Let's just say Lord Sutherland has cracked. He's planning to summon that giant shadow fury here and let it eat all the vampire shades. Needless to say, there's an obvious downside."

"You're telling me," said Aiden. "Keir, I'm bound to

your girlfriend, but it won't last forever. Also, this is a little weird, especially with the second soul on board."

"I'm not thrilled about it either," Evelyn put in.

"There are entirely too many people sharing my body," I added. "But we're all real. Ghosts included."

"Jesus," said Keir.

"I mean, I technically came back from the dead," said Aiden. "Wouldn't claim to be the next messiah, mind, but you never know."

Keir groaned. "You *sound* like my brother."

"There you have it." Aiden gave a self-important nod. "I'm real, but I won't be for much longer unless you evict the low-life who's walking around wearing my face. Did you see me? I mean, him?"

"Hey!" shouted a loud, shrill voice, drawing our attention.

Neil Sutherland marched up the steps from the house, his straw-like hair in disarray and his fancy clothes rumpled. A quick scan of the spirit realm confirmed no vampire piloted him—more's the pity.

"Fuck off," Keir said to him. "Go back into your hole in the ground."

"Seconded," Aiden said. "Neil, is it? I remember you crying and hiding when your father captured me."

Neil's face reddened. "Do I know you?"

"Probably not." Aiden sighed. "Does nobody remember me at all? Man, dying sucks."

"Next time I'll make sure you'll *stay* dead, vampire," Neil spat.

Keir moved towards him, but Neil raised his hands and sent a bolt of lightning at us. It bounced off the road, and my hair lifted with the static aftereffect of Neil's mage power.

Metallic hate coalesced on my tongue. Neil had nearly killed Keir once already—though, thinking about it, that was probably the moment Keir had turned into a shade.

Keir's face showed no fear, only irritation, as he snagged the mage apprentice by the front of his cloak and swung him over his shoulder. Neil landed in a crumpled heap. Keir gave him a brutal kick in the ribs when he tried to get up, and Aiden gave a round of applause next to me.

"You know, I don't appreciate it when people try to kill me." A knife appeared in Keir's hand. "Especially stuck-up brats with an ego complex."

Neil whimpered. Then the street trembled beneath my feet, unbalancing all of us. Neil fell flat on his back, avoiding Keir's knife, and a rumbling echoed along the row of terraced houses.

"Cut that out," I told Neil.

"That wasn't me," Neil gasped. "It was—"

A crack split the road down the middle, leaving Keir and Neil on one side, and me and Aiden on the other. More cracks splintered outwards like ripples on the surface of a pond. Roof tiles clanged loose, while more vampires emerged through the basement door in front of us, swaying like drunks.

"What the hell is that, the signal to attack?" I didn't think so, somehow. The vampires could barely keep upright, let alone walk in a straight line. "Or—the fury?"

"No," said Evelyn. "That isn't an Ancient."

The sound of glass shattering filled the air. Walls crumbled as the roads trembled, causing my teeth to rattle in my skull. Vampires tripped over one another as their survival instincts took over, clouds of dust from the collapsing houses smothering the basement entrance.

"Hey, my body's somewhere under there!" Aiden shouted indignantly. "Whoever's causing that earthquake, chill the hell out."

Earthquake. Like… an earth mage. "Neil, what is your father playing at?"

"I don't know!" Neil yelped, clinging onto the edge of the road for dear life. "I bet it's *your* people, trying to take what's ours."

"Doesn't look like he minds if he wipes you out along with his army," I remarked, my words lost in the thunder of collapsing houses. It looked like my suspicion that the foundations had never been stable was right on the mark.

I leapt over the crack in the road to reach Keir and pull him to safety. His feet were braced against the rocking street, his eyes on the vampires swarming to the surface like ants from a disturbed nest. One of them grabbed Neil from behind, dragging him away with a strangled cry.

Aiden swore, pointing ahead. "Hey, dickhead, get out of my body!"

Keir and I both spun around in time to see Aiden's body use two other vampires as leverage to climb out of the ruined house. He was covered in dust, his eyes aglow with the light of a vampire's soul.

Another quake shook the road, and Aiden stumbled over the edge. Keir caught him before he fell, locking his arms around his brother's shoulders. I jumped over to join him, helping to carry Aiden's body away from the crack in the road. He kicked and struggled, the vampire fighting for dominance. My grip broke, and magic sprang to my hands.

Evelyn appeared in front of Aiden. Magic flew from her to him, erasing the mark on his collarbone. The vampire's spirit came loose, flying at me.

Reaching up, I willed the vampire's life force to flow into me. Energy flooded my body, filled my veins with liquid warmth. The vampire faded, and Keir shouted from behind, "I banish you beyond Death, vampire!"

The vampire's faded spirit disappeared into nothingness. Keir held Aiden's body, freed from its immortal pilot.

I released a slow, shaky breath. Beside me, Evelyn hovered above the cracked road.

"Thank you," I whispered to her.

Keir's wide eyes sought me out. "Jas, is Aiden still with you?"

"Just about," Aiden's faint voice said from beside my shoulder. "Jas, you'll have to transfer me over to my body. I'm not going to last much longer."

"Which symbol do I use to return you to your body?" I wished I'd read that whole ritual magic book, but there was no *time.* I'd just have to trust in my skill as a witch and necromancer.

"Same as the one on you," Aiden said. His voice sounded quieter. "Since the body is already mine, it'll make the binding permanent."

The road continued to tremble, but Aiden's presence had dimmed to almost nothing. I couldn't lose him now.

"I'll help," Keir said. "Just tell me what to do."

"I think a witch has to do it." I pulled out the pen, pushing up my sleeve. Then I took Aiden's hand and exposed the pale skin of his wrist, pressing the nib to his skin. One touch and the ink ignited, but Aiden remained floating at my side even as I completed the symbol.

"You'll have to undo the spell binding us first," Aiden said.

Keir's eyes met mine across the road—steady, trusting. He knew I could do this.

I pressed the pen to my own wrist. My teeth rattled as the road gave another tremor and the pen pierced the skin, drawing blood. "Shit."

Aiden flew loose from my body—but not towards his own.

"Aiden!" Keir shouted, his eyes blanking out as he flew to catch his brother's spirit. On Aiden's wrist, the mark gleamed, but not brightly enough. I hadn't put enough power into it.

I caught Aiden's limp hand, pushing all the power I had into the binding symbol. Magic rippled from my skin to his, igniting the mark. A shuddering breath tore through his lungs. Blue eyes flickered open.

"Keir!" I shouted. "He's—"

Aiden promptly fell flat on his face. "Ow. I don't think I can walk."

"I can carry you," Keir said, "but we have to get off this street."

Cracks covered every inch of the road, and most of the houses were reduced to piles of rubble. Vampire-driven zombies climbed over the wreckage, but none of them seemed keen to leap over the gap in the road to join us.

"Hang onto me," said Keir, gingerly lifting his brother onto his back.

"Damn, Keir," Aiden said. "You grew up. You're not half as scrawny as you were when I left."

"Hold on tight," Keir said. "This whole street is going to collapse."

I jumped from one fragment of the road to another. "What the hell is Lord Sutherland doing, trying to rip open the earth?"

"I don't think he's summoning that fury," Evelyn commented, floating behind me. "Otherwise, we'd hear it. Maybe he's just throwing a tantrum."

I doubted it. "What in hell were you doing the whole time I was in the lab, anyway? Not summoning another dragon?"

Evelyn didn't answer. I didn't *think* she'd opened a spirit line again, but it wasn't worth arguing. She'd saved Aiden's life, after all.

Keir and followed an unsteady route through the cracked street, keeping an eye on Aiden in case he slipped. I held my breath every time the earth trembled, making a mental note to find out if there was a blood magic symbol for perfect balance if I ever got out of here alive.

"I'm going to tell everyone I run into that I haven't inhabited a body in nearly a decade," Aiden informed Keir. "Just to see their faces."

I snorted. "You're lucky your body isn't one of the zombies the mages burned."

"Otherwise you'd still have me hitching a ride alongside your creepy cousin," said Aiden.

"I'm not her cousin," said Evelyn.

"I think I'd have gone to hide in the spirit realm after a week of listening to you two bickering." I climbed over the street's single street lamp, which now lay on its side, still flickering. "It looks to me like the Mage Lord might have lost control of his magic."

"Not quite." Keir stopped walking. "Shit."

Lord Sutherland stood at the street's end, his hands outstretched, power rippling around him. Cracks spread out from his feet, deep into the earth, like the roots of an enormous tree.

I halted on an island in the middle of the trembling road. "I thought you wanted to protect the city, not destroy it, Lord Sutherland."

His positioning showed a startling lack of concern for his own safety, yet dark intelligence shone in his eyes. I was pretty sure they hadn't been grey-blue before.

"Not quite," he said, his voice soft and cold.

That wasn't Lord Sutherland's voice.

"Do I know you?" I said, a chill taking hold of me. *Oh, no. He didn't, did he? Please tell me he didn't.*

The Soul Collector's stare bored into me, pupils darting with madness. "You, Jas Lyons, will pay for what you did to me."

22

The Soul Collector and I looked at one another—or rather, I looked into his eyes, the only substantial part of him that was left. Not that the Mage Lord was much better off.

He was the god Lord Sutherland had chosen to summon to help him? And the price, apparently, was to become a vessel himself.

"Since the Mage Lord was unable to finish you off, I decided to take over," said the Soul Collector. "Which of your friends should I take first, Jas?"

"None of them." Lord Sutherland and Lady Anders were both mages with no necromancer ancestry that I knew of. In order to be possessed, either he'd died and been reanimated, used a ritual I didn't know about—or turned himself into a shade. "I should have known it was you he summoned. How'd you enjoy hanging out in limbo?"

His hands flipped over and the two houses on either side of him collapsed into rubble. Damn, that mage power was something else. Lord Sutherland must have been practising extreme restraint for the entire time I'd see him. It was a damn good job he couldn't crush a human in the same manner.

"You'll pay for that," he said, "and for taking my weapon away."

"I'd say you deserve it, considering all the people you killed." *At least he doesn't have the Ether Converter.* When Leila Hemlock had stolen it from the Hemlocks' forest and handed it to him, he'd left a trail of dead throughout Edinburgh, including Lady Harper.

"Maybe your psychic friends to start off with," he said through Lord Sutherland's mouth. "Or… yes, I think so."

The Mage Lord stilled. Then Aiden jumped off Keir's shoulders, baring his teeth. "Yes… this one will do. I want you to see your vampire friends take their final breaths, Jas. Witness their suffering."

"Nice try." Evelyn's hands splayed out behind Lord Sutherland, blasting him in the back with Hemlock magic.

Aiden fell forwards as the Soul Collector let go of him, moving back to his original host. "You," he snarled at Evelyn. "You betrayed me."

"I prefer to think of it as serving myself and nobody else," said Evelyn. "Would you like me to rip open the spirit lines and banish you to the deep once again?"

"Can you do that before I kill your friends?" His gaze locked on Aiden. "Interesting… this one has familiar thoughts. I wonder how you'd feel if I took him from this world so soon after he returned to life?"

"Don't you fucking dare," said Keir.

"I've heard enough from you," Evelyn said. "You don't

have your weapon this time. You're powerless, reduced to squatting in others' vessels like a vampire to survive."

"Aren't you little more than a lost soul yourself?" Lord Sutherland's mouth twisted. "You don't deserve the mercy of a quick death. I think I'll save you for last."

"Hey." Aiden pushed to his feet, leaning on Keir for balance. "I know you. You're the one who broke out of the lab after they destroyed your body, aren't you?"

The Soul Collector stilled, a dangerous light in his eyes.

My mouth fell open. "You… you were there, too? In the mages' lab?" That was how he'd got loose in Edinburgh? No wonder he'd been in such a weakened state, if the Orion League had used the lab to rip his soul from his body the same way they'd done to the vampires. And yet even *that* hadn't finished him off.

"I was alive before your world existed in its present form," said the Soul Collector. "I have endured worse than any mere mortal can ever inflict on me. You will wither away and die, as will all humans who play with the gods. We always win."

"Sounds like someone's holding a grudge." *He was in the lab.* That meant the shadow fury wasn't the only god the League had summoned. "I guess you lost your mind as well as your body and you couldn't stand knowing a bunch of plain old humans got the best of you. And now you're stuck inhabiting one of them."

My teeth rattled as Lord Sutherland's magic rode the wave of the Soul Collector's boundless rage. "This form is only temporary, until I regain what once was mine. He's not long for this world, regardless."

Aiden gave a laugh. "Yeah, right. You're not so different from us, Soul Collector."

The Soul Collector's mouth parted, and his glowing eyes shone even brighter in the spirit realm. While his eyes belonged to the Soul Collector, beneath lay the Mage Lord's own soul, fading away.

"You're feeding on his life essence," I said to the Soul Collector. "Aren't you?"

"Surprise," Aiden said. I heard Keir whisper an admonition to him, but the Soul Collector didn't move to attack. His hands lay outstretched, trembling a little.

"You're exactly the same as a vampire," I added. "But you can't stay attached to a host for long without killing them. Question is, which came first?"

"I am not mortal," said the Soul Collector. "I am endless."

"That's what you found out, right?" I said to Aiden. "Vampires are created when an Ancient is bound to a mortal. If the mortal survives the experience, then the effect on their spirit continues and they have to feed on others to survive."

"Pretty much," said Aiden. "Yeah, that's why the mages kidnapped me. They wanted to silence me in case word got out about their dodgy experiments. Wouldn't surprise me if the Ancients put them up to it so nobody ever found out we're your offspring."

"You are nothing to me," said the Soul Collector. "You're nothing more than a race of abominations who feed on human life essence to live."

"Uh, you're no better," I said. "Normally I'd be happy to let you chew on Lord Sutherland's soul for a bit, but I'm not a big fan of you destroying the city either."

"I'm with Jas," Evelyn added. "And unlike her, I'm perfectly happy to destroy that mage if it means taking you apart."

"Actually, I'm cool with it at this point." Magic flared to life in my hands, awakening the spirit line. One swift tug and he'd be lost… but given the fractured state of the veil, he might well come crashing back to earth again.

He gave a final, cold smile. Then he spoke a word.

The spirit realm cracked open, and I flew out of my body then crashed back into it. Red lights burned overhead, splintering the sky. A pair of jagged wings appeared from within.

My ears rang with the resonant aftermath of the word —the *Invocation*—he'd spoken. Calling the shadow fury into this realm.

The beast descended in a sweep of jagged wings. Evelyn sharply flew out of reach, and I scrambled to get a grip on my magic. If the shadow fury devoured either of us, that was it. We were done for.

The fury landed at a crouch, claws gouging holes in the tarmac.

I tensed. "Keir, get Aiden out of here!"

"Little difficult," he said, through clenched teeth, feet braced on the road—which was now trembling for another reason entirely.

The shadowy fury released a sound like a death rattle, and the surviving vampire shades fled. In another beat of wings, the shadow fury pursued them, snagging each vampire as easily as a human stamping out ants with a magnifying glass.

But it was the Soul Collector who deserved to be offered as bait.

Calling on my Hemlock magic, I leapt over the gap in front of me, crashing headlong into Lord Sutherland. He staggered, having not expected the direct assault, and I drove him to the tarmac, my hands locking around his wrists. Magic burned my palms, searching the binding spell he'd used. If I untethered the god from him, the Soul Collector would be a vulnerable target for the shadow fury. Lord Sutherland's scheming would end.

Not that that would stop the giant fury god flying over the city, grabbing vampire souls and dropping them into its gaping maw. Hands trembling, I pushed more magic into Lord Sutherland. As long as the Soul Collector was bound to him, he could only use the Mage Lord's power, nothing more.

"He can't kill us," Evelyn growled, adding her power to mine. Two channels of magic burned from my palms to the Mage Lord's wrists. The grey-blue sheen faded from his eyes, for an instant.

It's working.

The Soul Collector roared. Then he let go of his host. Lord Sutherland collapsed on top of me, unconscious.

"Hey!" I shoved at his dead weight. The road had stopped trembling, but the shadow-fury's roar echoed over the rooftops. We'd traded one threat for another.

I crawled out from underneath Lord Sutherland's limp body, letting it slide towards the gap in the road. Risking a glance at the spirit realm, I swore. The entire grey space was covered in deep cracks, which formed gaping holes in the endless void. Evelyn hovered beside me. She seemed unconcerned with the spirit realm's state, but then again, she still had a host. The Soul Collector didn't.

In a blur, he crashed into Evelyn, but she'd expected

the attack. She grabbed his transparent form, driving him towards one of the gaps in the spirit realm.

"I will find my way back, mortals," shrieked the Soul Collector.

"Have fun in the void," Evelyn shouted after him.

Then he was gone.

Keir whipped his head back to me. "He did that on purpose to avoid being eaten by the fury. Cowardly shit."

"What about him?" said Aiden, indicating the Mage Lord's unconscious body.

"Might be a bit late to call in the mages' emergency backup team." A shriek drew my attention to the fury, whose claws impaled three vampires at once, yanking them out of their hosts. My gut tightened. Some of those vampires might have been like Aiden, innocent victims. "I have to stop the Ancient."

"You can't kill it," said Evelyn. "We need to kick it out of this realm, otherwise the entire spirit realm will break."

"I'm sure the dragons will be thrilled." They'd be less than impressed with the Soul Collector falling out of the sky again, too. At least he probably couldn't possess any of them. "Can we fix the spirit realm?"

"We did it once already," she replied, hovering above the cracked road.

"Yes, but it wasn't this bad." And there wasn't a giant monster eating holes in reality as we spoke. Sure, the spirit realm would repair itself if we got rid of the shadow fury, but as long as the spirit realm remained in ruins, it wasn't going anywhere. Especially with an entire city of innocent souls to feast on.

"Jas," said Keir. "Don't you even think about sacrificing yourself."

"I won't," I said, "but I need to get into the spirit lines to heal the damage. Keir—please, get Aiden to safety. I—*we*—can do this, right, Evelyn?"

"Yes," she said. "Jas and I will fix this."

Keir's mouth thinned, then he gave a nod. "Aiden, I'm taking you with me. Can you keep an eye on that monster?"

I found a clear spot on the road to sit on and shifted out of my body to join Evelyn. At once, most of my exhaustion faded, and a renewed determination strengthened my resolve. *I can do this.* With Evelyn beside me, I couldn't—wouldn't—fail. No matter how depleted my spirit might be, my Hemlock magic shone as brightly as ever.

Power built, thrummed in my hands, mingling with Evelyn's. Reaching the edge of the nearest tear in the spirit realm, I willed it to close, to seal up.

"That way is too slow," Evelyn said. "The beast—"

The shadow-fury's head snapped in our direction, and it released an ear-splitting screech. The noise racked my body and soul, rippling down the fractured spirit line. Almost like Mackie's scream. Were the *psychics* related to the Ancients, too?

I spun head over heels in the air, catching myself against another ghost. Not a ghost. Ilsa clutched her talisman to her chest, her eyes widening at the sight of me. "Is that—an Ancient?"

"You've got it," I said. "He can't be killed. I was trying to seal the spirit lines, but he might undo them again."

Ilsa swore. "If you do manage to kill that bastard, it'll create a whole other problem. The blood of an Ancient has side effects on anyone who touches it."

"Like what?" I asked.

"Immortality."

Magic sparked from my hands and I yanked them away from Ilsa. Evelyn shot to my side, staring at Ilsa in open disbelief. "You *what?*" she said.

"Incoming," Ilsa warned.

The fury's scream died out and its wings spread, carrying it towards us. It was even bigger than it had seemed while squashed into the lab's corridors, despite its wings' skeletal appearance. It looked like someone had reanimated a dragon's giant corpse… which wasn't too far from the truth. Its tightly stretched skin shimmered oddly, almost like runes were drawn onto its skin.

"The beast that spawned the furies," said Ilsa. "How… pleasant."

"The gods aren't picked for their charm and personality," I said.

"I will devour you," the fury roared, its voice erupting a dozen new tears in the spirit realm. *Damn, it* is *causing the breach.*

"It's speaking English." I pressed my hands to my ears, willing the spirit realm to stop shaking. "Ilsa!"

Ilsa retreated, her talisman aglow. The fury's claw passed through the spot where she'd been hovering. I dropped in mid-air towards my inert body, relieved to see Keir had taken my advice and got Aiden to safer ground.

On the other hand, Lord Sutherland grasped the edge of the road, his legs trembling. *He's awake.* And staring in horror at the monster in the sky.

"Thanks a bunch," I snapped at him. "This is what you wanted, is it? You saw how the Whisper devoured your witch. You're no different."

"I am descended from a pure line of mages dating back to the twelfth century." He feebly pulled himself upright. "I am the last of my line, aside from my son, and I will not be forgotten. I will not die here."

"You can't fight that thing," I said.

"I don't need to," he said. "As you see, it's devouring the abominations as planned. It will not harm me."

Unbelievable. He seemed to be right, though—the fury had grabbed another vampire's soul, entirely ignoring the Mage Lord. As a living person, he wasn't of interest—yet.

Lord Sutherland pushed up both his sleeves, scowling at the marks on his wrists. One hand fumbled for his pocket, drawing a pen. Just like the one I'd used for my own blood magic.

"Don't you dare summon that Soul Collector back," I warned.

"I don't need to." He pressed the point of the pen to a gleaming rune. The symbol ignited, and the shadow fury dropped his vampire prey, changing direction.

"You're not—" I broke off. "You are. You're controlling the fury." I hadn't imagined seeing runes gleaming beneath its shadowy skin. The Mage Lord must have drawn them onto the beast during its captivity.

Recklessness seized me. I lunged at Lord Sutherland, knocking the pen from his hand and into the gap in the road.

"You foolish girl," he spat. "Without me controlling it, it'll have free rein."

"Not if I have anything to do with it." I took off, vaulting over another gap in the cracked road, my gaze trained on the fury's shadowy form. It continued to devour the unfortunate vampires, fuelled by Lord Sutherland's last order.

"What are you doing?" Evelyn yelled at me.

"I have an idea." A wild one, admittedly, and yet what was more audacious than claiming dominion over the gods?

Stopping on a stable-looking piece of ground, I drifted out of my body, waving my arms at the fury. "Hey! Over here!"

The fury turned to me. As his gaze locked on me, I shifted back into my body. "Evelyn, I'm gonna need your help. See those runes on his skin? I don't think they got there by accident."

"If we free the fury from the Mage Lord's control, that won't stop him from devouring every spirit it can find," she said. "Unless *you* want to control him?"

"No, I want to set him free." Who wouldn't be angry after being imprisoned and tortured? Perhaps the shadow fury might not be capable of seeing me as any more than a tasty snack, but if it didn't work, the element of surprise might at least buy us a little time.

I held up my arm, exposing the symbols etched into my own skin. Then with the finger of my left hand, I mimed erasing the runes.

The fury snapped out a claw, sending me flying.

"I'm not attacking you!" I caught my balance at the edge of the road. "I'm removing those runes controlling you. I'm not on the Mage Lord's side, believe me."

Maybe the fury didn't understand me. But when I mimed erasing the rune a second time, the monster stilled, wings beating.

Calling on all the magic I could muster, I aimed not for

the fury itself, but for the ink on his skin. The beast squirmed in discomfort, but it was too late to stop the flow of magic burning from my palms, erasing the runes, smothering the mages' marks. Not just the mages. There were years of pain written there on the monster's skin. An intelligence shone inside his eyes which was difficult to ignore.

Please, please don't kill me for this.

The last rune disappeared. The fury's pitch-dark eyes blinked, once, his body alarmingly still. Shock, or preparation to launch an attack?

"There." I lowered my hands. "It's done. You don't need to fight us anymore."

Evelyn cleared her throat behind me, jerking her head at the sky. A number of furies had gathered over the rooftops. Not attacking me, just watching me. I'd drawn an audience.

"You don't have to fight us," I repeated. "Any of you."

In a rustle of wings, the other furies neared, surrounding their larger cousin.

"You were..." I began. "You were looking for your master. Weren't you?"

A murmur ran through the group. Then with one final look at me, the shadow-fury beat his wings once more. The furies took flight as one, into the fracturing sky, swallowed by the clouds.

23

Half an hour of dodging questions—and vampires—later, I sank to a sitting position against the wall in the guild's lobby, stealing a moment of quiet among the chaos of the battle's aftermath.

The city was a shambles, and the guild wasn't much better. The vampires, once left alone, had taken to searching the rubble for their missing bodies or failing that, just grabbing any they could find. Isabel and Asher had volunteered to help the survivors remove the blood magic runes. Meanwhile, I found myself dragged from one person to another to explain what in hell I'd done to make the giant god go away.

No sooner had I found a moment to breathe than Ivy and Vance picked their way through the crowd to me.

"We cleared out the lab," Vance said. "However, we need a necromancer to destroy the spirit barrier and check there isn't anything left behind."

"It should be fine to bring down the spirit barrier now

the Ancient is gone," I said. "Most of the spirits will probably be able to move on without a fuss without the barrier there, and a necromancer can deal with the rest."

Not me, though. For all the praise she'd heaped on me, Lady Montgomery still hadn't offered me my old job back. Lord Sutherland might be on his way to jail, but the price on my head remained.

"Good," said Ivy. "I don't have the spirit sight, so I didn't see where the shadow fury went. It's not in this realm, right?"

"No, he went through one of the gaps in the spirit line," I said. "I doubt he'll come back. He feeds on dead souls, not living ones, and I'm pretty sure he'll feel more at home wherever the other furies live than on earth."

At least, I hoped so.

"I'm gonna take your word for it on that, Jas," Lloyd said, picking up a couple of candles from the floor of the lobby. "I still think you're bonkers."

"Hey, it worked," Ivy said. "She stopped the shadow fury from causing any more damage."

"The shadow fury was in chains, metaphorically speaking," I explained. "Once I got them off, he was happy to leave. Since he eats souls, I'd rather he didn't come back here, but I can't even pronounce the word the Mage Lord used to summon him."

"He's lucky he survived," Ivy said. "Normally, humans can't speak Invocations without being torn apart by the backlash, but he had another god's protection. I hope the others are keeping an eye on him."

"They are," Vance said. "He's chained in his own dungeon."

The last I'd seen of Lord Sutherland, his wrists had

been bound with the same spells he'd once threatened to put on every witch in the city. *Irony is a bitch, isn't it?*

"Good riddance," Lloyd and I said at the same time.

"And the spirit realm?" Ivy asked.

"It should heal itself," I said. "If not, Evelyn and I can help, but I can't promise there won't be any more furies. They should be less aggressive now I've saved their big brother, though."

"I think they *like* you, Jas," said Lloyd.

"Hey, I'm the hellhound whisperer, you're the fury whisperer," said Ivy.

What would Cordelia say when she found I'd been making friends with one of the Ancients? A grin crept onto my face at the thought and I laughed until my sides hurt.

"What's so funny?" asked Mackie, pausing mid-step.

"I think she's finally lost her wits," Lloyd remarked, shifting to the right as Morgan walked up behind Mackie.

"At least I'm in good company." I caught my breath. "I can't decide if I want a nap or a drink. Or both."

"Jas?" Mackie crouched next to me. "Is it true that—he survived? The Soul Collector?"

"Ah." My mirth faded. "Yeah, he did. He fled into the other realm, and he won't be coming back if he thinks the shadow fury is still loose in the city."

"He survived?" said Morgan. "Since when?"

"Since Lord Sutherland made a deal with him," said Mackie. "Where have you been for the last hour?"

"Cleaning up the mess you made when you screamed four zombies to pieces all over the stairs."

"You did?" I gave her a thumbs-up, deciding not to mention the remarkable similarities between her screaming power and the furies. I'd decide when, or if, to broach that subject later on.

"So the Mage Lord isn't actually the Mage Lord any longer?" asked Morgan.

"He is now," I said. "I mean, he'll be removed from his position, but the Soul Collector isn't controlling him. Unless someone else knows the Ancient's real name, there's no summoning him back here. Oh, and he doesn't have the Ether Converter."

"Damn right he doesn't," Ilsa said from behind Lloyd. "Jas, the boss is looking for you."

I rested my head against the wall. "No rest for the fury whisperer."

"Is that your new official title?" Keir caught my hand, pulling me to my feet. At his side stood Aiden, who'd been talking non-stop for the last hour. I didn't blame him, given the years of silent torment he'd spent in the lab.

"You're the real hero of the day," Aiden said to me.

"Lucky, more like," I said, resting my head against Keir's chest. "I'm just glad it's over."

———

"To Jas," said Lloyd, raising his beer glass and clanking it against mine. We'd barely managed to squeeze our entire group onto the pub's longest table, and I was crammed between Lloyd and Keir. "The fury whisperer."

"Please stop calling me that," I said, half-heartedly. After the whirlwind of the last few hours—Lady Montgomery profusely thanking me and offering me my old position back with a pay raise, mages queuing up to shake my hand, a dizzying stream of thanks from guild members I hadn't exchanged two words with before—we'd ended up at the Redcap's Cave. I'd barely managed to keep my eyes open through dinner, but the triumphant atmosphere was infectious. I tipped back my glass, the alcohol buzzing through my system.

Keir chuckled and tapped his glass against mine, too. "It's a compliment."

Keir seemed different, with his brother. More relaxed. He wore a wide grin and looked like years of stress had disappeared from his shoulders.

"Sure." I drained the glass and set it down. On Keir's other side, Aiden was in the middle of a play-by-play account of his last night out in Edinburgh which had somehow ended in a round of drunken poker with a group of ogres. Drake was hanging onto Aiden's every word beside an exasperated-looking Vance, an amused-looking Ivy, and even Asher had come along, at Isabel's insistence. Their voices washed over me, turning to a humming noise in the background.

I yawned, wondering if it would be bad manners to take a nap on the table.

"Wakey wakey," Lloyd poked me in the shoulder. "You can't fall asleep now. You have to join us for karaoke."

"I thought you said never again."

"After a few more of these, I will." He took another sip from his beer glass. "Life's short."

"Does that mean you're going to ask Morgan to sing with you again?"

Lloyd choked on his beer and glanced down the table, but Morgan didn't look up. He was in the middle of yet another recount of the fight to anyone who would listen. So, basically, Mackie. And Wanda, who was too polite to tell him everyone at the table had witnessed the fight and knew perfectly well he hadn't slain twelve furies single-handedly.

Keir's hand squeezed my knee. "Jas, you look tired."

I yawned. "I might lie down and take a nap."

"I can escort you home." Keir's hand brushed my wrist, and the witch mark tingled. I'd forgotten I was wearing it —and I'd also forgotten my plan to undo the binding between us.

I tilted my head up at him. "Might take you up on that."

He leaned in. "Good, because I haven't thanked you properly yet." His tone deepened, sending a quiver of need through me and momentarily banishing my sleepiness.

"Hey, don't start groping each other at the table," Lloyd said. "Another round, anyone? I'll pay."

"He's going to regret that," I said in an undertone.

Keir chuckled. "Aiden, Jas and I are going to head back home before she falls asleep on the table."

"Sure." Aiden stood to give his brother a one-armed hug. He was still a little unsteady on his feet, but after a few beers, everyone else would be, too.

"Sure thing." I waved goodbye to the others and walked out hand in hand with Keir. "I still have the guide to ritual magic. I think I know how to unbind your soul from mine, if you want to do it."

Keir's eyes widened in surprise. "Are you sure?"

"Yeah," I said. "Don't get me wrong, it's nice to be close to you, but I'd rather the *feeding on my soul* thing be optional. Just in case I wind up stuck in another realm again."

"It bothered you that Evelyn had to step in?" He trailed

a hand down my back, his vampire's touch whispering over my skin. "I like the idea of having you all to myself."

"Me too. Want to come to the guild, or to Lady Harper's place? Your choice."

"What about those awful relatives of yours?"

I stopped walking. "Uh… is it a bad thing that I forgot all about them?" Oops. In fairness, Evelyn had been quiet all night, so maybe she was already with them. Telling Cordelia all about how I'd made friends with the fury.

Ah.

"What d'you think?" Keir asked. "Want to get it over with?"

I released a breath. "I guess so."

I'd worried about the state of the spirit line leading to the forest, but the spirit realm was almost free of tears by the time we reached the bridge.

The instant we crossed over into the Hemlocks' place, we landed in the cave. Cordelia wasn't in the mood for ceremony, then. Neither was I, come to that.

"Jacinda," said Cordelia, looking down at Keir and me. "What have you done?"

"Ended the war before it started." As I'd expected, Evelyn floated in front of Cordelia's tree, not looking surprised at my appearance. Her eyes narrowed in a manner that made her look startlingly similar to the stony faces carved into the walls. "I got rid of the Ancient with minimal casualties, the former Mage Lord and his associates are in jail, and the spirit realm will heal. Oh, and the furies aren't our enemies any longer. I'd count that as a win."

"You made us all look like fools," she said. "You made an agreement with our ancient enemies—"

"The shadow fury was imprisoned and tortured in a lab for years, Cordelia," I said. "Besides, you know you can't actually kill the gods. If I'd tried, more people would have needlessly died."

"You undid years of our work, Jacinda."

"So what?" I threw up my hands. "After years of fighting, what's wrong with starting a clean slate? Just because your ancestors started a war with the Ancients doesn't mean we have to repeat the same mistakes."

"Jacinda," she said. "The Ancients are our natural enemies."

"No," I said. "They aren't. Not if we don't want them to be."

I had no more to say, so I, re-joined Keir at the back of the cave. Before we could get the hell out, Evelyn pounced. "You have some nerve walking away."

Her harsh words surprised me. "All I did was undo the damage the Soul Collector and the Mage Lord did. As a bonus, we have an ally the next time we get stuck in the Ancients' realm. It's hardly worse than setting a dragon loose in the city, and you can't solve every problem by breaking everything. If you and Cordelia realised that, you might be a lot happier."

This time, when I yanked the cave door open and walked out into the forest, she didn't follow me.

"She's pissed," Keir said, as we appeared on the hillside outside Lady Harper's house.

"I don't care," I said. "I'd have thought she'd be angrier about the Soul Collector escaping than the fact that I stopped the Ancient and the other furies from eating holes in the spirit realm. She knows perfectly well you can't kill a god. What else was I supposed to do?"

Despite the Ancients' escape, it was hard to see today's outcome as anything other than a victory. We'd saved Keir's brother and ignited the hope that I might bring an end to my coven's war with the Ancients. And as an added bonus, I held the means of understanding how my soul and Evelyn's had ended up tethered in my hands. If Cordelia had trusted me enough to tell me her secrets upfront, then perhaps she wouldn't be as mad at me for getting hold of that information by myself.

Yawning, I unlocked the door to the house, turning on the living room light. Once I'd discarded my coat and lit the fire, I pulled out the mages' ritual magic book, which they'd stolen from Asher... who'd also 'borrowed' it from the necromancers, or so it seemed.

Keir sat down on the sofa next to me as I skimmed through the pages. "What do you have to do, drain my spirit essence the same way you did to the shades?"

"Basically." I found the right page, reading the text. "Okay, hold out your hand."

I took his warm hand in mine, then tapped on my spirit sight. Keir glowed all over, and I shivered when his fingertips traced my palm through the spirit realm.

"Open the connection," I said. "I think you have to feed on me first."

"Sure." He reached through, and a heady sensation filled me, as though I was drawing power from him and not the other way around. Then again, I was, in a way. I kept one eye on our hands, seeing the glow around his palm as the energy transferred. Then I took that glow and pulled the energy back into me.

His eyes flew wide, but he held still. Carefully, I pulled

on the power, searching for the link. He exhaled sharply. "Whoa. I think that was it."

"Are you sure?" I released his hand, my veins fizzing with energy. "I definitely took something from you, but I think you'll have to try feeding on someone else to be certain it worked."

"It did," he said. "You know, the last few times I've fed on you, you've felt... less substantial than usual. Now, I don't feel that."

"Good," I said. "Maybe I'll actually catch a break now."

He took my hand again. "I can still feel you inside me. It's... electrifying."

His lips moved over mine, and I moaned, revelling in the echo of the spell through our blood. "Keir."

"I've waited so long," he whispered, trailing a hand through my hair.

"Likewise." I wrapped my arms around his waist, my mouth parting to let him in. His fingertips moved down my shoulders, my arms, tracing my outline as though to memorise every inch. Then his touch went deeper. Cooler, yet somehow more heated. I gasped.

"Don't worry," he murmured. "I've got it under control."

"Keir." I moaned as his touch flickered between spirit and real world, skimming my skin and soul until both sides of me were alight with need. His fingers tugged on the edge of my shirt, pulling it over my head. "You don't need to take my clothes off, you know."

"There are some parts of you I can't appreciate from the spirit realm." He unclasped my bra and lowered his head to my breast, tugging the tip into his mouth. His hand moved to my waistband, undoing the button on my jeans. I moaned as his mouth moved over the delicate skin of my nipples and then trailed down my stomach. By the time his hands worked off my jeans, my breath came in heavy gasps.

The carpet was soft against my back, his skin pleasantly cool against mine. He straddled me, pulling his shirt over his head, and I grabbed the waistband of his jeans and slid my hand inside. He was already hard.

"Fucking hell, Jas." Keir hissed out a breath as I withdrew my hand and tugged his jeans down his hips. He rocked back off me, removing his jeans, and pressed his mouth to mine again.

"God, yes," he breathed, delicately stroking the skin between my legs. I gasped as he flicked my clit with his fingertip. Then he did the same in the spirit realm. I gave a stifled scream, my spine arching. By the time I'd recovered, he'd pulled off his boxers and had a condom on.

"Do that again," he murmured, pulling off my underwear with one hand and using the other to stroke the wet heat between my legs.

"Encourage me." I rocked my hips against his fingers, and a smile tugged his mouth.

"So demanding." He removed his fingers and lowered himself onto me, sliding inside me with one thrust. For an instant, he was suspended above me, every muscle taut. Then he moved against me with agonising slowness, his pace quickening until we came together, touch on touch, in the spirit realm and otherwise.

I dug my nails into his shoulders as a second wave of pleasure rocked me from head to toe. He gave one last thrust and gasped as he came. Trailing kisses down my shoulder, he withdrew from me, whispering my name.

We might be severed, but I'd never felt closer to him as he lay beside me on the soft carpet, his longish hair falling over his face.

"We should go to bed," I murmured.

"Is it more comfortable than here?" He wrapped his arms around my waist, pulling me tight against him. His hands moved over my ribs. "You've lost weight. You should eat more."

"Are you offering to buy me breakfast?"

"Sure, but I'm afraid my brother will be there."

"I'll forgive you if you make tonight worth my while." I twisted onto my back, grinning up at him.

"Your wish is my command." He ran his fingers through my hair, and across my lips. "When did you take the piercing out?"

"Why are you scrutinising me?"

"Because you're sexy as fuck and I want to memorise every inch of you." He kissed my chin, then my lips.

"I could say the same to you." My fingers trailed through his hair. "I've never seen you look this happy."

"That's because I've got everything I ever wanted, Jas, even what I thought I'd never have again. And it's thanks to you."

"Keep plying me with compliments like that and I might let you stick around all night."

He grinned, straddling me. "Challenge accepted."

24

I came back to wakefulness slowly, my mind sluggish. My body felt like it'd been drained ten times over. Rolling over on the guest bed, I found Keir leaning over me, looking concerned.

"Ow," I said. "I think we might have gone overboard last night."

"Jas, what's that on your arm?"

Lifting my arm, I squinted at it, my vision fuzzy at the corners. "Just the blood magic runes."

His finger touched the edge of my wrist, beside a symbol I didn't recognise. *Did I draw that?*

"That wasn't there before." He propped up on his elbow. "Was it?"

"I… did I draw it last night?" I couldn't have, right? "Uh… Evelyn?"

No reply. I rolled off the bed and left the guest room we'd slept in, finding my clothes strewn around the living room. The fire was still alight, but there were no signs of Evelyn.

Keir followed close behind me. "Jas, what is it?"

I gave the symbol on my wrist another scan. "Did Evelyn possess me while I was asleep?"

"Why would she do that?" He picked up the ritual book from beside the fireplace and handed it back to me.

A gasp escaped, and the book fell from my hand. On the page was the same symbol I wore on my arm—the symbol I had no memory of inking on my skin.

"That's not an energy transfer spell," Keir said, reading the book over my shoulder. "It's either a binding, or…"

"Unbinding." I sank to my knees on the soft carpet. "She cut herself loose. She's not bound to me any longer."

The words on the page swam before my eyes. Evelyn had ripped herself out of my body, taking my magic along with her.

"She doesn't have a body of her own, though." Keir rested a firm hand on my shoulder. "I don't think she thought this decision through."

"I think she did." I twisted to look at him. "Tell me. When I did the energy transfer, did it feel like a vampire was feeding on you?"

"That—" He broke off. "Yes, it did, but not exactly."

"Because I don't need your life force to survive," I said. "Doesn't mean I can't transfer energy from anyone to me in the same way. No wonder Lady Montgomery kept it under wraps."

"But what has that to do with Evelyn?" His eyes grew wide. "Your spirit. She was feeding on you…"

"Until she got strong enough to go it alone." The image of her furious expression in Cordelia's cave came to mind. "I guess setting that Ancient free was the last straw."

"It's not your fault." Keir set about gathering our

clothes, and we dressed quickly. "Evelyn's incapable of thinking outside the box she's been stuck in all her life."

"Perhaps, but she's raging mad, and I don't think she should be allowed into the forest in that state. Especially without me to rein her in." Being without a body hindered her, yet the symbol on my wrist was more than an unbinding. She'd untethered herself from me, perhaps for good.

"Wise idea." He passed me my coat and I pulled it on, along with my shoes. I suspected I wouldn't be coming back here anytime soon. Packing Lady Harper's journal in my bag along with the book of ritual magic, I swung the rucksack over my shoulders and joined Keir by the door.

Once we set foot outside, I spotted her instantly, standing alone on the spot where the spirit line over-lapped with the hillside. From this distance, she looked almost solid. *How much did she take from me?*

"What the hell are you playing at?" I called, marching towards her.

Evelyn turned to face me. "I got bored watching you screw up, Jas."

"How exactly did you plan to get rid of that fury when nobody can kill it?" I folded my arms across my chest. "You'd have let it destroy half of Edinburgh, wouldn't you?"

"So what?" she said. "I told you, if you cared for those friends of yours, you'd have left them alone, Jas. If you had, the mage would never have been able to summon that monster."

"That isn't true," I said. "He figured out how to do it without my help. And I didn't mean to free the fury..." I trailed off. "It was you."

Her head inclined, a slight affirmation.

"You set the vampires loose," I said. "It was *you*. You went back into the lab without me there, set all the vampires and the fury free, and let me take the blame."

That wasn't all she'd done. She'd deliberately jumped into the river to shock me back into my body when I'd almost had Lord Sutherland cornered, breaking my phone to impede me from contacting my friends. Her secret meetings with the Hemlocks, too. How had I not seen it?

Because I didn't want to. Because I thought I understood her.

"I should have been chosen as heir," she said, "and if not for a freak act of nature, I would have been. It's time I took what's rightfully mine."

The forest took the place of the hillside, and magic swirled around Evelyn. Hemlock power, boundless and raw. My own magic ignited in response. *My Hemlock magic. I still have it.*

Evelyn landed on the forest path, the trees swaying on either side, leaves rustling together like a chorus of whispers.

"Don't," I warned. "Whatever you're doing—don't."

"Relax," she said. "The Hemlocks have plenty of magic to spare. You, however, won't be so lucky."

I don't understand. Why would Evelyn betray me now? She'd saved my life several times over, and I'd done the same for her. Maybe our goals would never be in exact alignment, but I hadn't thought she'd turn on me with no warning.

I called my magic to my hands, forming a rippling shield. "I'll protect the whole forest if I have to, Evelyn."

Her mouth twisted. "You shouldn't have any power left."

"I guess we were bound for too long." I raised my palms, and she bared her teeth. "Get out of here, Evelyn. Cordelia, back me up here!"

For a heart-stopping instant, I thought she'd take Evelyn's side, condemning me to my fate. Then a sharp current of power bolstered mine. Evelyn floated backwards, anger shining within her eyes.

"If I cannot take the power for my own, then you shall not either, Jacinda."

The mark on my wrist ignited. I screamed aloud as devouring pain pierced me, body and soul. Keir shouted my name, his arms around me—from the pain, my arm should be ablaze, my whole body burning from within.

Then it stopped. I lifted my head from the forest floor. Keir's steady hands helped me to my feet.

"She is no longer in the forest," Cordelia's voice said. "Find her, Jas."

"We will." Keir wrapped an arm around my shoulder. "She can't escape in the spirit realm."

I hardly had breath to speak, but the forest disappeared in an instant, depositing us outside the disused train station.

I sagged against Keir's side, and pushed up my sleeve. The mark on my wrist looked darker, a brand burned into my skin. The other marks had faded already. That was no ordinary witch mark.

I reached for my Hemlock magic and felt nothing. Not even the spirit line.

"She…" My knees buckled. "She took it. My Hemlock magic."

"She can't have," Keir said. "Cordelia kicked her out."

"And she kicked me out in return." I held up my wrist, which tingled with the aftermath of the intense pain she'd inflicted on me. "I can't sense any of it at all. Even…"

I turned on my spirit sight, relieved to see the spirit line still flowed overhead. My necromancer powers were in full working order. Yet without my Hemlock magic—

"Jas!" yelled a voice. I looked up to see Ilsa sprinting full-tilt towards the bridge. She skidded to a halt in front of me. "Jas… she stole my talisman. Evelyn did."

"Evelyn did *what?*" I lowered my hand. "She can't do that. She doesn't even have a body."

"The book is partly incorporeal." Ilsa's face was pale. "It shouldn't be possible, but through the spirit realm…"

"Shit." Horror coursed through me. "She stole your talisman because it contains the power of an Ancient."

Since Evelyn looked like me, the guild's defences would have let her pass without a fuss. She must have gone there the instant she got out of the forest.

"I let my guard down after the battle," said Ilsa. "Why would Evelyn steal from me?"

"I don't know, but she also took my Hemlock magic and broke our link," I said. "Even the other Hemlocks couldn't stop her."

Evelyn had always said the Hemlocks' magic went far beyond the magic in the forest. She'd made no secret of the fact that she wanted more, and the other Hemlocks had done nothing to challenge her ambitions. What had they been telling her during their secret meetings? What other advantages had they given her?

I won't let her win this.

"She's done holding back," Keir said. "You know that

time I nearly drifted through the gates of Death? I thought I saw you beforehand, but now I'm sure it was her. She was playing both of us. Even when she offered to let me feed on her when you were gone, she was trying to cover her tracks. To retain your trust."

"She's way too smart," I said. "She must have spent the last few months figuring out how to distance herself from my body until she was ready to separate altogether."

While helping my friends so I wouldn't suspect anything.

"But you still have your necromancer magic," said Keir. "You can stand against her."

"I bloody well hope so." I tapped the spirit realm, but of course there were no signs of her on the other side. She'd had months to learn how to hide herself. "All she needs now is a body."

"She can't control the book, though," said Ilsa. "It belongs to the Gatekeeper. How—how did she separate herself from you?"

"With this." I unzipped my rucksack to remove the ritual magic book, and a piece of paper fluttered out. Keir caught it before it blew away. "Ah. That's Lady Harper's map."

"Where'd that come from?" Ilsa peered at the map. "What's that writing?"

I took the map from Keir, upside-down, and a famil-iarity caught me in the chest. I *knew* that layout. "Uh… why does Lady Harper have a map of the Ancients' realm? Written in code?"

"That's not code," Ilsa said. "That's the faerie language."

I nearly dropped the map again. "You can *read* it?"

"A few words," Ilsa said. "Hazel—my sister—is better at

ancient languages than I am, but I do know the basics. Is that your mentor's map?"

"It was," I said. "I didn't realise it shows the Ancients' realm. The layout is exactly the same." I traced the lines with my fingertip. The old cathedral-like place was on the right, while the sloping hillsides were copied in detail.

"What does the X on the map point to?" Keir asked.

"I never found out." I peered closer, then turned the map over. "I think Evelyn knows, and she's heading into that realm herself to start a war on her own terms."

"You're joking," said Ilsa. "What are you going to do?"

I lowered the map. "I'm going to finish what Lady Harper started. And I'm going to stop the Hemlocks' magic from tearing the realms apart."

ABOUT THE AUTHOR

Emma is the New York Times and USA Today Bestselling author of the Changeling Chronicles urban fantasy series.

Emma spent her childhood creating imaginary worlds to compensate for a disappointingly average reality, so it was probably inevitable that she ended up writing fantasy novels. When she's not immersed in her own fictional universes, Emma can be found with her head in a book or wandering around the world in search of adventure.

Find out more about Emma's books at
www.emmaladams.com.